A X 5 0

AX50

MARK HELME

Matador
9 Priory Business Park,
Wistow Road, Kibworth Beauchamp,
Leicestershire. LE8 0RX
Tel: 0116 279 2299
Email: books@troubador.co.uk
Web: www.troubador.co.uk/matador
Twitter: @matadorbooks

ISBN 978 1838590 765

British Library Cataloguing in Publication Data.
A catalogue record for this book is available from the British Library.

Printed and bound in Great Britain by 4edge Limited
Typeset in 11pt Minion Pro by Troubador Publishing Ltd, Leicester, UK

Matador is an imprint of Troubador Publishing Ltd

INTRODUCTION

This book is narrated by different characters who describe their lives from 2021 until 2112. The postscript describes the world in 2112. Occasionally, a complex invention is mentioned. The explanation behind this is not necessary for the narrative, but if the reader is interested, an asterisk (*) will be appended. An explanation will be found in the appendix, in numbered order, at the back of the book.

Earlier that afternoon, I'd had my first 'big-air' experience on my mountain bike. I suspect it wasn't at all impressive but tingling fear turned to relief as my wheels reconnected with rock. I hurtled on down Hazard Peak track towards the azure blue waters of Morro Bay. We hit the sand, dropped our bikes, sprinted towards the Pacific and collected our kayaks, launching them for the second part of the race. My body hummed with adrenaline as I smashed through the breaking waves. At one point, a huge roller threw me against a rock. My left hand was bruised but not broken. In the end, I was tenth overall, but I was chuffed to be the fastest female.

I woke from this reverie as a waiter placed a plate of Puy lentil bolognese with sides of asparagus and roast peppers on the polished table in front of me. I tried, but failed, to ignore the stench of burnt flesh that assaulted me as steaks were served to my fellow students. We obeyed the rules; the soft slaps of covers hitting cell phones presaged an eruption of chatter and laughter as we ate.

I thought I heard a soft popping sound; no one else noticed. Concentrating, I heard it again, louder this time.

1

"What the hell was that?" I shouted.

Silence; everyone was staring at me.

"What the fuck, Max?"

"I heard something…"

And then everyone heard the unmistakable sound of a silenced gun.

"Oh my God, let's get out of here!" Pat screamed.

Chaos! The 'lockdown' room was beyond the approaching gun. Some students charged out onto the patio and across the grass of the gardens. Others chose to stay in the building and scuffled as they scrummaged through the door at the far end of the canteen. Some tipped over heavy oak tables and hid behind them. Panicking, someone had misguidedly pushed one of these tables against the door in the direction of the gunfire. It would be of little use as the door opened out of the canteen.

I'd forgotten about the pain in my hand as I leapt over the counter and into the kitchen. Screams failed to blot out the burst of automatic fire as the gunman entered the canteen. I sprinted through the gleaming kitchen, out of the back door and up the steep slope to the conifers that overlooked the school buildings. My heart was racing and I could hear the blood rushing through my ears. I dived behind a redwood trunk. Trembling, I peered out to view the scene. There were four students lying absolutely still on the grass in front of the canteen. They could almost be play-acting except for the blood oozing onto the grass.

Silence. The gunman must have been reloading. All the students were motionless, hardly daring to breathe, fearing they might be chosen as the next victim.

Then a single shot rang out loud and clear.

"He's down, keep me covered."

"No pulse, where the hell are the state police?"

My mind told me I was safe, but I started to shake uncontrollably.

Who the hell would attack our school?

I heard the unmistakable thrum of choppers approaching at speed, and somewhere in the distance, sirens growing louder.

The playing fields were swarming with heavily armed police charging towards the grounds in front of the canteen, automatic rifles leading the way. They checked the gunman was truly dead.

"No sudden movements, hands on your heads and step out slowly."

I thought for a moment they'd found another gunman, but they were pointing their automatic weapons at my traumatised friends!

"Move in a straight line toward the playing fields."

More police entered the school buildings. I heard muffled sounds of "clear" as they went from room to room. Two more lines of students appeared. I saw my friend Pat, his hands covered in blood.

Then sirens were blaring and ambulances screamed up the drive, halting in the yard. A swarm of medics rushed into the school and reappeared with injured students on trolleys.

I'd been missed during their cursory search of the grounds. I came out with my hands on my head, stumbling down the steep slope. As I neared the safety of the playing fields, the enormity of the situation hit home, and by the time I joined my grieving friends, I was sobbing my heart out.

Ten minutes later, the head teacher arrived. He was horrified that we still had our hands on our heads like criminals. He vouched for us all and led us off to the gym. I heard a single ringtone and then a cacophony of jingles as every cell seemed to go off. News of the shooting must have been broadcast. Mom phoned. I tried to remain brave, telling her I was fine but broke down as she kept saying how much she loved me and that Dad was on his way.

That was fourteen years ago, nearly half my life, and yet it's as vivid as if it occurred yesterday. After gaining a BSc in computing sciences from Stanford, I won a Rhodes scholarship to Oxford in 2028 which was to change my life.

In my first year, I met a guy called Dan. He was about my height (6ft 2in) with very short dark hair (he cut it himself with a no 2 spacer) and overlapping, crowded teeth. He had a squint; I never did work out which eye he was using. He was a strong, wiry guy with incredible energy and enthusiasm. His background was the polar opposite of mine. His mother had been studying history in Warsaw when she came over to pick strawberries in Hereford (UK) one summer. She'd met his father while waiting for a bus. He was from Lisbon and worked in a chicken factory. Dan was an only child, brought up in a small rented flat in Hunderton (a run-down suburb of Hereford). He wasn't impressed by my parents' enormous wealth (my dad owned one of the biggest electric car plants in the USA). He thought it must be hard to be so rich when many Americans were impoverished. He was a paid-up member of the Labour party and was studying PPE (philosophy, politics and economics), hoping one day to be an MP. He believed it was more important to follow your beliefs than to be successful. I told him about the animal and bird sanctuary that Dad and I had created in the grounds of our home. Like me, he loved nature and was incensed that human greed was causing so much destruction of natural habitats around the world.

Besides his love of politics and nature, his other passion was rock climbing. He belonged to the university mountaineering club and had climbed in Snowdonia and the Peak District. At the beginning of our second year, we moved out of St John's College and lived in a rented flat in Jericho. These were the happiest months of my life. Never for a moment did I imagine this nirvana would be so short-lived.

In January 2030, his club was going ice climbing in Cervinia. He was embarrassed as he confessed that he'd never been abroad before. He couldn't afford the trip, so I said it was to be my Christmas present to him, and while we were there, I would teach him to ski. I knew he would feel uncomfortable in a hotel and so I rented a little private Airbnb apartment in the old part of Cervinia. We were lucky as high pressure had settled over the Alps. Each night there was a hard frost, and dawn would reveal sparkling snow and bright blue skies. Dan would slip out of bed in the dark as they needed to start the ice climbs at first light to be safely off them before the ice melted. He returned in time for us to grab a quick bite before hitting the ski slopes where we would laugh as he kept falling in a heap of slushy snow. In the evening, we would sit on our balcony enjoying a cold beer and watch the Matterhorn glow red with the last rays of the day.

On the sixth day, by coffee time, it was warm enough for me to sit on the balcony in a T-shirt; apparently a 'Foehn' wind was blowing from the south. I feared that the snow would be very sticky by the time Dan returned. He was late for lunch and didn't answer his cell phone. By 3 pm, I was really worried. Soon after, a *polizia* car pulled into our narrow street.

That was the instant my life fell apart. The policewoman ːd to be compassionate, but there was no kind way of telling ː that Dan had died in a terrible accident. They'd all been ped up. Dan was the fourth and final climber. He had been ːsting on a narrow rock ledge as Ralph (who was leading) vas just cresting the top of the frozen waterfall. Ralph had ːo strike three times with his ice axe to get a good purchase. With his final attempt, there'd been an ominous crack and then the other climbers reported a surreal experience of falling while still attached to the ice with their crampons and axes. They'd all landed in a deep snowdrift, bruised and shaken but nothing broken. Tragically, Dan had been yanked by his rope and catapulted across the ravine and smashed into a rock face on the far side. His helmet had completely imploded and by the time the others reached him, he was long dead.

I collapsed. I don't think I actually fainted but my mind went blank, unable to assimilate the full horror of what had happened. I was vaguely aware of being encouraged to drink some *genepi* and hot black coffee. Thankfully, the police called a doctor who injected me with a sedative. I felt myself go hazy and blacked out. I woke with a horrible thick muzzy head; the dreadful reality flooded back. Guilt overwhelmed me, as Dan would never have come if I hadn't paid for everything. In the background, I kept hearing a muffled banging. Eventually, it dawned on me that someone was knocking at the door downstairs. I opened the door to find Mom standing there with arms ready to enfold me. I've never been so thankful to let her take over. I hadn't met Dan's parents. We'd been so immersed in our studies and love for each other that I had never found time to go to Hereford. I had his address, of course, and Mom phoned and told them she'd arranged return flights and a hotel for them. This will sound terrible but I forgot about them after that.

My parents' love helped me more than the inevitable counselling sessions. St John's College was understanding and said I could take leave for as long as I needed. Little by little, I came to terms with my loss and vowed to dedicate my life to aiding the poor and the environment in memory of Dan.

I returned to Oxford a couple of weeks late for term. My period was late but I knew that stress would frequently cause this and wasn't concerned. A few weeks later, when I started to feel nauseous, I bought a pregnancy testing kit. I have to confess that my first reaction to the positive test was one of horror. I wanted to achieve so much! What a waste of my life. Gradually, it dawned on me; this gift of new life was Dan's legacy and would be far more important than anything else I might aspire to. I knew then that I would keep and love this unborn child. I phoned Mom. She was overjoyed. She said that having a grandchild would give her life meaning. Petra was born at thirty-eight weeks in late September. She was cute, almost bald save for a few wispy pale hairs on her head, whereas the rest of her body was covered in fine brown hair that I learnt was called lanugo. She was slender like Dan but had my blue eyes. I loved her to bits, and great waves of warmth spread through me as her tiny lips latched on. My enormous engorged breasts threatened to smother her as she fed. Reluctantly, I weaned her onto a bottle so Mom could look after her as I returned for my final year at Oxford.

When Petra was two, I received a card from Dan's aunt informing me that Dan's parents had both died in a car crash. I know I should have felt sad or at least guilty that I hadn't even told them of Petra's existence, but in truth, I was relieved that I could now honestly tell Petra that her only close living relatives were my family.

Mom also looked after Petra while I completed my PhD at the AI department at Massachusetts Institute of Technology (MIT). I became acquainted with many postgrads in both AI and robotics and was determined to make use of these connections after receiving my doctorate.

Mom, Dad, Petra and I celebrated with a weekend together on Bonefish Cay (our private island in the Bahamas). On Saturday evening, while Mom put Petra to bed, Dad poured me a daiquiri.

"What are your plans now?"

"I want to continue my research in AI. I know loads of brilliant people who've been at the cutting edge of droids and robotic technology. I would dearly love to create a company that would produce and market these. I believe we could be world leaders very quickly."

"That's my girl, self-deprecating as ever! I like your style. You'll need to attract experience from other companies. Your friends are no doubt brilliant, but you'll need people who are business-savvy. Suppose I loan you ten billion dollars with no interest for the first two years. The banks should then look favourably upon you should you need to borrow more."

I wasn't expecting such generosity even though I was an only child! I bought a site just south of Anderson Lake in Silicon Valley. With good salaries and fantastic facilities, I was able to attract the brightest and best from around the world to join my contacts from MIT. I called the company Xantec. It took us a couple of years for our humanoid robots (we call them Xan-droids) to be the market leader. I'd taken personal charge of our AI development team. We used simulated axonal connections which grew stronger or withered as the 'brain' learnt. I was almost certain that this artificial brain was the most advanced form of AI on the planet, and we kept our methodology strictly confidential. I wanted to be the first person to crack the conundrum of making economically viable fusion power. I set my artificial brain the task of finding a molecule that would act as a catalyst to enable fusion of deuterium and tritium at a manageable temperature. (Until then, fusion had only been achieved at impractically high temperatures.) It came up with europium sulphate which has a most unusual structure. My fusion experts managed to get hold of a tiny amount. (It always was incredibly rare and expensive.) Amazingly, it worked! Of course, this had to be kept absolutely secret as it would potentially enable us to produce limitless cheap energy. I therefore needed to find a large deposit of europa. The other problem I'd been trying to solve was the overheating of my synthetic 'brain'. Even with advanced cooling fans which blew air over liquid nitrogen, it could only be switched on for a couple of hours at a time.

For the last three years, I've been working on a new form of AI using actual brain cells. This work had to be kept under wraps as it wasn't legal. I persuaded a gynaecologist to collect some of my eggs as I told her I wanted more children but didn't have a partner at present. I said I would store them as we had perfect storage facilities at our lab. This wasn't strictly legitimate, but she trusted me. I then persuaded one of my best friends from my Stanford days to donate fresh sperm. I told him I was working on a new male contraceptive. I used his sperm to fertilise three of my eggs and incubated them for five weeks. I put two into liquid nitrogen for long-term storage. From the remaining embryo, I extracted stem cells from the forming brain and incubated these with blood vessel stem cells[1]. I froze this brain when it was still only about a litre in volume. I planned one day to grow my daughter's 'brain' until it had the volume of an Olympic swimming pool. I named her Xanasa. She would need pumps and dialysis machines and so must grow where she would always live.

Petra was six and had turned into the most gorgeous, petite, fair-haired, rather shy girl. Her tutors told me that she was academically a year ahead of her peers.

I needed a place where my team could secretly mine europa and I could grow Xanasa's brain. The Chinese had found europa in Costa Rica but the President had refused them permission to mine it as he feared that they would harm the environment. I intended to try to persuade him to let my company move there.

———

I woke as the air hostess gently shook me. We were circling over lush dark green jungle as we came in to land at San José International. As Costa Rica had such a reputation for eco-friendliness, I was surprised by the smog hanging over the city. I was whisked through the capital to the edge of the western suburbs, where the President had invited me for an informal discussion at his home. I was amazed to find myself at an ordinary house without any obvious guards.

Juan Gonzalez anticipated my arrival and met me between hibiscus hedges that lined his front path. He was diminutive! I know I'm large, even for an American woman, but he can't have been more than five foot tall! He had greying hair, but his dark brown eyes sparkled like a child's. His soft, caring face lit up whenever he smiled or laughed, which he was prone to do. He took me to his back lawn where we talked under the shade of a tree that was covered in bright yellow flowers. The whole area was infused with scent from gardenia bushes. Brightly coloured birds sparred over fruit and grains that had been left out for them. Two malachite-green humming birds squabbled over an ornamental banana flower. This was my idea of heaven.

Fortunately, he'd done his research and knew about the 'animal sanctuary' that I'd started as a child. He also knew that Xantec had already donated generously to the National Parks of Costa Rica. We talked about my plans and I promised that if we were given permission to mine europa, we would provide his country with free electricity. Within five years, we would also provide free electric vehicles for his people on a car-scrappage basis.

"I've no idea how you could possibly achieve this without damaging the forest, but if your technical team can reassure me, then I hope we can come to some arrangement."

We spent another hour talking about his country's need for better hospitals, education and insulated houses in the mountains. I said that in time we would like to help him achieve these dreams.

I flew home hoping that I'd finally found a place where I could fulfil the vows that I'd made after Dan's death.

ZILGRIM MCMANUS
WRITING FROM 2049 TO 2058

Fourteen years later

My college campus was a remarkable creation of teak and glass built over a bay on an island off the west coast of Costa Rica. In the restaurants and social areas, we could watch the colourful reef fish swimming just beneath the glass floor.

Everyone studied psychology, history and the art of government. The brainy students chose between science, engineering, robotics, artificial intelligence, law and medicine. I studied sport science and combat, which allowed me many hours each week for fitness training. There were about 20,000 students aged between eighteen and twenty. When the sea was calm, I would ride my wave-skimmer home. My parents (Ethan and Avril) had built a sensational home cut into towering red cliffs. The large living area has a ten-metre plate glass window cantilevered fifty metres above the ocean, providing magnificent views of the sun setting over the Pacific. My parents' lives hadn't always been easy. My twin sister, Elli, had been brain damaged at birth. Even though we were twins, Mom had demanded a natural birth.

After I was delivered, Elli became stuck. It must have been very hard for my parents, not only having to bring up twins, but one of them was late to be potty trained and indeed was slow at everything. Mom had given up work to look after us. We moved to Costa Rica when we were six, and my parents had a small house and two women from the local village to do housework and look after us. It was then that Max Spitzen (our leader) decreed that all Xantec employees should have large families. Eight other siblings came along in quick succession and our new home was built.

When I was seventeen, Mom and Dad allowed me to move into my own apartment and gave me my own droid for company. I remember my excitement as she arrived. She was completely hidden by holographic wrapping. My hand trembled as I reached for the button to reveal her. Instantly, she appeared. I couldn't believe my luck. Standing before me was the likeness of a beautiful twenty-year-old Spanish girl with deep penetrating brown eyes. She wore a jasmine necklace which gave off a beautiful perfume. I called her Jasmine, which I soon shortened to Jas. She greeted me rather formally, saying, "I hope to be of service to you, sir." She turned out to be a fantastic cook and has always kept my home spotless, ready for friends. She now knows me far better than my parents. At night, she used to lie on the floor at the end of my bed, rather like a well-loved dog. If I wanted a cuddle or to have sex, she would join me in bed. She has a body temperature of 36.5 degrees and is soft and cuddly. I preferred sex with my fellow students or with one of the Costa Rican girls as they'd chosen me, whereas Jas had no option.

The person who I really fancied was Petra, Max's daughter. She is nothing like her mother, who is cold and intimidating. Max has been a close friend of my parents ever since they all went to Stanford together. I gather from Mom that Dad was infatuated with her when they first went to college, but he gave up when he realised she was in a different social league. Max had always been a natural leader. In those days, she was wild and held the most outrageous hedonistic parties. They say this all changed when she met the love of her life at Oxford. He died before Petra was born. When they all met up again at MIT, she was a serious, hardworking single mother. Petra is stunning with fine sun-bleached blonde hair and sparkling blue irises flecked with tiny white streaks. She's shorter than me and as slim as a sylph; such a contrast to her tall, muscular mother. Petra was in the year ahead of me at college even though we're roughly the same age. She's brilliant but very shy. She was allowed no privacy. Her mother insisted that a bodyguard was with her at all times, even waiting outside when she needed the bathroom. Occasionally, we used to meet in the canteen for lunch. I'd an inkling that she might be keen on me, but no one was allowed to date her, so it made no difference. I hadn't seen her during my last year at college, as she'd already left to start work.

Then, two weeks before college finished for the year, Petra turned up under the pretext of visiting her old tutors. We met in the canteen. As we were leaving, she passed me a book. I thought this odd as she knew I wasn't an avid reader. I took it home that night wondering if she was trying to turn me into an intellectual. (*Little chance of that*, I thought.) I opened it and noticed that the cover didn't sit flat. Inside, I found a letter.

Dear Zig, (that's what everyone calls me)

I hope you won't mind me writing and forgive me if I've read you wrong. If you're interested in me (I hope you are), I've discovered somewhere we could meet. I think you know our private beach. (Actually, I know you do because I've seen you watching me from your wave-skimmer beyond the boundary patrolled by my guards.) Mom has created a special room for me inside a cave. I use this for changing or reading in the heat of the day. The great thing is that my bodyguards never enter it as they believe that I can be safely guarded from the beach. I thought that was the only way in, until yesterday when I explored the back of the cave and found a very narrow gap that I could squeeze through. No one of an ordinary build could possibly get through there, and certainly my guards wouldn't stand a chance. The narrow dark channel steadily opened up and then I noticed a glimmer of light and smelt fresh air. A little further on, I came to an area full of vines and small trees where a sinkhole must have caused the roof of the cave to collapse. It is about fifteen metres deep. I could see a large wild fig tree growing near the edge. I guess it must be about fifty metres from the shore. If you would like to meet me, I'll be there at midday this Saturday. Of course, you'll need a rope and climbing gear, but I'm sure the drop would not be a barrier for you. Hope to see you. Petra.

I couldn't believe my luck, but I was worried that her fiercely protective mother might somehow discover our tryst. I was filled with excitement and fear in equal measure. However, I would risk anything to spend some time with Petra. I was fascinated to discover what lay behind her mysterious veneer.

Saturday was even hotter and stickier than usual. The rope and caving equipment was heavier than I'd expected. I had to fight my way through the jungle for the last half-mile. I arrived near the place that she'd described bathed in perspiration. I couldn't see the sink hole anywhere. It was dark under the dense high canopy. Eventually, I spotted a massive strangler fig tree that was full of chattering birds and spider monkeys enjoying the ripe figs. I still couldn't see the sinkhole. I parted some of the undergrowth and nearly fell to my death as it was right beneath me. A minute later, I had tied the rope to the tree, removed my sweaty shirt and was abseiling through the hole. Fortunately, my Petzl stop was in good working order as I was soon abseiling down the walls, thankful for the cooler air. I couldn't see the bottom but was confident that Petra's estimate would be correct. I felt some ferns brush my legs and almost immediately was standing on solid rock.

"I knew I could rely on you," came a soft voice from the dark.

My eyes slowly adjusted and I saw Petra approaching, diffident at first, but as she saw my smile she opened her arms to embrace me. I felt overwhelmed with delight as her cool arms clasped me tight.

"We don't have long as Mom said she'll meet me for a swim in an hour. She's the only person allowed into my cave. I hope you don't mind us staying here as you couldn't possibly get through the gap."

So our first 'date' was enjoyed in a gloomy, dark sinkhole standing on slippery, wet rocks! I was ecstatic as she told me how she had dreamt of this moment from the day that I first started college twenty months ago. We kissed and I could feel every movement as she explored my body. My initial excitement waned when she said her mother wouldn't allow her to have boyfriends.

"Mom says that my research is too important for boys to get in the way. I do love her, but sometimes I wish she would relax and let me have fun!"

Petra promised to come to my twentieth birthday party which was arranged for the week after the end of term. She warned me that we would have to be incredibly circumspect as she would be chaperoned by her bodyguard, who would report everything back to her mother.

"When you have your Xan-link implanted they will also operate on you and insert a chip[2] around your right femoral artery. This is detectable by satellite unless the individual is deep within a thick-walled building or a cave. You need to know this because Mom will be able to track your movements if she suspects that we're trying to meet."

My hour was nearly up and, feeling demoralised, I started to prusik (a climbing technique I had learnt at college) back up my dangling rope.

———

Sometimes, I envied my twin sister Elli as she didn't have to attend boring college lectures, but most of the time, I felt sorry for her as her life was pretty dull. To celebrate our joint twentieth birthday, Elli had a small family gathering in the afternoon, while I'd been allowed to invite all my friends to our barn at the edge of the jungle where Crestor (my favourite band) played.

My parents had been wonderful. They'd provided loads of spicy food, all manner of drinks and had gone to stay with friends for the night, taking Elli and all our younger siblings with them. The noise was overwhelming as our bodies pulsed to the beat of the colossal speakers. I kept looking out for Petra but feared that her mother had intervened. She arrived about an hour late, sandwiched between two massive bodyguards. I offered them all drinks, vainly hoping her minders might let their hair down. Petra sipped her wine as the sober guards watched our every move. We danced, but Petra kept her distance. Anyone watching wouldn't have thought we were special friends, but she whispered such words of love that I was left in no doubt about her feelings. I hated her mother for being so unreasonable.

She whispered, "I must leave you now and dance with others to confuse the bogeymen."

I rejoined my friends and tried to avoid looking at Petra. I spotted her dancing closely with another man and felt intensely jealous, wondering if I was being duped.

Soon after this, she departed. I drank far too much trying to blot out my frustration and suspicion. I'm ashamed to admit that after dancing and flirting with a girl called Maria, we must have ended up back in my rooms as I woke with her thanking me as she got out of bed to return to her village.

Two days later, my Xan-link was to be implanted. Mom said, "It's nothing to worry about, Zig. You'll have a small operation where a radio transmitter is positioned under your brain connecting it to Xanasa's brain. After about a week, the bruising around your eyes will settle. In due course, you'll be left with a minute scar between your nose and left eye. Only Commissioners (the adult offspring of Xantec employees) have one. It gives you instant access to Xanasa's brain and stored information. It will also enable you to calculate and be fluent in any language."

I was beginning to get the feeling that this 'perfect' world that I lived in was being extensively monitored in secret ways. I didn't like the sound of being permanently linked to Xanasa. Would she be reading my thoughts and dreams and passing this information on to Max, who would therefore uncover my desire for Petra? Could Xanasa control me? I knew the surgeon who was going to perform the op as he'd coached the water polo team when I'd been captain. We'd become good friends. I persuaded him to fit a switch in my Xan-link so that I could turn it off. He agreed but said I must NEVER tell anyone, and warned me that Xanasa would know instantly if I did turn it off. To disconnect my Xan-link, I would need to place my X-talk[*3] on my forehead for one second and then remove it for five seconds and repeat this twice.

I knew my link would only become active once the bruising around the nerve junctions had settled down. During this week, I was required to choose between five different careers:

1. Administrators. These were involved in strategy and management. Twelve were chosen by Max to form the Board that effectively governed the Central and South American Region (CASAR). My dad was a member of the Board.
2. Doctors/Surgeons and Judges.
3. Engineers/Architects.
4. Researchers at Costa Rica Central (CRC). Petra and my mother worked in this division.
5. Reactors. They worked with armed droids and cloned soldiers sorting out any disturbance or serious crimes in the whole of CASAR.

There was never any doubt in my mind that I would be a 'Reactor' as I wasn't clever enough for the other roles. I would only start work once my link was switched on.

———

Dad invited me up to his hideaway which he'd built high in the jungle canopy. He used it to escape from his job and high-tech life. He'd filled it with retro gear – binoculars, telescopes and cameras for observing birds and other creatures. I suspected that the comfy chair was used for sleeping much of the time when he escaped there.

He said that in order to grasp the importance of my job as a reactor, he would give me a brief résumé of the history of the organisation. "CASAR was once a collection of relatively poor countries riddled with corruption, drugs and violence. The USA had been the destination for much of their drug trade. Fourteen years ago, Max and her company had been invited into Costa Rica by the President, and within six years, they'd transformed the country into a thriving success story. This was due mainly to our fusion reactor providing free electricity. We also devised a toothed tunnelling device that used industrial diamond teeth which were replaced automatically as they wore down (called shark-moles). These laid steel tunnels as they went. As our engineers extracted europa from inside the mountain, the slag was washed down these tunnels and created a new island in the Caribbean. On this, we built factories that produced all the electric vehicles, robots and droids. These were provided free to the people of Costa Rica and were also sold internationally. Shark-moles were also used to create a nationwide hyperloop[*4] system which linked all the major cities of Costa Rica. Modern homes, schools and hospitals were built. The working week was cut to thirty hours, allowing the Costa Ricans time to attend to their gardens, fiestas and other hobbies. The smog of San José disappeared, wildlife thrived and tourism boomed. Once the neighbouring countries saw how successful Costa Rica had become, they invited us to assist them. This is how we've gradually become responsible for the whole of CASAR."

He concluded, "I don't mind if you forget this history, but there is one thing I do want you to remember. When you go into action, by all means take droid soldiers with you as decoys, but never go into danger without at least two clone soldiers."

I wanted to make the most of my last carefree days. My best friend, Charco, (who was a month younger than me) was free, and so we flew in our drones to the Cocos Island where my dad has a live-aboard diving vessel. My droid, Jas, and his droid, Cooli, came along to look after us. The dive and sailing droids always kept everything in perfect condition in case Dad arrived unannounced. We enjoyed swimming with hammerheads and then ventured deep into a volcanic tunnel which led to a secret vibrant coral reef in a shallow cove. It was a brilliant holiday but at night I couldn't sleep as I felt guilty about waking up with Maria after my party, and I yearned to see Petra again.

I'll never forget the moment my 'link' was switched on. Suddenly I only had to think about something I wanted to know and the answer appeared as if by magic. Even mathematics became simple.

As Dad and I climbed into a drone to take us to the hyperloop station, I asked, "What was the point of college when our Xan-links are so brilliant?"

"It's a fair point, but knowing and understanding an answer are two different things."

We arrived at Costa Rica Central (CRC), and Dad introduced me to my boss Sinto (who had the rather grand title of 'Ambassador to Chile'). He showed me round. First, he showed me the Great Hall. This gigantic hall was able to accommodate 250,000 people. It was rarely used. At present, there were only 140,000 Commissioners, but this number was growing steadily by 5,000 each year.

He led me deep into the mountain down a corridor cut into solid rock. We had to prove our identities using iris scanning, fingerprint and facial recognition to gain access through a stout steel door. Finally, an enormous heavy lead door opened hydraulically for us, and we were admitted into Xanasa's presence. I felt my skin prickle as I peered through bulletproof glass to watch blood being pumped through large transparent pipes that fed into her enormous stainless steel enclosure. Droids were monitoring the sterile liquid glucose containers that connected to these tubes. I was stunned to think that this living brain was the main reason that half a billion people lived in peace and comfort.

Sinto said, "Her vast memory banks are cooled deep inside the mountain. Science and calculation are simple for her, but she is less good at deciphering human motivations. She finds ethical, emotional and political decisions difficult. That's why Commander Spitzen and her board of advisers are so important."

I was shown the lift which led to the research areas and fusion reactor, but these were off-limits to me.

We then went down to the coast to see the robot-controlled factories on the artificial island. This was still growing as slag continued to be washed down from the mines. Off the southern coast of the island, I was taken to a lift where Commissioner visitors were allowed to descend in glass spheres to a depth of twenty metres. There I marvelled at corals that had been artificially seeded onto sunken rocks thirteen years ago and were now teeming with colourful creatures. On the west side of the island, I was shown a fenced-off area where the army barracks was sited. Sinto explained how the clones, who lived there, came into existence.

"Xantec was asked by the USA to investigate whether there were any blood or DNA changes that could explain why some soldiers exhibited more bravery and loyalty than others. Of course, there were no such simple explanations. We were given many fresh blood samples linked to specific soldiers with their known characteristics attached. One happened to be from a highly intelligent navy seal who had been awarded the 'medal of honour' after dying trying to save a colleague in Afghanistan in 2035. We used cells taken from his blood to produce clones. These embryos were then carried by paid surrogates. There are now thousands of these clones who are our policemen and soldiers. You'll often be on missions with droid soldiers and clones. Never rely on droids as they can't react quickly enough to rapidly changing situations. They are expendable as they come off the production line every day. The clones are human and take twenty years to develop and train. You'll not be popular if you lose any of these great warriors."

"That's enough for one day. You'll be in Chile for three days from tomorrow."

I returned home full of enthusiasm. I enjoyed a glass of Malbec with Dad as we discussed my future as a 'reactor'. I told him I was going to Chile for three days to get a feel for the country. He gave me his take on Chile.

He concluded, "Enjoy your introduction, Zig, but Mom and I worry that you will soon have to deal with some serious criminals. Try to find some clones you trust and then form a close bond with them for your mutual protection."

I retired to my apartment and experimented with my Xan-link. If I thought hard about a place, vivid pictures would appear. I could zoom in and out at will. I guessed that Xanasa was connected to hundreds of geostationary satellites with very powerful cameras.

I concentrated on my friend Charco, but nothing happened, so perhaps it only worked on humans if they had a chip inserted. I tried Petra; blank. I guessed I wasn't able to spy on other Commissioners. I then tried Maria. I felt I was prying; but curiosity overcame guilt. I wish that I hadn't looked as I was overwhelmed with shame as a handsome man handed her a crying child which she proceeded to breastfeed. Why on earth had she agreed to come back to my flat that night? Had I forced her? Was she afraid of a Commissioner's power? I was angry with myself for getting so drunk that I'd no recollection of the latter part of that evening. I vowed never to get so drunk again, and I would never sleep with non-Commissioners in case the girls felt coerced.

My thoughts drifted to Petra and I wondered what she was doing. Of course, I couldn't contact her over my Xan-link as her mother would be onto that in a flash. I longed for her to get in touch. I could only wait as she understood the intricacies of the CRC surveillance system. It was with sadness and remorse that I requested Jas to cuddle me as I drifted off to sleep.

The following day, Sinto told me that I would be staying with three different Chilean families to help me understand the people that I would be trying to protect.

The first night, I stayed with a wheat farmer in the Lake District. They welcomed me into their modern comfortable house. They were very pleased to have free electricity. Mr Fernandez continued, "Before Xantec came to Chile, we used to live in an old rustic farmhouse. It may have looked quaint, but the roof leaked and it was draughty and cold. Thanks to the new GM seed, we now produce more wheat than ever and we only use half of our land. We plan to create a wildlife reserve on the remainder. This area has a river running into a lake situated near the mountains in the east. We will eventually build eco-lodges and welcome tourists to this park."

"Do you have any children?" I asked.

"Just Christobal; he's eight. He has to travel fifty kilometres to school twice a week. The rest of the time, he attends a virtual school. He'll be home soon. It's a shame that they have to travel so far, but most of our friends are only having one or two children. All the local schools have closed."

I checked with Xanasa and indeed, on average, the population of CASAR was falling by 2% a year. The ageing population were now largely looked after by droids, who of course did most of the menial work as well. Factories were largely automated, so society could cope. However, in these isolated places, I thought it must be hard for children to find enough friends to play with.

The second night, I stayed with a family whose menfolk had once been fishermen in Valparaiso before the fish stocks plummeted. The old town had been lovingly restored and was now a tourist mecca. Their thirty-year-old son, Juan, had upgraded his trawler to take tourists whale watching and sport fishing. The father ran a tilapia farm. Both businesses were thriving.

Mrs Herrera complained, "It's all very well for them to be out happily enjoying themselves, but where are my grandchildren? I wish Juan would find himself a wife."

My final night was with the President who lived in a tall tower block overlooking the metropolis of Santiago. From his front room, the snow-capped Andes appeared to be gold tinted, reflecting the evening sun. I felt privileged to have the benefit of his assessment of the country's progress. He felt genuinely grateful for the help that Xantec had provided.

"I love to watch the different seasons with the sun providing light shows on the tops of our lovely mountains. Before Xantec arrived, they were a ghostly presence, glimpsed, if you were lucky, through thick smog. Xantec has been good for us, but I fear we are getting lazy and fat as droids and robots do all our hard work. I fear for our health and self-esteem."

I returned to CRC and reported back to Sinto. He said that obesity was a growing problem throughout CASAR. Xanasa and the Board had decreed that by 2053, all roads in CASAR would be converted into walking and cycle tracks. The roads would be sealed in recycled plastic mixed with rubber. The Board's plan was to scrap electric cars, forcing people to use bicycles for local journeys. There would be drone taxis to take them to hyperloop stations. Processed food would be low in fat, sugar and carbohydrates. The Board hoped that these measures, combined with intensive education, might reverse the obesity epidemic.

The next day was a harsh introduction into working as a 'reactor'. A new drone factory in the Atacama Desert had been attacked by protesters. The droids at the factory had repaired the surrounding fence and had the line functioning once more, but the perpetrators hadn't been apprehended. The ambassador replayed me satellite images overlaid with the chip locations of the vandals. Initially, they sped off towards Chacarilla in two 4x4s. They stopped in the middle of nowhere, and within two minutes, their chips disappeared. During the previous night, Xanasa had used infra-red imaging from space. Although many animals showed up in the area, there were no humans.

"Something of a puzzle, Zig. I've found in the past that a reactor on the ground can often sort this out. How do you fancy taking a look?"

It turned out to be a rhetorical question. As there were three saboteurs, I was advised to take twenty droid soldiers. Remembering my dad's advice, I asked for and received permission to take two clone soldiers as well. I was assigned Gregor and Sandy who, of course, looked identical, distinguishable only by their name tags. We took the hyperloop to Iquique. As I travelled, Xanasa informed me that there were no known caves or mine shafts in the area. We took off in three drones and were soon landing in a swirl of sand. Suffocating heat enveloped us as we left the air-conditioned aircraft. The 4x4s were still there, but empty. The whole area was barren and deserted. I remembered from my history lessons that in the Vietnam War, Americans had sometimes stepped over camouflaged tunnel entrances and were mercilessly killed from behind. If there were deep tunnels, then their chips wouldn't be detectable. I set the droids to bang the area with their gun butts to see if they heard metal which might be manhole covers under the sand. The clones clothed in their 'stealth' suits (which took on the appearance of whatever lay behind them) looked like sand ghosts watching over us. They'd chosen to stay by the drones. Sweating like a pig, I went back to collect ground-sonar equipment. I was just lifting it when I heard gunfire, and four droids were turned into a load of scrap. I hadn't expected automatic fire. Sandy shouted at me to get into the drone. Gregor grabbed my outstretched hand and hauled me in. With maximum thrust, we were soon high above the area, watching helplessly as the rest of the droids were mowed down. I could now see some bushes at the base of a cliff that had previously been hidden by a dune. My database said there was some limestone in the area, and I surmised there might be a cave, possibly caused by an underground stream that still fed the bushes. I scrambled to get my own stealth suit on as I asked Sandy how we should deal with this. He clearly deferred to Gregor who answered.

"No problem, sir, we'll land at the top of the cliff. You circle round one way and Sandy will take the other side. As you both pin them down, I'll abseil down the cliff and throw a sonic bomb into what you believe will be a cave."

Shit! I wished now that I hadn't sounded so certain about the cave. I didn't want to muck up my first mission.

I'd no choice, "Okay, let's do it."

We jumped out as the drone hovered perilously close to the edge of the cliff. As my feet hit the ground, Sandy was already circling downwards and left. I sprinted off, realising that we needed to open fire simultaneously. I cursed as a thorn bush ripped my leg as I charged down the steep slope. I'd never been so fired up in my life. I stopped and carefully rounded the base of the cliff. I could just make out a dusky yellow spectral presence crouched down beyond what I hoped was a cave entrance. Behind the bushes were barricades, on top of which I could see three gun barrels pointing down to where the droids were still burning. Acrid smoke filled the air as their 'skin' smouldered. Binoculars and some black hair appeared just behind the barrier. High above, a sky blue phantom was starting down the cliff. I gave the signal and a barrage of fire splintered the barricades. The guns disappeared. We continued to fire until Gregor was above the cave entrance, and watched as he threw a canister inside. There was a second of absolute silence and then a deafening boom shook the ground, sending rocks crashing down the cliff. Dust filled the air. I found it hard to breathe and my eyes were full of grit. I was deafened by the blast but forced myself towards the swirling dust that was spewing out of the cave. Sandy and I rounded the barricades. As the dust slowly settled, we saw the shapes of dun-coloured limbs poking out from a pile of rocks and debris. Clearing the rocks, we found the three men, along with their ancient AK47s. They all had dribbles of dusty blood coming from their ears. Two of them looked relatively intact. The third had a shaft of wood sticking out of his right calf. Without a moment's pause, Gregor had whipped this out and stemmed the rhythmical spurting of arterial blood with a tourniquet. He injected him with antibiotics.

"Sir, we need to get them cuffed. They'll wake in a few minutes."

Sure enough, they woke soon after but were completely dazed, deaf and unable to support themselves. The clones were immensely strong and soon manoeuvred them into the drones.

———

Back at CRC, Sinto praised me. "A good first day's work; I'm sure you know that we'll deduct the cost of those droids from your pay cheque."

I was incensed by this callous injustice, until I noticed a glimmer of a smile.

"Get yourself home; you've earnt your xanacea. Make sure you're fully awake tomorrow."

I'd heard about xanacea, which was said to be the most awesome mind-blowing drug, and which was distributed after dangerous missions. It was held securely in CRC and ambassadors had to sign it out. My Xan-link informed me that it attached to opiate receptors and simultaneously blocked the reuptake of serotonin. I now understood what Dad had meant by getting information without being any the wiser.

That evening, I couldn't relax. Images of the terrifying destruction of the droids kept repeating as if on a continuous loop of film. I was apprehensive about taking xanacea. I requested Jas to stay with me in case I became ill. I settled down with some music to discover how I would react. Absolutely nothing! I was enjoying the music and was trying to decide whether to turn in early, when I was overcome with the certainty that I was loved and valued by my parents, siblings and friends. Suddenly I was transported to the banks of a crystal clear river filled with beautiful fish that cascaded down a waterfall, plummeting into a deep, cool pool surrounded by jungle. Petra lay naked on a bed of moss in a nearby shelter and beckoned me to join her. I woke with Jas shaking me hard, saying I would be late for work. She gave me brist (xanacea's antidote) and coffee to wake me up.

No hangover! Indeed, I was brimming with enthusiasm. If I get xanacea after each dangerous mission, bring them on!

At CRC, they'd given the prisoners veritax. This induces sleep and causes their brains to relive the pivotal events of the last three days as if the subjects were dreaming. While they sleep, a PET scan[5] of their brain function is taken. Xanasa interpreted the scans and was able to give us a good idea of what they'd been doing and their motives. It was a boring morning while we waited for the results, but it gave me a chance to get to know my colleagues. I was pleased to learn that Charco had been appointed to the Chilean division and would join us in a couple of weeks.

Xanasa's interpretation was ready. There was nothing that we didn't already know about the attack and the battle. However, we learnt that they were being forced to make the attack by the owner of an electric car plant who was afraid that the use of taxi-drones would put him out of business. They'd been too afraid to tell us as this man was holding their cousin hostage. They were in no doubt that their cousin would die if they grassed on their bullying employer.

Once they were fully awake, Sinto interrogated them. He invited me to sit in. He was surprisingly kind and sympathetic. I'd expected him to throw the book at them for destroying our droids and trying to kill me.

"I fully understand why you did this. If someone threatened to kill my cousin, I would've done the same. We'll set you free with no punishment as long as you help us capture your tyrannical boss and free your cousin."

"That'll be impossible. Our cousin is held in a secure cellar with a steel door. There are always four armed guards in the house and two are always awake."

Carlos Santos, a renowned bully, was the owner of the car business. They pinpointed his house in the hills overlooking Santiago. From satellite images, we could see a modern monstrosity surrounded by a considerable garden. Sinto thanked them and told the droid guards to fetch them whatever food they wanted.

Back in the Chilean control room, we observed a holographic image of the house and grounds. It was a huge rectangle made of steel and bulletproof glass. There were only four chips (meaning four legal adults) showing up in the house. Either one of the guards was absent, or the cellar with its reinforced ceilings and door blocked transmission from the chip that belonged to our prisoners' cousin. On balance, we thought the latter was most likely. It was lunchtime and Carlos was probably elsewhere. There was no time to lose as he must know that we'd captured his saboteurs, and their cousin would now be in imminent danger.

"Would you like to take this on, Zig?"

"Sure, as long as Gregor and Sandy are free to help me."

I'd decided to dispense with droids as I feared they would just get in the way. I radioed ahead to have a suitably equipped drone waiting for us. As we were approaching Santiago, Sinto, who had remained in CRC, informed me that a fifth chip had appeared on his screen. Ten minutes later, the drone delivered us to the grounds of Carlos's house. It was a very clear night and surprisingly chilly. We switched on our night vision glasses and with our gear on our backs, we crept silently towards the house. From my Xan-link, I'd been checking on the movements of the chips. Downstairs, two were stationary and so I guessed they were asleep; the other two only moved occasionally and must be the duty guards. Upstairs, there was another motionless chip, which I hoped was Carlos, asleep. We would need two access points. Gregor climbed onto Sandy's shoulders and I passed up the laser cutter. This silently melted the steel wall adjacent to where we reckoned Carlos was sleeping. We repeated this downstairs, hoping that the guards wouldn't smell the molten metal. We heard a scrape of a chair through the hole we'd made. I feared for a moment that the guards had rumbled us, but then we heard the unmistakable slap of cards hitting a flat surface. This time, I stood on Sandy's shoulders; Gregor, meanwhile, was by the ground floor hole. We slipped sonic bombs through the two holes simultaneously and sprinted towards the bushes. We were deafened as the blast shattered the bulletproof glass.

Sandy was smiling. "We brought the most powerful ones, sir; we didn't want any of them feeling like a battle."

We carefully climbed through the remains of one of the ground floor windows and soon had all five safely cuffed. I left Sandy guarding them. Gregor and I took the key from one of the guards and let ourselves into the cellar. The stench was disgusting. It was pitch-black until we threw the switch. The poor guy was sobbing, lying curled up in a foetal position on the cold, damp floor. Thanks to Xanasa's instant translation, I was fluent in Spanish and was soon able to calm him with reassuring promises. We wrapped him in a warm blanket and our drone delivered him to his family in Santiago a few minutes later.

As we climbed into our hyperloop pod, I was on the point of collapse due to exhaustion. I asked, "How can we guard these guys on our way back to CRC?"

"No problem, sir. Sandy and I have already taken amphetamine. We'll be fine; you take this tablet and we'll make sure you get home safely."

I woke in my bed with no recollection of how I got there. Jas said that Gregor had carried me in.

There was a brief trial the following day at CRC. Carlos Santos was sentenced to life in the maximum security prison. The henchmen, who were the guards at his residence, were also coerced by threats of violence to their families. They were given community service and were warned that they would be closely monitored for the foreseeable future. They were escorted home, along with the three 'saboteurs' of the factory who were not charged at all.

I was given a week off. Jas gave me an enquiring look as she handed me a note that had been delivered by a girl from the nearby village. I opened it. It was typed: *Meet me, usual time and place tomorrow*. I wondered how Petra knew I had time off, but I really didn't care. I was thrilled to think that she still wanted to see me.

As I forced my way through the undergrowth, I started to worry. I now knew how easy it was for Max to observe where my chip was located. Once I was underground, we would be safe. Petra embraced me as soon as my feet hit the ground. I so longed for us to be able to meet without all this subterfuge. When we finally disentangled ourselves, I told her my fears.

"As long as Mom doesn't suspect you, she won't be looking. Even she can't watch everyone! But she might set Xanasa a task of seeing if anyone repeatedly comes anywhere near our home. I think we'll have to find a different place to meet up. I can't say when, but I'll let you know."

With that, we parted, and I made my way home, wondering when the next secret message might be delivered. I was really enjoying my new life, but I'd been dealt a duff hand falling in love with someone I was forbidden to see. I spent the following week hanging out with Charco, telling him about the exciting life that was waiting for him once his Xan-link was working.

I was apprehensive when Max asked to see me as soon as I arrived back at CRC. I prepared my excuses and decided that I would promise to never see Petra again. Sweating nervously, I frantically tried to come up with some plausible explanation as to why I'd been hacking through the jungle near her home. I was shown into her office, which was flooded in light which came pouring through large windows, giving a bird's-eye view over the forest canopy. I was blown away by the beauty; so different from the artificial views that were used to brighten our offices. She was frowning as she read a report behind her large polished teak desk. I hated the way she controlled Petra but, for a moment, I felt sorry for her as she looked overburdened with worry. As I waited, I noticed a quiet hum at a frequency that I knew I'd heard before. Eventually, it clicked; it was the sound of the motors that pumped the blood around Xanasa's brain. We must be near Xanasa, and perhaps Max had a secret passage through the rock so she could reach Xanasa in an emergency.

"Thanks for coming in."

She wasn't shouting and didn't look angry. I didn't relax, as I'd heard how devious she could be.

"Should you ever breathe a word of what I'm about to tell you, including to your Mom and Dad, it'll be considered high treason. Do you understand me?"

"I do."

I began to relax as this didn't sound like a preamble for a dressing-down.

"Xanasa believes there's been a security leak. Ever since we discovered the secret to nuclear fusion, she has scanned all internet messages for the words europium sulphate. To begin with, there were occasional scientific references about the strange structure of this compound, but these gradually dwindled as supplies ran dry. This is thanks to our agents buying all the europa as soon as it comes on the market. Xanasa has just intercepted an encrypted email from the CIA asking the director of science to secure some europium sulphate ASAP."

She continued, "I guess that could be innocent, but why send it encrypted? Somehow, the CIA have got wind of how we've cracked fusion power. It's impossible for a foreign spy to have accessed this building. The only way in is via the hyperloop with its tight security. The jungle surrounding CRC is mined, and anyway, these are the only windows and they don't open. Drilling the rock would show on our seismograph recordings. There are turbines in the air vents but these are constantly working, and the air tunnels are monitored for movement by laser sensors. All the corridors are covered by CCTV. Water only comes through small-bore high pressure pipes. The cooling water for the fusion reactor which then takes away the slag never enters the building. It is sampled via a two-cm diameter channel which has been drilled through solid rock. Our sewage is liquefied and pumped out under high pressure through a ten-cm channel, also drilled through the rock."

"My conclusion is that someone with access to information about our fusion reactor has passed this on to the CIA. As you've only just joined us, you're the only person who couldn't possibly be involved. Hence, I need you to investigate this and try to work out who the traitor is. I'm the only person you can discuss this with. I'll adjust your Xan-link so that you'll have total access to Xanasa and all her surveillance. Any questions?"

"Do you have any suspicions?"

"Not really. I mean, what motive would someone have? All Commissioners have built their architect-designed houses with no expense spared. They've access to anything they want when they're off duty. No one has to worry about money or inheritance. Frankly, I'm at a loss to think of a motive. You'll work in the office adjacent to mine."

With that, I was dismissed and went next door to ponder this impossible task. There had to be some motive that Max hadn't thought of. Initially, I narrowed my suspects down to the engineers, researchers and the Board. They were the only Commissioners who had access to the fusion reactor plans, and without these, europium sulphate would be worthless. This still left 25,000 people so it really didn't help much. It occurred to me that the information must have been delivered face-to-face or at least by a handwritten note as otherwise Xanasa would have picked it up. I asked Xanasa to check which of the 25,000 had visited the USA last year. This reduced the number dramatically to 556. I then removed visits that were specifically for family funerals and I'd whittled it down to eighty-six.

The following morning, I told Max my line of thought, hoping she might be impressed. If she was, she hid it well. Ignoring my conclusions, she said, "I remembered last night that there was one person outside of our organisation who knew about europa. But I don't think he ever knew about the need for the sulphate compound. Anyway, you'd better check it out. He was the president of Costa Rica in 2035, Juan Gonzalez."

Xanasa informed me that he was in an old people's home, apparently suffering with dementia. I needed to confirm this in person. He was a charming, smiling little guy and, to begin with, I thought the nursing home ploy was a smokescreen. I soon changed my mind as he kept repeating the story about how he'd entertained Commander Spitzen in his garden. The nurses said he'd been seriously demented for five years. This put him in the clear.

I reported back. "We can forget Juan as he's been nursed with dementia for five years. I've had another idea. Suppose someone wanted to stage a coup? They might sell secrets to the USA in return for them invading CRC and killing you. They have enormous firepower, and their bunker-busting bombs would smash your bulletproof glass windows as if they were made of rice paper."

"Nice try! I should have mentioned that once Xanasa was fully functional, I contacted the US President and said that I would like to demonstrate her ability without causing any loss of life. He was intrigued and I suggested that he fire a ballistic missile into the Pacific and I would ask Xanasa to destroy it. He knew how far we were from Seattle and was confident it would land in the ocean before we could hit it. It took off and within a hundred metres it turned into a fireball. The video and explanation went viral. No country has ever threatened us because they know Xanasa can hack into any control system whatever cyber-protection and clever firewalls they've used."

Feeling humiliated, I went back to my room to think how I could pin it on one of the eighty-six suspects. The drug veritax was of no use as it only brought up memories from the last three days, and the leak had occurred prior to this. I could interrogate them, but it would be impossible to know whether they were lying. The evidence that lie detectors are effective is dubious.

That night, I thought of another possible motive. Could someone want to leave CASAR because of a terrible crime that was yet to be discovered? They might persuade a foreign government to give them asylum and a new identity in exchange for valuable information.

I suggested this to Max and for the first time I saw a glimmer of a smile! "I think you might be onto something there, Zig, check it out with our justice department. Take this signed letter to give you full access."

It was a small department. Crime in CASAR was rare, perhaps due to the intense surveillance. I spoke to the judge in charge of the Supreme Court. I showed him the eighty-six names and asked if he had any suspicions about them. He glanced through the list. With a quizzical look, he asked me how on earth a young lad like me was looking into the affairs of these important Commissioners. I told him I was not at liberty to say. At this, he left me, and I heard him speaking on the phone: "Max, have you really given this lad authority to investigate so widely?" I couldn't hear her reply.

"Very mysterious," I heard him mutter as he returned. "I'll keep this list overnight under lock and key. I'll ask my colleagues if they've heard any rumours and will let you know tomorrow."

The next day, he called me in.

"Not much, I'm afraid. One of your list was accused of murdering his wife, but there was no evidence. His alibi seemed sound, and anyway, that was four years ago. None of the others have ever come before the judges. There are rumours, but I must stress nothing more, about the head of our secret service who is also on the Board. Have you heard of Karl Johansson?"

"Is he the tall fair-haired guy who rather fancies himself?"

"You've got him. He travels around CASAR picking up information from informants. There is talk of him taking very young girls back to his hotel. They are always just over sixteen, so nothing illegal. There are no rumours about anyone else on your list, which, by the way, I would like you to take away with you."

I mentioned Karl to Max. She dismissed it. "He may be a creep, but he's the second most powerful person in CASAR. He owns half of a beautiful island. He would never do anything illegal. I would be very careful if you're planning to watch him; he's extremely clever and if he discovers you're investigating him, he'll never forgive you."

Then we had a breakthrough. What looked like a routine report arrived in the diplomatic bag of our embassy in Washington. The clerk had spotted that the typed letters weren't as sharp as normal and had sent it for analysis. A microscope revealed numerous random characters that were hidden within each alphabetical letter. We gave this information to Xanasa who quickly cracked the code. The symbols were Mayan glyphs. The decoded letter said, *I have the detailed picture/design. I will bring this when I come for my grandfather's funeral. Meet me there.*

Only the Board have access to the diplomatic bag. So it didn't take Xanasa a moment to inform me that Gretchen Holloway was the only member whose grandfather had recently died. However, that didn't give her a motive. She'd worked with Xantec from its inception and was now head of research. Max said I must check her out but thought her an unlikely suspect. I asked Xanasa to investigate her relatives in the USA to see if any of these were in trouble, in case that explained her treason. She discovered that a nephew was in gaol following an armed robbery to fund his cocaine habit. Gretchen could be planning a plea bargain to get him freed. I felt I had enough and asked permission to have her arrested. Max reluctantly agreed. Gregor, Sandy and I arrived at her house as she was sitting down for breakfast. She invited us in for coffee. I gave the reason for her arrest. She looked absolutely flabbergasted. She was either a remarkable actress, or I'd made a terrible mistake. Without any attempt to escape, she came with us but demanded to see Max. I'd anticipated this and Max met us at CRC and took Gretchen into her private office. Afterwards, she readily agreed to take some veritax and be scanned. To my surprise, there was nothing to suggest that she'd written the encrypted letter, although she'd been making arrangements to go to her grandfather's funeral.

Someone must have planted this letter as a wild goose chase to distract us, but who? All the other Board members had unblemished records. When Xanasa checked, none of them had any relatives in trouble in the USA. I couldn't officially investigate Max. Might she be double bluffing by asking me to investigate, thinking that such a young, naïve guy would never dream of suspecting her?

I asked Jas to arrange for a girl to take Petra a bunch of orchids and to deliver a note as she handed the flowers over. The following Saturday, with great anticipation, I landed on the floor of her sinkhole. She was obviously thrilled to see me. As we separated, instead of a relaxed smiling face, I noticed she was frowning.

"What's wrong?"

"I'm worried that Xanasa will have spotted the same chip disappearing in the vicinity of my mother's house on three separate occasions."

"Petra, each day, I think of you countless times. I lie in bed thinking of where we could go on holiday and how I would like to marry you and have children. Finally, I've decided that I don't care if we're discovered."

I thought she would be thrilled that I cared so much and had in effect proposed to her. Instead, she was frowning and her lips started to quiver. I spotted a tear running down her cheek.

"What's up?"

"Mom will ruin everything. I should've told you. I once had a boyfriend before. He was working on the same research project as me. Mom had him banished to Argentina to work in the embassy there. She can be much harder than you might expect. I'm afraid for you, and if we're lucky this time, please wait for me to contact you in future."

I enfolded her in my arms and gradually she calmed. Her tense muscles relaxed and for a while she seemed to melt into me as we became one.

"What should we do?" I whispered.

"I don't have any answers. I love you more than you realise. Something will work out. I have to join her for lunch now. I'll arrange to see you soon."

I didn't want to break the spell but I just had to ask before I left, "I'm so sorry if I've messed everything up by coming again. Before I go, may I ask if your mother has any relatives left in the USA?"

"There's only Grandad, her father. Since my grandmother died, he lives alone in a mansion near Santa Barbara. I visit him occasionally. He's a lovely old boy with a wicked sense of humour."

"He doesn't sound a bit like your mom. I hope we can see him together one day."

I left feeling utterly demoralised. I shouldn't have suspected Max, and now I'd put my relationship with Petra at risk. I was making a terrible hash of this investigation and wished I'd never been forced to take it on.

I asked Max, "I'm getting nowhere; could someone with more experience assist me? If that's impossible, please could I have a few days' holiday as I feel I need to recharge my batteries?"

"Zig, I would if I could. The trouble is that I can't trust anyone who was already a Commissioner when this leak occurred. If you really want someone to help, you could take Charco on holiday and get him up to speed. You must tell him it would be treasonable to talk to anyone else about the operation. At the end of the holiday, if he's still interested, you could work as a team."

―――――

Two days later, Charco and I arrived at Cuidad Del Carmen, which is the tourist half of the Mexican island where Karl Johansson lived. He owned the eastern half and had put an electric fence across the isthmus that links the two. We had booked a private pod in the hyperloop, and before we arrived, we put on latex head masks that we'd borrowed from my local theatre. These extremely realistic masks made us look like two young Mexicans so that we could blend in with the tourists. That evening, there was a fiesta. We had a drink in our room and then donned our masks. At the end of the parade, we invited a couple of young men to join us for a drink at a bar. After they'd had a skinful, I asked if they thought there was any truth in the rumour about Karl Johansson and young girls. They stared at us, looking terrified. It was obvious we had hit a raw nerve that spelt danger for them. We apologised, paid up, and retreated to our hotel.

We had to eat breakfast wearing our masks, which were rancid from yesterday's sweat. As we finished, we were told someone was waiting at reception. It was one of the lads from the previous evening. He asked us if we'd like to go for a walk in the park. Once out of the hotel, he said that the hotel had 'ears'. He'd followed us there last night to check that we weren't Karl's spies.

"I wanted to tell you last night how evil Karl Johansson is, but it's too dangerous to say anything in public. He regularly sends his heavies to abduct young girls, who are taken back to his mansion. They are given sweets and drugged before being forced to take part in sexual acts. The girls are often as young as eleven. I'm telling you this as my cousin was abducted when she was twelve. She's never recovered. She used to be full of fun but now is withdrawn and miserable. I hate that man and would gladly kill him if I had the chance. Where do you come from?"

"Costa Rica."

"You'll be safe from his clutches there. Could you tell the Xantec authorities what's going on? Maybe they'd start watching him."

We were walking back to the hotel when our Xan-links simultaneously went off. Max wanted us back in CRC directly. I wasn't supposed to be investigating Karl. She must've got wind of us being on his island. Trouble ahead!

When we arrived, I was told that Max wanted to see me on my own. I entered and she ignored me while she appeared to be busy looking at a large hologram. She was scowling and clearly angry when she looked up.

"You have disobeyed me twice! I could forgive you checking out Karl as long as you were discreet, but you've also been seeing Petra against my command. You've no idea how important her work is. She's at present nearly finished work on a project that's going to transform all Commissioners' lives. She's destined for great things and you must never distract her again."

"In fact, this isn't why I recalled you early. Xanasa has discovered that 100 grams of europa have been taken from the reactor on two successive days. You know that the fusion reactor is housed deep inside this mountain. Security there is paramount. Only three teams of two Commissioners ever enter that area. The droids never leave the area. The Commissioners are scanned each day as they leave through the only passageway that connects the reactor to the outside; it would be impossible for them to smuggle anything out."

Another conundrum. "I'll try to solve it, but nothing springs to mind."

I told her about the island and Karl.

"That's abominable! I'll order his immediate arrest."

Back in my room, I remembered that water was sampled through a long, narrow passage bored through the rock. Had one of the Commissioners put the europa down there? I told Max.

"That's worth checking out, Zig. I'll get the CCTV that films this process looked at, and the six Commissioners will be given veritax and scanned forthwith. There is some good news, though. Karl has just been detected travelling to CRC on the hyperloop. I've ordered ten clones to arrest him as he arrives."

Finally, we were close to ensnaring this nasty pervert. I went to the station to watch the arrest. It had been cleared of passengers, and eight clones blending in with the walls of the station had taken up their firing positions. Two, not wearing stealth suits, were ready to confront and arrest Karl. The pod arrived; I was tense with anticipation. The doors swung open. The pod was empty! I ran across to check there was no possible way out or hiding place. It was then that I saw a minuscule silver chip on one of the seats.

I rushed back to Max to show her. "The clever bastard! He must've had his chip surgically removed. We'll deal with that surgeon later. I bet he's fled and this was another clever ruse to distract us. Xanasa, play us satellite images of any boats leaving his harbour over the last four hours."

There were three small boats and one large cruiser that left almost simultaneously. Of course, without his chip, we'd no idea which of these he was on or indeed if he was on any of them. They might all be decoys.

"Xanasa, follow any drones that have left his mansion today. Arrange for soldiers to intercept the small boats and any relevant drones.

Zig, I want you to go with Charco and your two pet clones and take the hyperloop to Tampico. I'll arrange for a speedboat to be ready for you at the harbour. I'm sure he'll be in the fast cruiser and will expect us to intercept via Tampico. I suspect Karl will turn east and head in the direction of Tampa. You must arrest or if necessary kill him before he can rendezvous with anyone."

When we boarded our boat in Tampico, I was pleased to learn it was furnished with a powerful electric jet engine. (It used to belong to cocaine smugglers.) Xanasa kept us informed of the cruiser's position. Max had been spot on; Karl had turned east. Xanasa predicted he would hit the Florida coast about ten minutes before us. We took the opportunity to sleep while the captain maintained full throttle.

I was woken by Xanasa, who had spotted four wave-skimmers being launched from Karl's boat. One of the riders had no chip! Excitement banished sleep as I maxed out my skimmer. I was catching him. He was going so fast that if he turned to check my progress, he would almost certainly crash. He was too smart for that; he turned towards a tourist beach. He crested a wave and I hoped that might topple him, but he was cautious and chose to slow down to match its speed. I jumped the waves. Something hit the water. Too late, I realised it was my gun. I carried on, hoping for a miracle. I was about a hundred metres behind him as we raced across the beach towards some sand dunes. He changed direction, heading towards a wood beyond the dunes that would provide cover, to prevent Xanasa tracking him using satellite images. By now, I had calculated that the clones and Charco should have reached the jetty at the far side of the wood. He'd disappeared among the dunes and I followed, running as fast as I could, keeping my head as low as possible. I heard what sounded like firecrackers. Sand exploded just behind me. I dived into a deep depression at the foot of a dune and spotted a gully leading from it. It was a dried-up riverbed. I sprinted along it, thankful that the stones gave me better traction. I reached the woods and hid deep in the shade. I'd no idea where Karl was. I heard a chopper approach; it hovered above the trees.

A heavily amplified voice rang out. "Drop your guns; come out into the open with your hands held high. You are surrounded by armed police." I hoped this might stop him shooting, but if he was in cahoots with these police then he would have succeeded in giving them the europa and our secrets. Shit!

I heard the steady thrum of a sonic stun gun and then absolute silence. I moved towards the dunes with my hands up high.

"On your knees, hands behind your head!"

I was roughly frisked and cuffed.

"Where's your weapon?"

"I have no weapon. I was being shot at by an American who was chasing me. I was in a boat well inside international waters when this American approached us on a wave-skimmer and then started firing at us for no apparent reason. My brother and his children were on board, so I jumped on my wave-skimmer to draw him away from the boat. He nearly caught me, and then when we got near the woods, he opened fire."

"Okay, smart ass. If this American guy was firing at you, where is he now?"

"I've no idea; I was scared stiff and lay absolutely still, hoping not to be shot."

They didn't seem to buy my story and dragged me off to the police station, where I was fingerprinted, photo'd and iris scanned. I was swabbed for gun residue and left to stew in a tiny cell. It seemed like an eternity until the door was opened by a surly officer. "Okay, you were clean and your story has been backed up by the tourist on the beach who called us in. I've been told to put you on the next flight to Cancun."

———

As I arrived in Cancun, Max contacted me to say that Karl had been captured by the clones. I'd expected some thanks, but got none.

"We're still in a real mess. Karl's veritax scan showed that he'd buried a canister of europa by a large stone just after he'd fired at you. He has told his CIA contact that it's hidden there. The CIA have promised Karl that they'll attack CRC and release him as soon as they have the canister. Apparently they told him that they have ballistic missiles that Xanasa can't hack. Of course, this is rubbish, but it's imperative that we pick this canister up before the CIA locates it."

I'd been hoping for xanacea, sleep and a holiday as reward for my efforts. Instead, I commandeered a drone to take me to the port where Charco had left the boat. Fortunately, it was still there. I woke the captain and emphasised the urgency of our return trip.

As I settled down to sleep, Max interrupted.

"Xanasa has sent an encrypted message to the Chief of Tampa Police. It will appear to have come via a secure link from the head of the FBI. It reads:

The gunman who evaded capture in the woods near St Petersburg is part of a drug smuggling gang. The FBI has reliable 'intel' that the gang is returning tonight to collect their hastily hidden cache. They'll be heavily armed and masquerading as FBI agents complete with badges and authentic numbers.

Xanasa's message concluded with the advice:

You should assemble a large armed unit to arrest them all.

This should provide some confusion while you find that canister, Zig. Good luck!"

The captain woke me with coffee as we approached the beach. I jumped onto my wave-skimmer wearing night vision glasses. Xanasa guided me to the position where I'd hidden from Karl. I'd no idea where he'd fired from, and Xanasa couldn't help as Karl had got rid of his chip and was under the cover of the trees so that he couldn't be seen from space. I systematically searched along the edge of the trees, slowly moving deeper into the wood. I still hadn't found the stone when I heard a helicopter with bright searchlights approach. This was soon followed by a heated exchange as two groups of men wearing head torches started shouting at each other. I methodically continued my search and noticed a pale shape amongst the undergrowth just a couple of yards ahead of me. I hoped that this was Karl's rock. The men had stopped arguing and now formed a line systematically searching the undergrowth and heading my way, the searchlights from the helicopter creating a swathe of brilliance a few yards ahead of them. Anxiously, I felt around the base of the rock and touched a cold object almost completely buried in the sand. The helicopter's light was only about thirty metres away and closing rapidly. I unscrewed the top and flung the powdered contents deep into the undergrowth, filled the canister with sand, screwed the top on and replaced it near the rock. I then took twenty quick paces away from the light and hid in the undergrowth. I'd hoped they would stop at the rock and I could sneak away while they were preoccupied with their search. It was all going to plan until one of the men moved away from the rock, turned his head torch off and stood about a metre from me. He unzipped and started to piss. I must have subconsciously shifted to avoid the splashes. He switched on his torch and looked straight at me!

"Don't move an inch!"

I froze as his automatic rifle rose into a firing position.

"Hands in the air."

I was used to the routine now.

"On your knees."

I was soon cuffed and roughly bundled into the chopper.

I was shoved into the same spartan police interrogation room as last night. I had a few moments to collect my thoughts. A furious CIA interrogator threw open the door and made me sit on the floor while he took the only chair. He made the policeman last night seem like a wet nurse.

"You have no rights at all. The president of the USA has personally given me permission to ignore the Geneva Convention. This time, I want the truth, not the load of bollocks you gave that idiot policeman last night. If I don't like what you tell me, I'll leave you to my friend."

At this point, a heavily tattooed thug of a man made his perfectly timed entrance.

I paused for a moment, hoping that Xanasa was listening in.

"I lied yesterday. I was chasing an employee of Xantec's; there was no American involved. The man I was chasing is called Karl Johansson. He fired on me, not the other way round. We know Karl has paranoid schizophrenia with grandiose delusions. He was once an important Commissioner on our board of directors, but for the last 4 years, he's been locked away in a secure psychiatric hospital. Well, I say secure, but clearly it wasn't as secure as we'd hoped. We knew that he'd escaped and had access to a gun. This is why we were trying to apprehend him yesterday; we didn't want him to cause an international incident by harming an American citizen. We should've informed you and for this I apologise. After we captured him and returned him to the hospital, he told us that he'd been in communication with someone from the CIA. He'd apparently told them that he'd hidden a canister with valuable material in it. We suspected that this was all part of his delusional state, but I was sent back to try to find the canister. I'd found nothing by the time your roughnecks arrested me."

"Frankly, that sounds even more ridiculous than the bullshit you concocted last night. We've found the canister and its contents are being analysed as we speak."

He glared at me as he went to leave, passing me with only a few inches to spare. I thought he might kick me. As the door slammed shut, I was thankful to have got through the first interview unharmed. I must've fallen asleep on the floor as I woke to the door creaking open. A distinguished-looking man in a crisp suit was towering over me.

"I'm Craig Leporte. I'm a barrister hired by Commander Spitzen to defend you. Come take this seat; I'll happily stand for a moment. The contents of the canister turned out to be dry sand. The only crime you've committed is illegal entry. Commander Spitzen has assured me that she'll pay the fine. If you are okay with pleading guilty, I'll get on with arranging a plea bargain. You should be home within forty-eight hours."

True to his word, I was back at CRC the following day. I learnt that Karl would be held for the rest of his life in the high security prison deep within the mountain at CRC.

Charco and I were given a three-week holiday, partially as reward, but mainly to allow us to recover from our ordeal. It was late January and the weather was set fair in southern Chile. We set off to trek through the Torres del Paine National Park.

The American election of 2052

On our return, we were told that Commander Spitzen had summoned all Commissioners for a meeting in the Great Hall. It was empty and bleak when I'd seen it before. It was now full of energy with exuberant Commissioners chatting to their friends. A reverberating Tibetan gong was struck, and as its vibrations diminished, we all turned to the podium. Silence descended as Max entered.

"I've four announcements to make today. Eleven years ago, our research teams successfully nurtured monkeys in incubators from embryo to delivery. Our scientists have overcome the problem of these babies having sterile guts. The newborn monkeys have a syringe filled with their mother's liquidised faeces and vaginal fluid squirted down their throats. Since this modification, they have remained perfectly healthy, and have indeed lived rather longer than the control group. At that time, it had become increasingly difficult to find women willing to be surrogates to carry our clones. For the last ten years, all our clones have been successfully nurtured in similar incubators. We've been able to produce thirty thousand a year. In six years' time, the first of these clones will be fully trained.

Secondly, many of you know that Xanasa is infused with chemicals that prevent her from ageing. I'm proud to announce that my daughter's research team have perfected the dosage of these medicines for humans. Clones that are over sixteen have been given these for five years with no ill effects. The clones don't appear to have aged at all in that time. Our scientists believe that humans taking these drugs will age slowly because of solar and background radiation, but this should be at less than a tenth of normal ageing speed. You are the elite who both control society and improve it through research. The more experience you have, the better it is for everyone. Therefore, from tomorrow, you'll all have a weekly injection to slow ageing.

Thirdly, many years ago, I allowed some of my researchers to have sabbaticals to work with other advanced AI projects around the world. They were instructed to place hidden viruses in the AI programs which Xanasa could activate remotely. Yesterday, Xanasa reported that AI systems around the world have been irreparably damaged. We have taken this step to ensure that no other countries will be able to develop AI that could compete with Xanasa. Because of this, we should remain safe from a military attack for the foreseeable future.

Finally, the US presidential elections occur in just under nine months' time. You'll be aware that the Democrat candidate, Sophia Mezvinsky, has made it clear that if elected, she will be inviting us to make the USA as successful as CASAR. At present, the polls are predicting that Sophia will win with a landslide. We have to be ready if this translates into reality. The Board has been preparing for a year. We'll have our shark-mole drills and robots ready, should she win.

None of this will work unless we have won over the hearts and minds of American citizens. This is where you all have such an important role. Now that CASAR is stable, we believe that 10,000 Commissioners can administer it. We'll need our 30,000 researchers to continue at CRC. This leaves 100,000 of you to persuade the people to vote for Sophia, and if she wins to help them adapt. You must prepare them for a complete cessation of carbon fuel within two years. By then, the hyperloop tunnels will be complete; all cars and drones will be electric. There will only be three airports for international flights. Commercial airports will be converted into factories. Boats, farm machinery and factories will be powered by electricity.

At the end of this meeting, Xanasa will inform you which state you've been allocated to, who's in charge of your state and which area you're responsible for."

———

Two days later, I was flying into JFK Airport. I'd never been to the USA before. When I arrived in New York, I found the noise and exhaust fumes very unpleasant. Everyone was rushing about their business. I couldn't read people like I could back home; they seemed very unfriendly. I was rather scared, especially as I knew it was legal for people to carry guns. I wanted to see the Museum of Modern Art as Petra had said how much she'd enjoyed it. I was just walking out of Central Park when I saw a group of men who all had the most startling green hair that was stiffened with some sort of gel so that it seemed to shoot straight out of their scalps for about ten inches. This had to be photographed.

My cell phone must have flashed as one of them shouted, and suddenly they were all charging in my direction. I reckoned they were not about to praise me for my artistic flare. I turned and fled down a side road. I was soon gasping for breath; noxious fumes filled my lungs. I turned into a narrow alleyway and nearly tripped over a drunkard who was sprawled across a hot air vent. It was a dead end but, thankfully, the second door I tried opened. I found myself in a cold, damp, badly lit stairwell. There was a fire exit on the second landing. I opened this revealing a rickety old iron staircase. Down beneath was another road heaving with cars. I was just turning to go back inside when a glimpse of green on the sidewalk caught my attention. Too late, I'd been clocked. I shot up the stairwell and at the top found a ladder and trapdoor. I'd just pulled the ladder up after me when I heard footsteps charging up the stairs. It was a huge building that must have extended for fully one hundred metres. I ran across the open roof hoping to find another fire escape. I'd almost reached the end of the building when I skidded on a frozen puddle, coming to an abrupt halt as my foot hit a metal bar held rigid in the ice. I fell and avoided cracking my skull by taking the impact on my shoulder. Just then, a green head appeared from the trapdoor, and soon there were nine of them rushing towards me. I noticed something glint in the weak sunshine. I was completely unarmed and my coat would offer little resistance to a knife. Then a shot rang out. I didn't hang around. I looked over the parapet, spotted a balcony about three metres below and leapt. I landed and heard my ankle snap. I screamed in pain. A door opened and an elderly lady's head appeared.

"Where on earth have you come from?"

"Please, I'm being attacked! Can I come in?"

I'd just hopped through her door as a flash of green appeared above me.

I was shaking with cold and terror.

"They tried to shoot me and are carrying knives! Am I safe here?"

"Totally safe. I have bulletproof glass and the doors are triple locked.

Who was chasing you and how have you upset them?"

"I've never met them before; in fact, I've only just arrived in New York. I don't know why these green-haired young men took against me. I was only taking a snapshot."

As soon as I mentioned the green-haired men, she hit an alarm on her wall.

A moment later, "How can we help you, Mrs Yarpole?"

She was clearly talking to the police, and as soon as she mentioned a gunshot and green hair, she was interrupted.

"We'll be there pronto."

"Who are these men?" I asked.

"They are a notorious gang of cocaine dealers called the 'Southsiders'. Locally, we know them as the 'Green Hedgehogs', but no one would call them that to their faces."

Feeling more secure, I looked around. It was a cosy little flat and a white cat was sulking in a corner. She looked miffed as I'd obviously invaded her territory, and I was now sitting in her chair, judging by the white hairs that were stuck to my trousers.

The police arrived. Once they'd heard my story, they wanted to see the camera shot. The image wasn't great, but they reckoned it could be enhanced at the station while I was getting my ankle treated.

By the time I was escorted to the station, they'd gone to arrest the gang. My picture had apparently shown them passing two small 'dog tags' joined by a chain. Earlier, a soldier had been shot by a gang member. They must have suspected that I had incriminating pictures on my camera. Having given my statement, I said I'd be in Pennsylvania for a couple of weeks if they needed me.

At the hospital, they fitted me with a lightweight, strong but remarkably thin cast to secure my sprained ankle.

———

Two days later, I was riding in a horse and trap, bumping along a dirt road in Mifflin County, Pennsylvania. Jacob was sitting next to me controlling the reins. He was a friendly, tanned, middle-aged man with long brown hair flowing from under a broad-brimmed hat. He looked like a cross between a hippy and a medieval peasant. I was going to stay with his family who belonged to the Nebraska Amish. I was thankful to get away from New York and felt peace wash over me as we slowly journeyed through this beautiful tranquil land. The sun was shining, but it was bitterly cold as the only canopy was uselessly situated behind us on the buggy. Thankfully, I was well prepared, having bought a down jacket and sheepskin-lined leather boots (bigger than normal to accommodate my cast). We arrived at Jacob's wood-framed farmhouse and were soon surrounded by a swarm of children and his sturdy, no-nonsense wife. She wore a black kerchief on her head which looked rather odd. I was shown in, and the welcome warmth from a log burner greeted me. There was no electricity and later Jacob showed me the outdoor bathroom. I didn't plan to linger in that freezing hut!

The warmth, chatter and friendliness of the family reminded me of gatherings from my childhood. Jacob said I should dress like one of them. He lent me a white shirt, a thick woollen coat and scratchy brown pants that he laced up at the back for me. I came downstairs to howls of laughter from the children. Even so, I was pleased to be treated like one of the family. It was hard work lifting hay and feeding the cows. Digging the vegetable patch finished my back off. Thankfully, my cast kept my ankle pain-free. After a week, I felt completely accepted, even though I couldn't share their faith and religious practices. I was more relaxed than I'd been for ages.

In my report, I suggested that these farmers living in harmony with nature should be allowed to continue their traditional way of life as no fossil fuels were burnt. I never imagined that this idea would have such profound consequences for the future of the world.

———

When I returned to work at CRC, I found a curious typed note in a sealed envelope underneath my coffee mug. It said *Meet me at 4 pm today in the meditation room at the back of the canteen.* I was intrigued and postponed my meeting with the Philadelphia Chief so I could be there. I was slightly worried as there was no CCTV in the meditation room as people had to change into their yoga kit there. I feared that I'd angered someone in my investigation leading up to Karl's arrest. If I was attacked there, the perpetrator could disappear into the crowds who work at CRC without trace. It was with some trepidation that I opened the door at 4.05 pm, ready to run if I didn't like the look of the person who'd sent the message.

Petra sprang from the floor and leapt into my arms. I was relieved and thrilled as I hadn't seen her for months. She hung onto me for ages. I looked closely; she looked pale, thin and her right eye had developed a twitch. Altogether, she didn't look at all well.

"Are you okay? You look exhausted."

"I've been worried about you doing all this secret stuff. I would be much happier if you had a desk job here. I'm also worried about Mom. She has been working all hours preparing for this American election. To make matters worse, she's become paranoid ever since you uncovered Karl's plot. She doesn't trust many of her old friends now and has become increasingly dependent on me. I hardly get any time to relax as she wants to bounce her ideas off me as soon as I get home."

"Plenty of time to discuss that; I'm just so pleased it was you who sent me that note. Let's concentrate on each other. You stroke my back and I'll stroke yours. Once we are both properly relaxed, we can work out a solution."

In truth, I'd no idea how to solve this conundrum. I was just playing for time and enjoying the experience. A few minutes passed and then I had an idea; "When did your mom last take a holiday?"

"None for at least ten years."

"You both like skiing, I think. If she's racing down black runs, she can't think about work. Why don't you both fly in her private jet to the Austrian Alps? She'll be away from the USA and there's great skiing there. I think she still trusts my dad. He could deputise while you're away. If she wants a personal bodyguard, I'm always available."

"Not a bad idea, but forget about the bodyguard. You're still *persona non grata* and have been ever since she found out about us."

"How did you get that message to my room?"

"A good friend of mine is having a secret relationship with a man in your section. I think this may come in useful, so I hope it continues. I told my boss that I was feeling ill and had to leave early. I can't use that ruse too often, but we should be able to meet here from time to time.

I've frozen some eggs, by the way. As we're taking the weekly injection, we should live for hundreds of years. One day, I hope we can start a family, but I can't say when. Are you prepared to wait?"

That took me completely by surprise.

"Of course I'll wait."

Deep down, I wasn't really sure I could cope with these infrequent secret meetings for years to come.

Half an hour later and feeling totally in love once more, we unlocked the door and went our separate ways.

The succeeding eight months were spent visiting the USA, making friends and generally persuading voters that we would increase their wealth as well as making their country a safer and better place to live.

The Democrats' manifesto had been agreed with Spitzen and the Board.

The salient promises they made if they were elected were:

1. Xantec would provide free electricity, and their advanced robotics and hyperloop system would transform travel and industry.
2. Within one year, there would be no tax, and health care would be free for all.
3. The USA would stop spending vast amounts of money on military, foreign aid and world policing.
4. All guns and ammunition would be banned, and all armaments would be surrendered to the police within ten days.
5. All army personnel would help the police deal with this gun amnesty and with eliminating all drug trafficking.
6. Drug users would report to hospitals for detox.
7. We would aim for a fair and equal society.

For those who wished to have no part in this fair society, they would be free to negotiate citizenship with other countries. If they left within three weeks, they would be allowed to keep their bank assets and shares but would forfeit their properties to provide homes for people without satisfactory accommodation. After three weeks, they would forfeit all their assets.

On Election Day, the exit polls gave Sophia Mezvinsky a commanding lead. However, we were all on tenterhooks until Richard Bush conceded defeat just after midnight. Sophia gave an impassioned speech, talking about a new beginning for the American people.

We all knew exactly what to do and where to go. The same could not be said for the general population. There was panic and pandemonium. Airlines offered to buy back tickets from people who were travelling abroad for ten times their value. They smelt money as the super-rich wanted to leave. Police cells were full of guns awaiting destruction by the army. Surprisingly few people left the armed forces, and the supply of drugs rapidly dwindled. Hospitals were overwhelmed by drug addicts demanding relief from their 'cold turkey'.

I was soon enjoying the peace and quiet of Mifflin County and the friendly welcome of Jacob's family. They were delighted by what they'd gleaned about the revolution that was affecting the country. It was soon clear that I wasn't needed there as the Amish continued to live as they'd done for hundreds of years. I asked to be transferred to New York. I know it was petty of me, but I really wanted to put the rest of the 'Green Hedgehogs' behind bars.

Tracking them down wasn't as easy as I'd hoped as of course they weren't chipped. I went to the police station where I'd been interviewed. They were too busy with the gun amnesty to give me much assistance, but they gave me the addresses of the remaining seven members. I got Xanasa to keep a watch on their flats via satellite. I requested assistance from my old clone friends, Gregor and Sandy, and asked them to bring their sonic blasters and bombs. In the meantime, I did get to visit the Museum of Modern Art.

Two days later, Gregor, Sandy and I were settled in a hotel suite in the Green Hedgehogs' patch. Xanasa interrupted me and showed me the live satellite feed. Six 'Hedgehogs' were entering a surprisingly dingy-looking flat. I couldn't see any guns but felt sure they'd all be carrying one. I asked Xanasa to keep a record of everything I viewed until this operation ended. We found an abandoned flat with a good view of their hideout. What looked like dingy apartments from the satellite, on closer inspection looked more like a heavily defended fort. The flat they were meeting in had thick plated steel on the inside of the windows as well as a steel door. To our dismay, every one of the flats that surrounded this one was similarly fortified. Gregor checked around the back. There was no fire escape and no air conditioning vents. They must have some air purifying device inside the buildings. If they'd gone to so much trouble, they would surely drink bottled water to prevent us poisoning their water supply. Gregor came up with a possible solution, and with no better plan, we agreed to give it a go.

The police agreed to lend us two cars with sirens, and an old work van. They also lent us a cocaine sensing and measuring device, a set of old overalls and two police uniforms. Gregor wore the overalls and parked his van at the back of the 'Hedgehogs'' flat. He'd spotted a manhole cover that gave access to the sewage system. Sandy and I (in the police uniforms) waited for fifteen minutes and then drove our cars with sirens blazing and screeched to a halt in front of the block, ran up the stairs and started banging on the reinforced door. In the meantime, Gregor had unloaded his remote controlled miniature submarine and attached a sonic bomb with a cocaine sensor to it. He then guided it up the sewage system, following the ever-increasing concentration of cocaine. (We had banked on them flushing their cocaine down the toilet as soon as they knew they were being raided.)

I was beginning to panic as I feared that the door would be flung open and we would die in a hail of bullets. Just as I was about to abandon the mission, there was a muffled explosion from within.

"Shit, what a bloody mess! The door is locked and we need to get them cuffed before they come round or we'll be dead meat!"

"No problem, sir. I know you didn't ask us to bring weapons, but I brought this MP5K just in case."

With that, he blasted the lock on the door and we were in. Scattered on the floor of the living room were a veritable arsenal of guns and seven 'Hedgehogs'. They were all deeply unconscious. I feared they might be seriously damaged as the steel plating had exaggerated the force from the sonic bomb. I summoned both police and ambulance. Mission accomplished.

———

The chaos of the first few weeks gradually resolved. In the end, less than 100,000 people fled the country. Their mansions provided good homes for over a million poor Americans. Within a year, fusion power was providing free energy, and the economy was thriving as advanced robotics boosted the productivity of the country. The air quality improved dramatically as carbon-guzzling cars became electric. Tourism flourished as the world realised that it was once again a safe, quiet, clean place to visit. As agriculture became more efficient, considerable tracts of land were given over to nature.

Four years later, Canada and the whole of continental Europe, including Turkey, asked Commander Spitzen for her assistance. Canada was relatively simple as there were fewer people, and our shark-mole machines were already on their borders. By spring 2058, continental Europe was also transformed and their armies had been disbanded. The aristocracy and many wealthy people from Europe joined the rich refugees from the USA who had mainly settled in Australia and New Zealand.

THE APOCALYPSE 2058-2060

By 2058, trade throughout the whole world was booming. The population was falling except in Islamic countries and Africa, where overpopulation was leading to deforestation and increasing dependence on imported food. As oil and gas were no longer used in Xantec-controlled countries, there was a world-wide glut. Russia, the Middle East and other oil producers suffered. India and China were the new superpowers outside of Xanasa's empire.

Global warming had peaked with a rise of 2.5 deg centigrade. Low-lying atolls and the coast of Bangladesh had repeatedly flooded, but it hadn't been as catastrophic as many had predicted. The Taiga (the largest forest on Earth) was extending northwards into the tundra. The Amazon and other forests, under the guidance of Xantec, were growing fast, more than compensating for the destruction that was still occurring in the Congo and Malaysian forests. The future of the world was looking bright, and life expectancy was the highest in history.

China had been the world's most powerful economy for forty years, thriving on world trade following the success of their 'one belt, one road' strategy. However, their ageing population and demand for high wages was now hampering their growth. Meanwhile, India's young educated middle class were driving their success in tech start-ups, military equipment, cheap robots and droids. India was predicted to overtake China's GDP within the year.

China was offering cheap training in technology for their trading partners around the world. While in Beijing, some trainee Pakistani workers had been brainwashed into believing it would be honourable and patriotic to attack Kashmiri Indians on their return to Pakistan. This skirmish eventually spiralled into a conventional war between India and Pakistan. As India was about to invade Lahore, Pakistan threatened them with a nuclear attack. India called their bluff and continued regardless. A calamitous nuclear exchange followed, leading to millions dying in Lahore and New Delhi.

Meanwhile, Syria took advantage of the fact that Turkey had demilitarised under instructions from Xanasa. They attacked Kobane, which Turkey had held ever since the Syrian war ended in 2019. Within five minutes of the launch of the air attack, Xanasa had caused the planes to crash and had disabled the rest of the Syrian air force and army.

Knowing that the Syrian air force was grounded, Saudi Arabia took the opportunity to invade Iraq (Syria and Iraq had a mutual defence alliance). In turn, the Shia government of Iraq called on their allies in Iran for assistance. The Ayatollah sent a message to be delivered at Friday prayers in Shia mosques in Riyadh to warn all Shia Muslims to flee the city before midnight. At 1 am, Iran simultaneously hit Riyadh, Saudi air bases and the Saudi army in western Iraq with nuclear strikes. This attack on innocent Sunni civilians caused the Wahhabis to attack any Shia they could find; an orgy of murder and rape ensued.

After this slaughter, Iraq, Iran and Bahrain (all majority Shia countries) declared war on Saudi Arabia.

Egypt, Jordan, Qatar and Afghanistan (all majority Sunni countries) formed an alliance with Saudi Arabia, but it was too late. Without their air force and most of their army, Saudi Arabia was quickly overrun. A world-wide 'civil war' between Sunni and Shia ensued. People who had once lived happily alongside their neighbours started attacking each other.

Taking advantage of the ensuing chaos, North Korea ordered a pre-emptive nuclear strike against Seoul and the South's air bases. They then invaded with over a million soldiers. Initially, due to the surprise and shock of the nuclear strike, they made rapid progress into South Korea. Japan, which had created a high-tech military force once the USA had disbanded its military, helped S. Korea drive this army back. China had the excuse it needed to sweep in and take the whole peninsula. They signed a peace treaty with Japan and then invaded Taiwan.

While China's attention was focussed on the Far East, India joined the Uighers and Tibetans as they invaded Eastern China.

The United Nations had disbanded once the USA, Canada and Europe stopped funding it. Armed African UN forces became local warlords. A severe drought in the Horn of Africa led to starvation as the World Food Organisation no longer existed. A migration of starving people moved from east to west across Africa. Worse was to come. An Ebola epidemic began in Gabon. The virus had mutated and the vaccine was now ineffectual. The refugees from East Africa turned south as they heard rumours of the epidemic. Tragically, many were already infected and soon the disease was rampant throughout the continent. The world powers decided to ruthlessly contain it within Africa. Australia sent naval boats to patrol the Indian Ocean. Israel invaded the Sinai Peninsula and patrolled the eastern bank of the Suez Canal. Xanasa sent boats with armed drones to destroy any vessels on the north and west African coasts. Xanasa also disabled all African aeroplanes. Africa turned from a booming vibrant economy into a stinking rotting hellhole.

I grew up in a friendly, happy, colourful fishing village called Kodimunai on the very southern tip of Kerala. We were poor Catholics of the Mukkuvar untouchable fishing caste. I never knew my mother as she died a few days after I was born. My aunt, an English teacher, had a daughter called Leah who was like an older sister to me. At their home, we were only allowed to speak English. My aunt cooked for us as well as her own family, and I would collect supper each evening for Father and my younger brother Tom. Some might think that without a mother I would have had a very sad upbringing. On the contrary, my early memories are full of laughter and happiness. I enjoyed school, where I excelled in English and history. At the sound of the bell signalling the end of classes, we would rush to the beach to play football and other games while waiting for the blue fishing fleet to return with the day's catch. There would be great excitement as women came to inspect the fish. Local traders bought any large specimens. If Father sold a lot, he would give Tom and me a few rupees to buy treats. Once the nets were all stowed away and the boats heaved above high tide, we would return home. After bathing, we would sit down for grace before our evening meal. It was literally a lifetime ago, but still as I remember those meals of fresh succulent spicy fish, my mouth fills with saliva.

After the evening meal, my father (Ignatius) and Grandad Tom would sit under the shade of our tamarind tree enjoying the evening breeze, while discussing the world, politics and family. I would often listen, hidden by the tall leaves of our ginger plant. They would often be joined by Father's best friend, Naheed Abidi, who would arrive in a cloud of smoke belching from his clapped-out old car. Father would often tell the story of how Naheed had saved his life years ago. Father's boat had capsized in a fearful storm. As he surfaced, he was picked up by an enormous wave that flung him onto his drifting boat. He smashed into it with such force that his arm was broken and he had a severe nosebleed. The blood attracted unwanted attention. His next recollection was seeing a large dark fin cutting through the waves. Within seconds, Naheed arrived, took an oar and kept hitting the shark with all his might until it swam away. Naheed dragged Father to safety and pulled Father's boat behind him to shore.

In the summer of 2058, laughter became a thing of rarity as we listened to the news of war brewing in Kashmir. Father believed that Iran's secret service was behind the shootings in Kashmir. He couldn't believe it when an army was despatched to invade Pakistan. Fortunately, we were too far south to get any fallout from the nuclear carnage, but the huge dust cloud blocked the sun and our harvest was poor. Worse was to follow when civil war between Shia and Sunni Muslims erupted all over the world. About a quarter of our population was Muslim, the majority being Sunni. Unfortunately, Naheed was Shia. There'd never been any quarrel between the factions; indeed, many of Naheed's friends were Sunni. All this changed after the nuclear attack on Riyadh. To begin with, old friends just stopped seeing each other. It got really nasty after a Shia man was clubbed to death by a gang of Sunni men. A Sunni girl was raped in retaliation, and after that, all hell broke loose.

Dad, Grandpa and Naheed continued to meet in the evenings, but their talk was very subdued and sombre. Naheed was a farmer and his crop had failed. The nuclear dust was clearing, but it was too late for his rice crop. We weren't much better off as our vegetables hadn't grown well and for some reason the fish catch was poor. Naheed said that his six-year-old daughters were losing weight and he was distraught when he heard them trying to stifle their hungry sobs. Dad and Naheed pondered the possibility of sailing off to find somewhere better to live. The Maldives were suffering badly as the tourist trade had dried up. There were no stable countries to the east until one reached Australia. They'd heard that Ebola was waning in Africa, but that length of journey was out of the question in our little fishing boat. So they resolved to stay and somehow survive for three months until the next rice crop would be ready to harvest.

One evening, when I was listening, Naheed looked more troubled than usual.

"Ignatius, I have a terrible dilemma." He paused.

"Okay, spit it out."

"Some young Shia men have got hold of sniper rifles and are living in the hills above Eraniel. They are executing Sunni in the area one by one. I think this is despicable. My problem is that I've been offered a million rupees by a rich Sunni man if I tell them where they're based. One day, after Friday prayers, I gave a lift to one of the sniper's sisters. When I dropped her off, she walked towards those hills by Eraniel. I know there's a cave there and I'm sure that's where they're hiding. I've been given 100 Lakh and I'll be given the rest when I tell them the location of the boys' hideout. Although I believe the snipers are wrong, I'm reluctant to hand them over to be lynched. My problem is that I know this money would feed my family for years to come. What should I do?"

I never heard Father's answer as a neighbour's dog started barking. That night, I lay in bed thinking about how much food you could buy with 100 Lakh and I wondered what he'd said.

The following night, he looked even more stressed.

"I told my wife. She said it was obvious that I had to take the money for the sake of our girls. The problem is that I can't bring myself to betray these boys."

The next night, he didn't show up. Then at about 11 pm, I heard someone banging desperately at our door. I looked out and saw Naheed dripping with sweat and gasping for breath. Father let him in. I listened through the open door.

"I took the 100 Lakh back to the rich guy at his home, telling him that I'd failed to discover where the boys were hiding. I thought he would understand and would praise my honesty for bringing his money back. Instead, he tried to grab me. He's a mountain of a man. I dodged his grasp; terrified, I ran for my life. A gang of his neighbours, armed with clubs, screamed insults as they chased me. I reached my car just in time. Thank goodness it started first time. My wheels spun, kicking up stones as I accelerated away. They must have thrown something as my rear window smashed as I sped off down the road. I thought I heard gunfire and then I saw a grenade rolling under my car. I realised, too late, that it was a cricket ball. A moment later, I felt a sickening thump as a small child bounced off my bonnet, smashing my front windscreen. I know I should have stopped, but I panicked and put my foot to the floor. I left my car at Eraniel station, bought a ticket to Karakorum and ran here as fast as I could. I'm sure they'll see through my ploy and will be here soon. What should I do?"

Father paused briefly to think.

"Years ago, you saved my life, and now it's my honour to repay you. We'll leave by boat as soon as possible. Fetch your family as they'll otherwise be killed in revenge. While you collect them, we'll pack what little rice we have, put together some warm clothes for the nights and fresh water to drink. Now go, they'll be here soon."

Naheed briefly clasped my father and ran off to fetch his family. I was excited, if a little nervous, at the prospect of this adventure. I feared that I'd not be seeing my friends for a very long time, and was sad that Grandad wasn't coming with us.

I'd just sneaked my mother's beautiful hairbrush that was in-laid with mother of pearl into the packing when Naheed rushed through the door. He was closely followed by his wife and two girls. They looked scared, dishevelled, and the twin girls were whimpering quietly. Father took control and we were soon marching towards the sea. It was a cloudless sky with a warm easterly breeze. If the situation hadn't been so dire, it would've been very beautiful with the stars and a slither of moon reflecting off the calm sea. I was just enjoying the gentle susurration of the little waves when in the distance I heard the high-pitched scream of an engine, driven to its limit. Father made us push with all our might to get the boat launched. We jumped in; our outboard engine spluttered into life. The car screeched to a halt and six men ran down the beach. I heard a terrifying staccato noise, and ten yards behind the boat, the calm sea was turned into a churning maelstrom. We were soaked with spray.

"What on earth's that?" I shouted.

"Nothing to worry about; we're out of their range."

The village lights were soon a distant glow.

I gave Layla and Maryam a shawl each as they were shivering, whether from the stress of the situation or the cool wind that the motion of the boat was creating, I wasn't sure. They clung to each other, too frightened to talk. Tom, who was ten, two years younger than me, seemed to be revelling in the drama.

"Where are we going, Father?" he asked.

"At present, we are steering south-west, aiming for the Maldives in a couple of days. It's time for sleep; Naheed and I will take it in turns to steer the boat."

I woke in the middle of the night as Naheed and Father were arguing in clipped whispers.

"You must be joking! If we sail without light, we'll surely hit a rock."

"There's nothing between us and the Maldives. If we use a light, those ruffians will know exactly where we are."

"How do you know they're on that boat?"

"Why else would a fishing boat be out at this time of night?"

"They might be planning to use lights to attract fish."

"You know that's rubbish! Anyway, I would prefer the tiny risk of a collision than have them shoot our children with their automatic."

"Fair point. Okay, I can watch the compass with my torch. The breeze is blowing from the north now. If we hoist our sail and turn the engines off, we'll hopefully be out of sight by dawn."

That really had me scared. I thought we'd left them behind on the beach, but it seemed that my father was convinced they were following us!

The gentle rock of the boat must have overcome my fears and I woke with the sun blazing down. Any worry about being cold was long gone.

Fatimah, Naheed's wife, was cooking some fish they'd caught, and we were soon enjoying this with a meagre helping of rice. I looked around, thankful to see the ocean was completely empty. I didn't say anything for fear of upsetting Tom and the twins.

Father's boat was in reasonable condition. It was his pride and joy and was painted a lovely ultramarine blue, including the small cabin in the centre of the boat. This wasn't big enough for us all to sleep in, but there was plenty of space on the small foredeck. He'd added a small mast and simple sail after the time he'd run out of fuel on a fishing trip and had rowed for hours to get home. However, we females clearly had a problem. There was no toilet on the boat as the fishermen would normally just go over the side. Eventually, they found us a bailing bucket and a sarong slung over two poles for privacy.

To occupy the children, Naheed suggested that each of us hold a line with the heads of the breakfast fish attached. Nothing seemed to bite and then suddenly Tom shouted, "Help! Something's pulling me in!"

Naheed was over like a shot and reeled in the fish calmly and steadily until it was exhausted. Finally, he landed a small tuna.

That afternoon, we saw a low-lying island on the horizon. It took ages until we were sheltering under the shade of the plentiful coconut palms. It soon became apparent that it was very small and uninhabited. The only water we found was stagnant and infested with mosquitos in an empty coconut shell. The dry brown coconuts could be used to flavour our food, and the green ones at least quenched our thirst. We piled both types into the boat. We still badly needed fresh water.

We pushed off, setting a southerly course. We had to use precious fuel as the sea was flat calm with not a breath of wind. We were totally bored. Fatimah suggested we play mancala using coconut shells and some seashells she had collected from the beach. Tom and I enjoyed our contests, but Maryam and Layla were too young to get the hang of it and were restless. Maryam shrieked as a hermit crab climbed over her knee with one of our shells still firmly attached to its back. Time dragged as we drifted past abandoned islands. Many of them had been tourist atolls but were now lifeless, their artificial, soulless luxury slowly decaying. At last, Father spotted someone who must have been a retainer left behind to guard a particularly opulent development. We chugged over.

"Sorry, I've got no spare water. I have to get it from Male where there's plenty as they have a solar-powered desalination plant. Normally, I collect water when I pick up tourists, but I haven't had a single visitor for three weeks."

Layla started to sob, and with this, his heart melted. He gave us a little water, wished us well and gave us directions for Male and a description of the desalination plant.

We felt better and for a while I enjoyed watching creatures in the water. We caught glimpses of little grey fish, and some silver flying fish jumped over the boat, presumably escaping from a predator. The best bit was when a pod of dolphins joined us, surfing our feeble bow wave.

The next morning, we arrived at Male. We were given directions for the water plant and jostled our way through the busy, narrow streets. It felt strange to have so many people all around us after the seclusion of the last few days. I noticed that they were moving slowly and looked rather thin and wasted as they watched our odd little band walk by. We were thankful when Father spotted the large corrugated iron building covered in solar panels that we were looking for. We were met by a friendly man who greeted us and waved away our offer to pay for the water.

"We have more than we can possibly use and it keeps pouring out for free. You're not from round here, I think. Where are you from?"

Naheed tried to evade the question. "It's a long story; we won't bore you with the details."

"I'm interested as there were some scoundrels getting water yesterday who were asking about a group of people who might just fit your description. Come and have some food. We're fed up with the monotony of our present life."

With that, Aariz filled our canisters and we followed him to his ramshackle abode. His wife greeted us and prepared a meal of fish, rice and okra from their small vegetable patch.

While we ate, Naheed told our story.

"We've heard of the troubles between Sunni and Shia, but we've been spared any of that here. We believe that we're all children of God. We're Sunni, but we welcome you and want to free you from those horrible thugs."

"Thanks, but how can we lose them? We can't fight them as we know they have at least one automatic gun."

"First, my son will help me move your boat to a locked and covered boathouse. None of you must leave my house. They know they can't shoot you here for fear of being lynched by my neighbours. However, they'll be watching and as soon as you leave they'll look for an opportunity to attack. I'll tell you about my plan when we get back."

Father worried that although Aariz seemed friendly, could we really trust him? Would we ever see our boat again? We were relieved when they returned. We spent that afternoon making some effigies of ourselves by stuffing straw into different-sized hessian sacks and dressing these in Naheed and Father's well-worn *lungis*, Fatimah's colourful *shalwar kameez* and our T-shirts and trousers that the Sunni gang had seen us wearing. These were all put in a wagon under a tarpaulin and taken to the family's boathouse and hidden inside our vessel. At dusk, we all left, advertising our departure by walking slowly and talking loudly as we made our way to the boathouse. We left the harbour and could see two small atolls about a mile out to sea. Aariz described how in good times he would take tourists for an 'authentic' experience out to the northerly island, where he had built a shelter and cookhouse. The tourists would then row around to the southerly atoll which was tree-covered on its near side but had a secluded golden sand beach on its far side. While the tourists lounged on the beach, the family would prepare a feast to be served with chilled wine for when they returned. In reality, this couldn't be less authentic, as all the inhabitants of the Maldives are teetotal and would never choose to eat western-style food!

We had a snack in the shelter and then, using a torch, we left our manikins, propped upright, looking away from the wooded island. We used the rowing boat to return to Aariz's home. Father was fretting that his precious boat was being left unattended.

The following morning, Aariz went down before dawn to the harbour, pretending to work on his boat while he watched what was happening out at sea. Sure enough, he saw a dimly lit vessel landing on the far side of the southerly atoll. Ten minutes later, at first light, a blast of rapid automatic fire shattered the peace. The firing stopped. He watched as a boat disappeared out to sea.

He was overjoyed when he returned to give us his report.

"Why didn't they check that everyone was dead?" Naheed asked.

"They may've been afraid to go to the northern island in case they were ambushed. It's possible they ran out of ammunition. Anyway, I think that'll be the last we see of them. Good riddance! What are your plans now?"

Father paused, and frowning, replied. "We can't go home. We hope the Ebola epidemic has burnt itself out as we plan to sail to Africa."

Aariz's face fell. "That's more than 3,000 kilometres! You'll never be able to carry enough fuel. I noticed that you've a mast and sail on the boat. Your only hope is to use the trade winds, but the sea can get very rough and your boat might not survive a bad storm."

Father countered. "I agree, but we've no choice, we'll go when the trade winds begin. I've been told that the sea isn't too bad early in the season."

Hearing this, I pleaded, "Surely there must be somewhere nearer than Africa?"

"Sorry, Sarah, we've no choice. Aariz will help us get everything organised as the trade winds will arrive any day now."

They disappeared and we were allowed to explore the town and harbour until evening.

During our evening meal, Aariz told us about a voyage he'd made long ago. "A friend and I were getting paid to sail a luxury yacht to Pemba Island. On delivery, the owners paid us handsomely. We blagged a lift on a trading boat to mainland Tanzania, and from there, we hitched lifts to Lake Malawi. This place was so beautiful that I wanted to stay forever. The lake was full of fish and the water crystal clear. The soil on the shore was fertile and maize grew abundantly. The people were happy, well fed and welcomed us as if we were long-lost friends. I couldn't stay as I was engaged to my darling wife. If I were you, I would aim for that lake."

That certainly lifted our spirits, and Father resolved to find the lake. We woke as the giant orb of the sun appeared above the coconut palms; we couldn't thank Aariz and his charming wife enough for rescuing us. I had mixed feelings about boarding our newly stocked boat. Was this going to get us to our promised land, or would it be the vessel taking us to our watery graves?

We raised our sails to the faintest of breezes and slowly drifted out of the harbour.

As we rounded the end of the island, the wind picked up and we set our course, due west. We had a relatively peaceful week with gentle winds. It was quite cloudy, which meant we didn't have to drink so much. We had plenty of water and green coconuts. Regardless, Father was strictly rationing everything as he said we didn't know what lay ahead.

The next day the clouds gradually thickened, developing into a towering black thunderstorm by evening. The wind blew us ever faster in a westerly direction. It started to rain, gently at first. The boat was lit up by occasional flashes of lightning. We used a basin to collect fresh water from a tarpaulin we'd strung across the front of the boat. About an hour later, the waves began to crash over the boat as the wind howled around us. Father ordered us to tie the containers to the handrails. The sail was furled around the mast which we laid flat in the boat, securing it with rope. We crammed into the little cabin, sitting on the floor for stability. We'd only just taken up this horribly cramped position when the boat smashed into a massive wave. It was dark, but the water broke with white coruscating flashes of phosphorescence. Pale green balls were silhouetted against the light, washing over the side. That was the end of our coconut water. We were terrified as the waves continued to crash over the boat. I was sure we were all going to drown. Father and Naheed struggled with the wheel to avoid getting broadside to the waves. Fortunately, the cabin was watertight and the waves that washed over the deck were draining well through the scuppers. Fatimah had terrible cramp, which was a nightmare in such an enclosed space. The twin girls slept through in blissful ignorance.

Morning finally came; the clouds were less thunderous, although the wind and waves still propelled us at a frightening speed. Thankfully, we were all used to being on boats and no one was seasick, which would have been quite unbearable. By midday, the wind and waves abated and we were able to venture on deck to survey the damage. Thanks to Father's foresight, all the water containers, the sail and the mast were intact. We were able to erect the mast and with the sail up made good progress. That night, Father took a bearing from the stars and declared that we were well south of the equator; using his watch, he reckoned we had about 1,000 kilometres to go.

The sun shone relentlessly; water was running low. Fatimah made a makeshift shelter with the tarpaulin as we couldn't fit comfortably in the cabin. Days drifted one into another, and we started getting sores from lack of clean clothes and wooden planks for seats. After another week, we were completely becalmed. Father started the engine, but after about twelve hours, it spluttered and stopped. We were out of fuel. The top of my tongue was so dry that it stuck to the roof of my mouth. I feared we would die shrivelled up like dried tomatoes.

Morning broke with a slight breeze which picked up through the day. That afternoon, Tom spotted an island on the westerly horizon.

We arrived that night on a white sandy beach. Along the shore were some rickety old houses and what must once have been grand hotels; all completely deserted. The taps were dry. All the properties had been looted. Mangy cats stalked the alleyways. Father steered me away from a bed where a human skull was resting surreally on a grubby pillow. We found an abandoned army barracks and discovered a journal; its last entry January 2059. The journal had the rather grand title, *The President's Rifles of Lamu.* At least we knew where we were! We found a map in the barracks that showed we were 900 kilometres north of Lake Malawi. Father's makeshift sail could not be used to tack and so we couldn't use his boat any longer as the wind blew steadily from the east. Naheed had spotted an old dhow tied to the jetty. He went to check it over and returned with the news that it looked seaworthy. The sails were ripped, but nothing that we couldn't repair if we could find some tough needles and thread.

Just as we were all going to have a closer look, an old, stooped black man with snow white curly hair shuffled out of one of the houses. I thought he was using a stick, but I realised my mistake as he raised what was now obviously a gun into the firing position.

"Get away from my boat. What the hell are you doing here?"

He was clearly angry, but at least he spoke English and we could understand him.

Father told him what we'd been through to get here. The old man softened and lowered his gun as the story unfolded. We probably all looked near to death.

"Well, I guess you'll be wanting water, a shower and something to eat."

He led us into what must have once been a grand house, but was now in a sorry state of repair. We rudely gulped down great quantities of water. He took us to various houses to rummage through their dead owners' belongings to find some clean clothes. He'd fixed up a shower that worked from a rainwater sump. We used this in turn and it felt marvellous to be free of sweat and salt. We sat down to a meal of plantains, fish and some yellow moist doughy stuff he called mealie-meal. We'd never eaten anything like it before. It wasn't great but at least it filled our stomachs as we'd run out of rice a week earlier.

That night, I slept for twelve hours, thankful to be on dry land and in a bed for a change.

The following morning, Fatimah prepared mango, banana and papaya for breakfast. I was surprised that the old man had gone for a swim. When he returned, he told us that the island had once been a tourist mecca, but that it had suffered terribly when the drought hit East Africa. Then Ebola had swept through, killing the few who were left. He was the last survivor on the whole island. He said, "Nearly everyone has died in Kenya, and wild animals have taken over farms and towns. I suspect it'll be the same all over Africa. I've been thinking about it. That old dhow is of no use to me as it takes two to sail her. We could repair it together. Once you have gone as far south as you want, you will still have a long walk inland to Lake Malawi. You'll need a gun and some ammunition to protect you from wild animals. There are plenty of guns in the old barracks, but only a few bullets. I need to keep some, but I reckon you could have three, which should be enough to see you through."

Thankful for this generous offer, we set about mending the sails. After another good night's sleep, we loaded our water containers, mealie-meal and plantains on board. We thanked him profusely, winched the sail up the mast and cast off. Slowly, the rather heavy boat lumbered out to sea. The sail was enormous compared to our old fishing boat, but we made slow progress as the wind was very light and coming across our bows. Naheed felt we would be safer only visiting islands, and so we island-hopped down the east coast of Africa. We stopped at Pemba, which was like Lamu but bigger. There were rather more people alive and we didn't feel welcome. We filled up with water and set sail for Zanzibar. I'd read about this island at school and looked forward to seeing the old town. The shores were covered with tourist thatched huts built over crystal clear azure waters. After a bit, we found the old town, but it seemed rather wretched and forlorn. Stray cats wandered through magnificently carved wooden doorways. A monkey gazed down at us from a rickety colonial balcony as an old man limped through the arch of the stone fort. We still had water and so sailed to the south of the island. Having moored the dhow on a tourist jetty, we walked towards a modern hotel. Two pretty young African women suddenly appeared from behind a pillar.

"Sorry to pounce on you," the older one apologised, "we were checking that you didn't look dangerous."

They'd been working at this hotel when the troubles hit, and everyone else in the resort had either left or died. There were large vegetable plots that they tended behind the complex. We stayed with them for a few days, enjoying the comfortable surroundings. They even had electricity as the roof was covered in solar panels! I pleaded with Father to let us stay, but he was determined that we should reach our 'promised land'. We offered to take them with us, but once they knew of our planned trek, they opted to stay. They were from Tanzania and reckoned we should try to get to Lindi, which was about 300 kilometres down the coast on the mainland of Tanzania. If we were to then take a compass bearing west-southwest we should hit Lake Malawi. They gave us loads of fruit and vegetables and wished us well.

After the troubles in Kerala, I was thankful for the kind people who had helped us. I had no idea that our luck was soon to run out.

———

Ten days later, as the sun rose behind us, we arrived at Lindi where, having collected our few belongings, we abandoned the dhow. Lindi had once been a colonial town, but now its buildings, including an old Arab fort, were dilapidated and largely deserted. We started our long march inland. I had hardly walked at all for ten weeks and my legs were hopelessly weak. Within ten kilometres, I developed a blister on my left heel which hurt horribly, even though I limped to reduce the pain. The twins complained constantly and even the grown-ups looked exhausted. It was silent except for birdsong and an occasional troop of monkeys crashing through the branches. Just before dusk, we saw a most unusual tree towering above the scattered acacias. It had a tall, straight, smooth brown barrel-like trunk with little branches stuck on the top that looked like the incongruously small arms of a tyrannosaurus rex. Behind this was a collection of houses clustered around a small rusty chapel under the shade of avocado and mango trees. It turned out to be an old mission station. A hunchbacked elderly white man with a wrinkly, weathered face opened his door and bade us welcome.

"I'm Nathaniel; you appear to be lame, young lady. Have you hurt yourself?"

"I think it's just a blister."

"If you would like to wash in the bathroom, I have a few plasters left. You are welcome to have one."

I soaked and then peeled off my sock, which was stuck to the raw, weeping blister. Father applied a plaster, and after water and homebaked bread, I felt almost human again.

I don't know whether he was more amazed by our story or the other way round. He had lived there for fifty-five years. His only daughter had gone to university in Warwick and had sadly died of a drug overdose. He and his wife had never been able to come to accept this terrible loss, and for a while, he'd completely lost all faith in God. His other relatives in the UK were long dead. He was heartbroken when his wife succumbed to Ebola. He told how he'd prayed to be taken too, but however many people he cared for and buried, he never contracted the disease. Two people he nursed did survive and they'd formed a small community that worshipped in his little Methodist chapel.

"Are you aware that you have 300 kilometres to walk before you reach the lake? It'll be hard going as there are few roads and you'll have to climb some mountains covered in forest. Even if you're fortunate enough to reach the lake, you may find other people living there. You may not be welcome. I beseech you to stay. We have plenty of houses and the soil is fertile. It would be wonderful to have you all join our little community."

I knew Father had set his heart on reaching the lake, and I knew he was as stubborn as a mule.

I tried reasoning. "Please, Father, I think this place is perfect. At least let us stay for a year or two and then, when we know the country better, we could move on to the lake more safely."

As I feared, he wouldn't budge, but at least he said we could stay for three days to give my blister a chance to heal. Naheed and Fatimah chose to accept the offer as they feared the twins would never be able to walk so far.

Tom and I were devastated, but no amount of tears or persuasive arguments would change Father's decision. We enjoyed our stay with Nathaniel, who seemed to know every animal, bird and flower in the neighbourhood. He had some books with pictures of the local flora and fauna, which I found interesting and scary in equal measure.

It was with great sadness that we said goodbye to our friends, who'd become like family during our odyssey. We thanked Nathaniel, who had kindly given Father an old rucksack for our few possessions as we set off once again. The land was rolling scrub, but there always seemed more climbing than descent. At one point, we heard a deep rumbling sound which soon changed to loud trumpeting and crashing branches as a herd of elephants caught our scent on the breeze. I was thankful for the gun, but although Father raised it in readiness, the herd settled and we shrank away into the long grass. My muscles ached but I felt stronger than on our first day's trek and at least my blister was comfortable and nearly healed.

We started to look for somewhere to spend the night. There were no missionaries to rescue us this time. We came across occasional villages, but any thatched huts had completely disintegrated, and the more modern houses with galvanised roofs had broken windows. Human bones were commonplace, both inside these ruins and often scattered on the ground where animals had left them. Father kept hoping we would find an intact house and ignored our request for rest.

As we were walking along an overgrown dirt road, we came across three graves marked with crosses situated just outside an old wall. There was a gate that was locked. Father knocked, even though we could see that the house was twenty metres away. Of course, there was no answer. He called out. Silence. In the end, he lifted me up and I climbed over the gate and opened it from the inside. It was a single-storey house built with breeze blocks and a corrugated iron roof. We knocked on the door. No one came. Father tried the door. It too was locked. The strange thing was that there were vegetables and maize growing in the garden. We walked around the back of the house, looking to see if a window had been left open. Sadly, they were all locked shut. Inside looked clean and I could see four inviting beds. We rounded the last corner and were met with a double-barrelled shotgun being pointed at us by an elderly black woman.

"Get your hands up and stay where you are. I don't take kindly to trespassers. What are you doing here?"

I was pleased she too spoke English. She sounded fierce but looked like a frail grandmother with only a couple of wonky teeth which must have been worse than useless.

Father tried to mollify her, speaking calmly. "I'm very sorry we've intruded. We didn't know that anyone lived here."

"The gate was locked; didn't that give you a clue?"

"You're right. We're entirely in the wrong. We are trying to walk to Lake Malawi and I was looking for somewhere safe for us to spend the night."

"Where have you come from?"

"India."

"Well, you can't have walked from there."

"No, we spent three months living on a small boat before we landed at Lindi."

I was pleased to see her lower her gun.

"Well, you'd better come in and I'll get you some water; your children look fit to drop!"

We learnt that she'd lost her husband and two children to Ebola. She had no neighbours and was understandably afraid of looters who might harm her, hence her unfriendly welcome.

She'd once been a teacher and was able to give us some guidance about our route ahead. She said it would be tough going but worth it in the end; Lake Malawi was beautiful.

That was the end of our good luck. From then on, we had to accept any place we could find. The houses or huts all had their windows broken and had been taken over by all manner of insects, spiders and giant centipedes. That was the least of our worries. On three occasions, the heavens opened and we were soaked through before we could find shelter. Walking in wet clothes caused our skin to chaff in our groins. We often had to remove human bones before we could settle for the night. One of the huts was very dark, and as I was checking the bed for bones, I heard something large scuttling into the next room. I feared it was a monstrous big rat and screamed for Father to come and sort it out. I stayed outside as I have a morbid fear of rats. He started to laugh. I could hear him moving towards the entrance and was relieved to see he was preceded by a foot-long monitor lizard. Two nights after this incident, I was getting out of another disused bed in the night to go for a wee when I felt a needle stab my foot, followed by agonising pain; my foot was on fire. I must have screamed; Father rushed in and used our precious torch to find the culprit. A dun-coloured scorpion. I'd read in Nathaniel's book that the venom can cause numbness around the body and vomiting. Fortunately, I didn't get this but had a miserable painful night nevertheless. By mid-morning, the pain and swelling had subsided enough for me to get my shoe on and we set off once more.

At least the walking became easier as our fitness improved and my feet toughened up. Tom enjoyed looking out for birds and animals when the weather was fine. We often saw antelope and could easily have shot them for food if we'd had more ammunition. We foraged for fruit and maize that was growing wild in people's abandoned gardens and fields, but we never found enough and always felt hungry.

Roughly two weeks later in the afternoon, we saw a mountain range in the distance blocking our way to the lake. My heart sank. As we approached the foothills, I heard beautiful harmonic singing; moments later, I saw smoke and then people dancing in a circle around the fire. Oh, what joy and surprise to find a happy community still in existence! They can't have seen us approach as we were within a hundred metres before a tall, bare-breasted lady turned, pointed at us and started shouting. They all stopped dancing and stared in our direction. They were arguing loudly in some strange tongue and gesticulating wildly. Were they going to kill us and add us to the pot that we could now see boiling above the fire? Finally, someone who seemed to be in authority indicated we should move towards him. Using signs, it was clear that we were being invited to sit down and join them eating and drinking. My fears rapidly subsided as they brought us meat from the pot. I feared it was some form of bushmeat, but whatever it was, it tasted wonderful. We drank thirstily and felt better. They indicated we should join the dancing. We gladly obliged, thinking that this was the least we could do to repay their kindness. They were soon rolling on the floor in hysterics at our clumsy attempts. Three of them came over to teach us the steps and body postures. It turned into the most enjoyable evening. I think Father was a bit tipsy from the homebrew that all the men were drinking in copious quantities. We never learnt how they'd survived the epidemic as no one spoke English.

The following morning, we pointed to the direction that we wanted to take. They understood and showed us a hidden path that was well used at the point it left the village. It took us steeply up the mountain. At one point, the jungle cleared and the sun warmed our backs. Tom was in the lead and shouted that a large grey animal was blocking our path. Father ran past me and grabbed Tom and indicated that we should stand still. A buffalo was grazing quietly in a clearing. It was steaming slightly in the early morning sun; a red-beaked oxpecker was hard at work eating ticks just behind its enormous curved horns. I'd read that buffalo were very dangerous but thankfully he stared at us for a few seconds and then nonchalantly resumed his grazing before moving away into the thicket. Tom resumed his lead position and was looking up at the branches, hoping to see monkeys or birds in his usual way. Due to his upward gaze, he completely failed to spot a yellow and black snake that was sunbathing on the path and stepped right over it. Father grabbed my arm and pointed it out to me.

"Keep walking, Tom, and stop by the big tree. Stay still, Sarah, it's a puff adder. I'm sure it's more frightened of us than we are of it, be patient."

Sure enough, it soon slithered into the undergrowth, and we joined Tom.

"For God's sake, Tom, look where you're putting your feet!"

Father was clearly getting stressed out by the dangers as he never normally took the Lord's name in vain. From then on, he insisted on taking the lead and Tom sulkily walked with me.

Because it was so steep, we made slow progress. Eventually, we must have reached the top of the ridge as we started to descend, but couldn't see any view as the canopy was too thick. By late afternoon, we came upon a massive rock, and climbing onto this, we found we were standing at the top of a cliff. There beneath us was a vast shimmering silver lake, so enormous that we couldn't see the shore in the west. We wanted to reach the lake that day, but the path was steep and dangerous. We were still a long way up when dusk quickly turned to night. Fortunately, we stumbled upon a small cave at the foot of a rock face in which we could spend the night in relative safety. We lit a small fire at the entrance to ward off wild animals.

The next day, we reached the shore and found a deserted fishing village. It had no land for growing vegetables as cliffs rose up almost from the water's edge. There was an island a few kilometres into the lake. We found some abandoned fishing boats tied to an old jetty. Two of the boats had hopelessly ripped sails, but the third was relatively intact. It was big enough for three of us and had oars in case the wind dropped. Father decided we would take it and explore the island.

As we approached, we could see the island was flat and fertile around the shore but a forested hill filled the centre. As we rounded a headland, we saw maize fields that looked well tended and beyond them a collection of rondavels with smoke coming from a cooking fire. With happy memories of our last evening spent by a fire, we sailed round to the beach near the village. As we approached the shore, a band of young men came running down the beach shouting and waving spears and clubs. We obviously weren't welcome. Then a great gust of wind caught us unawares, and before Father could control the boat we suddenly lurched towards the angry men on the shore. Too late, I saw one raise a gun. I shouted; a shot rang out and Father cried out as he collapsed. I grabbed the rudder and forced it hard over. Fortunately, the wind caught our sail. I pulled this tight to harness the wind and we were soon racing away from the shore. Tom was hysterical. Blood was pouring through Father's trousers; he was obviously badly wounded. I made Tom take the rudder and found some thin rope to use as a tourniquet and pulled with all my strength to stop the bleeding. I got Father to put his finger on the knot and tied it double, hoping I'd done enough. It carried on oozing but at least the main flow had been stemmed. Father was very weak and felt faint. I laid him flat in the bottom of the boat. He suggested that we let the strong wind take us west and hope to find the distant shore. He drifted in and out of consciousness, but after an hour, he stopped moaning; I hoped the pain had abated.

As the sun began to set, I saw trees and then land. We made rapid progress and the hull was soon scraping up a sandy beach. Again, I heard singing. This time, I located it in a primitive church with a rusty corrugated iron roof. I left Tom with Father and ran, as fast as the sand would allow, towards the church. As I entered, the door creaked and eight heads turned to stare at me. They stopped singing and a kind-looking lady ran over, looking shocked to see me covered in blood. "Tell us, child, what on earth has happened?"

"My father's been shot."

"Where is he?"

"Please come quickly."

They all ran with me to the boat where Father lay slumped as I'd left him. He woke as we approached and ignoring my entourage, he took my hand and said, "Thank you, Sarah. I can see fields and this beautiful beach. You have brought us to our promised land."

An imposing regal lady, with big brass earrings stretching her lobes, stepped forward.

"I'm Grace Malongwi. I'm a qualified nurse. Are you in pain?"

"None whatsoever; my daughter has done a wonderful job, saving my life and bringing me here. Thank you for asking. I'm Ignatius Theakumkal and these are my children."

"Good. It's still imperative that we get you to our clinic and clean that wound up. There's an old door behind the church. Rubber, please fetch it, we'll use it as a stretcher."

He ran off. I thought his name was rather odd but didn't say anything as Grace was trying to look at Father's leg. It was getting too dark to see accurately, but as she felt the tightness of the rope, she grimaced. She stood as Rubber returned, carrying the door as if it was made of balsa wood.

"Okay, Rubber, take his shoulders. Samuel, take his good right leg and I'll take his left leg. We'll move him onto the stretcher at the count of three."

We were soon at the clinic, which had electricity due to solar panels. I was thankful to see that it was spotlessly clean.

"Rubber, you take the children, while Samuel and I sort this wound out."

I realised then that Tom was also covered in blood. We'd been travelling in these clothes for two weeks without washing and must have smelt awful. Grace had two children: a girl called Precious and a boy called Blessing who were about our age. After a makeshift cold shower, they lent us some clothes. Their home also had a solar panel linked to a battery which supplied a small LED light in every room.

Fresh fish, vegetables and mealie-meal were prepared for us by a motherly lady called Sweet. It was wonderful to have a proper meal after our last two weeks of slumming it. She introduced us to Angel and Easter, who were her foster children. As we ate, I told of our adventures. Sweet relayed how they'd all fallen in together. "Grace has lived here for years running the clinic. She nursed many patients with Ebola, including her husband, who died. She's sure she and her children, Blessing and Patience, are immune. She saved my life when I caught it. Angel was a baby when her family succumbed. Easter stumbled out of the bush on Easter Day two years ago. He can't have been more than four at the time. We assume that his family died and he found his way here by God's guidance. Rubber and Samuel have both lost all their relatives. We are all one happy family now."

I couldn't restrain myself any longer.

"Why is he called Rubber?"

Sweet laughed. "I'd forgotten how strange that name must seem. To us, that's just what he's called. We enjoy giving our children names which may have special relevance to the parent, like Blessing or Precious, or occur in the Bible, like Samuel, or sometimes they're just amusing. Rubber's surname, you see, is Banda."

I heard approaching footsteps and then Grace appeared.

"Tom and Sarah, come and see your father. His wound is cleaned, but no blood is reaching his leg. I'm sorry, dears, but this isn't good news."

I felt myself dissolve as the truth of what she was telling me slowly sank in. A consoling arm embraced me, but I was beyond being comforted. We walked slowly to the clinic. I wanted to be brave for Father's sake. In the event, Tom and I both broke down while he smiled as if nothing was wrong.

"Don't cry, my dear children. I'm not in any pain and you're in the care of some truly wonderful people here. We're all very lucky. Now you must let me get some sleep and I'll look forward to seeing you both in the morning." I kissed him as I tried to stifle my sobs.

As we appeared for breakfast, I could tell by the sadness on everyone's faces that I should expect bad news. Grace put her arms around both of us and hugged us tight as she spoke. "My dear children, your father is comfortable but he is very poorly. Sadly, we can't save him. He may not last the day."

I was devastated when I saw him sweating profusely, mumbling rubbish in his delirium. There was an unpleasant odour in the room, which I feared boded ill.

That afternoon, I held his hand, although he seemed to be deeply unconscious. Grace had filled the room with freshly picked frangipani. This did little to disguise the dreadful smell. After about an hour, his eyes suddenly opened.

"Thank you, my darling girl; you must look after Tom now."

With this, he slipped back to sleep, looking more peaceful.

Later that evening, I could see a faint pulse beating rapidly in his neck, but he looked deathly pale. Grace came in, took one look at him and left immediately to fetch Tom. About an hour passed. His breathing became quite irregular, shallow and bubbly. There was a pause and then he took one last breath and was silent. Tom ran over to me. Grace embraced us as our tears flowed freely.

That night, I went over and over the last few days, trying to think how I might have saved Father. I kept coming back to the grimace that Grace made when she felt the rope round his leg. Had I pulled it too tight or not tight enough? I had no idea and didn't want to ask. If only we'd never gone to that island, we would've arrived here safely. As it was, I felt very lonely. Tom was my only relative in this whole vast continent. We had no hope of ever getting home. I crept over to his bed and snuggled up to him, crying myself to sleep.

It all turned out much better than I'd feared. They were a happy, friendly community. While the men went out fishing, the rest of us all mucked in with the planting, weeding, harvesting and cooking. I loved singing while we worked. Soon Tom and I learned the words and joined in. In the evening, we would often play what they called Bao, which was like Mancala.

I became very friendly with Rubber. He told me exciting stories about life in his village as he grew up. I still don't know whether they were true or not. He taught me how to milk cows and to spot where the chickens hid to lay their eggs. He was immensely strong and could carry Tom on one shoulder, with me perched precariously on the other. Then he would run into the water and throw us into a deep pool. Sometimes, he'd pretend he'd seen a crocodile or hippopotamus coming towards us and we would shriek as we ran out onto the beach. It was true that there were hippo and crocs in the area, but I never saw them on our special beach, which was called Nkhata Bay.

About six months after Father died, Tom complained of a headache as he was going to bed. He said it wasn't too bad. I checked his neck wasn't stiff. (I must've learnt that in first aid.) I said it was nothing to worry about and if it wasn't better in the morning, we would tell Grace. I went to sleep thinking about harvesting and drying the maize crop which we were due to pick the following day. I woke with the morning sun already beginning to bake our little room. Tom was still asleep, which was odd as he was usually awake before me and would leap onto my bed as soon as he heard me stir. Once I was dressed, I went over and shook his shoulders. His eyes remained firmly shut but he was breathing normally. I began to panic, remembering his headache, and thumped him with no response. I ran out and shouted for help. Soon everyone gathered round his bed as Grace examined him. He had a high fever, was deeply unconscious, but otherwise looked remarkably normal. Once Grace had heard about the headache with no neck stiffness, she said she feared it was cerebral malaria. I'd never heard of such an illness. I'd read about malaria in history books, but it had been eradicated in India long before I was born. Grace said she would try to syringe some liquid quinine down Tom's throat, but they really needed to give it via a drip. Tragically, they'd run out of this option over a year ago. He never regained consciousness. Three days later, he died, leaving me totally alone. He'd been my greatest friend all my life. I felt so angry that God had caused me so much misery!

About a year after we arrived, I was in Sweet's bedroom where she'd taken me for privacy. She had noticed my breast buds and was just telling me about periods when we heard a thunderous knocking at the door. No one ever knocked as we never had visitors. By the time Sweet and I appeared, everyone else was outside talking to two huge identical white men who were carrying some strange weapons that looked a bit like wide-barrelled guns.

"Hi, don't be alarmed. We're here to give information. Are you all present and do you all speak English?"

Samuel replied, "We are and we do, but come on in. We still have some tea, or would you like fresh milk?"

"Thanks, we've walked ten kilometres to get here and would be grateful for water, if you have some."

They came inside, thankful to sit in the shade after their long march.

After some polite preamble of names and asking how we'd all survived and met each other, one of them told us why they'd come.

"We're soldiers and have been sent by the new leader of the world to discover where survivors are living in Africa. Your new leaders can offer you comfortable homes, free electricity, clean tap water, schooling and health care. You'll be given grain and enough land to grow fruit and vegetables. You can keep chickens and cows. There'll be work to do, but you'll have plenty of free time for recreation and holidays. In return for this comfortable lifestyle, we'll determine where you live, ask you to surrender any weapons and obey the law. You'll be vaccinated and have an anaesthetic while a bone marrow sample is taken.

"Alternatively, we've seen your church. You can live here if you're prepared to share your land with other Christian folk. The area that has been designated for Christians in Africa extends from here to the game parks of the Shire, Luangwa and Zambezi Rivers. Because of the dangerous animals in these parks, your area will be surrounded by a high electric fence which you'll not be allowed to cross."

Grace looked surprised. "Who's going to pay for this shiny new future? You must realise that Africa is completely bankrupt."

"You're right. Africa has been through unimaginable horrors, and most people have died. Our leader believes that Africa has a wonderful future. The country is amazingly beautiful and full of wonderful animals and birds. Tourists will flock here once modern hotels have been built. Of course, none of this is feasible right now. In answer to your question, Xantec, which is the name of the company that now rules the world, will pay for the reconstruction of Africa. We'll leave you with a detailed leaflet explaining everything. You'll have six months to think about it. Around that time we'll return to hear your decision.

I'm sorry we have to be so brief, but there are only a few thousand of us to cover this vast continent. Please would you tell us who your nearest neighbours are?"

"We only know about a group of people who live on Likoma Island on the eastern edge of the lake. Be careful, as they've been known to shoot strangers. They survived the Ebola outbreak by preventing contact with other people."

When they left, we read through the leaflet, pondering what this meant and trying to decide which way we should jump. We were all very suspicious of the fence. They said it was for our safety, but we all thought it sounded more like a concentration camp.

Samuel, who hadn't joined in, said, "No need to decide straight away. We should all pray about it. I suggest that we keep our thoughts about it to ourselves for about a week and then we'll meet to vote on it."

I didn't know what to think. I didn't like the sound of this anaesthetic. Was this all a ploy, like in the Second World War when Jews were told they were going to have a shower before poisonous gas poured from the ceilings? On the other hand, having free food, houses, electricity and holidays sounded fantastic. In the end, what mattered to me was to stay with my new family, and I'd go along with whatever they chose.

Later that night, we heard what sounded like an explosion. It reminded me of the quarry in Kerala. It came from the direction of Likoma Island. If they'd just killed them all, the regime must be ruthless. I hoped my new family would choose to live in the Christian enclosure.

That week lasted forever. I noticed several of my friends walking, lost in their own thoughts, as I'm sure they were all trying to decide what to do. To be fair to Samuel, during his Sunday address in the church, he didn't try to push one way or the other. He just said we should listen to Jesus.

The day that would determine our fate arrived. Samuel placed an old cracked bowl on the floor in front of us. He said we should each write our decision on a piece of paper and put these in the bowl. If there was disagreement, we would listen to everyone's view in turn.

As Samuel opened the papers, I feared a rift might split us.

"All the adults and Precious have agreed to stay where we are and join the larger Christian community. Sarah has said she would go with whatever the adults chose. Of course, the young children didn't vote, but Blessing has expressed his wish to join the new society."

Grace's mouth hung open, her eyes wide in disbelief. She turned white and I feared she might faint. Samuel's calming, melodious voice cut in.

"Blessing, we appreciate that the promises those soldiers made must seem attractive. We fear that this is a trap that will lead to you being enslaved while you are unconscious from the anaesthetic. You are a good, brave boy, but I believe it is too hard a decision for an eleven-year-old to make."

I watched Blessing's face with fascination as this speech went on. The kind, smiling face that I'd come to love contorted with anger.

"You're not my father and you've no idea what I would like and what would be best for me!"

With this, Grace's face resumed its usual stern appearance. She marched across the room, took Blessing by the arm and dragged him, snarling with humiliation, into his bedroom. Ten minutes later, he reappeared and apologised to Samuel, and agreed to stay with everyone else.

———

Those six months flew by. A week after opening the votes, Samuel and Grace announced their engagement. The great day came; the church was decorated with bougainvillea and frangipani. Samuel couldn't marry himself so Rubber stepped in to do the honours. Afterwards, we had a feast as Rubber had used one of our bullets to kill an impala which we roasted on a spit. It tasted fantastic and there was plenty left over. We ate a lot during the next few days, while the remainder had been cut into thin strips to make biltong in the hot, drying sun.

When the twin soldiers reappeared, Samuel informed them that we would like to continue to live in our little community, even though we understood that we would be joined by other Christians inside a fence.

"About a hundred thousand Christians have opted to join you. They'll start arriving in a few weeks. People and robots will come and drill boreholes. These will be solar powered and will fill large reservoirs on high points in the area. From these, water will be piped for drinking and irrigation. Enough simple houses will be built. You've been allocated a vast area and that should give everyone more than enough land to feed themselves.

As soon as your area is settled and completed, new towns will be built outside the fence."

I was apprehensive, wondering what these other Christians would be like and whether our happy community would be irreparably disrupted.

In 2060, China moved its army west to confront India and its allies. Both superpowers were equipped with the latest drones and droids. They also had sophisticated anti-aircraft missiles that effectively negated the use of air strikes. The result was a mass of destroyed hardware with few human casualties; a stalemate had ensued.

They were saved from this wasteful charade by a ceasefire, followed by a conference in Moscow arranged by Australia and New Zealand. India and China signed a peace agreement and spent the next few days in discussion with leaders from around the world. Commander Spitzen and her Board were then invited to join them.

Black joined me as we watched the press conference.

The imposing Australian President took the podium. "I speak on behalf of all nations outside of Xantec control. The world has suffered carnage for two years. Trade has virtually halted, shares have plummeted and our people are impoverished. We would like to invite Commander Spitzen and her Xantec organisation to assist all our countries. Africa is devastated and has no working governments; we propose that Xantec helps them too."

Max joined him. "If invited, we will gladly help any country as long as we are allowed to take absolute control. It'll take time to improve everyone's standard of living, especially in Africa, which I understand is a complete disaster at present."

———

Commander Spitzen called all the Commissioners to a meeting in the Great Hall.

I thought she looked older, and certainly her face looked tired and weary under her silvery grey hair. I suppose it must have been the strain of her work, as I assumed she was having anti-ageing injections like the rest of us.

She took the platform. "We've been asked to govern the remaining countries of the world. This includes the continent of Africa, which has become an anarchic morass of poverty and disease after the Ebola epidemic. We believe that Africa needs to be firmly stabilised by our clones and Commissioners before we can modernise it. In two years, I want the whole of the world to be thriving. The Commissioners who were previously based in California and Pennsylvania will be assigned to Africa. The rest of you will be notified of your tasks tomorrow."

I saw Petra talking to her mother and hoped she would arrange to meet me before I left. I'd never been to Africa and was fearful of what we would find. Horrible images of stinking piles of dead bodies being scavenged by hyenas sprang to mind.

In the event, everything moved too fast; we had endless briefings and meetings. Two days later, I was in an advance party flying to Israel. From there, Gregor, Sandy and I crossed the Suez Canal and used a petrol-powered 4X4 to drive to

Cairo. We didn't see anyone along the road, and even Cairo was practically deserted. The few people we glimpsed rapidly disappeared, scuttling away down bright alleyways. It became apparent that no one lived in the city; these people were looters. My faithful clones ran and caught one of these shifty miscreants. I learnt that the few survivors now lived along the banks of the Nile, where they could irrigate their crops. They said it was relatively peaceful, although very primitive there. He showed us to the airport, which was in good condition but covered in a thick layer of sand. The only bulldozer we found needed diesel and I cursed that we only had petrol. There was no choice but to use shovels. I found the midday sun unbearable and was embarrassed to keep stopping and recovering in the shade. In the meantime, Gregor and Sandy continued working through the heat of the day.

A few days later, the first planes landed. We set up base in what must once have been a very plush hotel; it was now empty and bedraggled. The first planes brought food, water purifying equipment, mattresses, tables and chairs. Most importantly, they sent us enough solar panels to light the place and charge our equipment. There were thousands of abandoned cars and 4x4s in good condition, just without any fuel. We ordered tankers of petrol as well as diesel to be brought in from Israel.

Ships carrying clones and Commissioners would investigate the coastal areas of the continent. The centre of Africa would be reached initially by clones in 4x4s who would prepare airports so that Commissioners and supplies could be flown in.

I was fed up with sitting around in the hotel. My boss must have sensed this. My clone friends were going to prepare airports in the Sahara and the Sahel in a 4x4 with a backup oil tanker. He allowed me to join them. Our first mission was to open the airport of Benghazi (Libya) so that experts could be flown in to get their oil fields functional once more. This struck me as ironic as Xantec was still committed to ending the use of fossil fuel.

Libya was even more tragic than Cairo. At least Cairo had some beautiful old buildings; Libya's towns were still bombsites from the civil war that occurred after Gaddafi was deposed. Having prepared the airport, we travelled along the coast and then turned south through the empty desert of Southern Algeria. It was December and we huddled close to our campfire to keep warm during the evenings.

Xanasa guided us to an oasis. This blew my mind as it seemed unbelievably green after the sandy wastes we had driven through. Crops were thriving and weaver birds were chattering as they fed their young, ensconced in their intricate upside-down nests. Most surprising of all, it was full of people. I asked them how so many of them had survived.

"We'd heard about Ebola on our mobile phones and set sentries to prevent anyone visiting our oasis."

They had solar energy for their base station and some of their mobiles were still working. They knew that Ebola had burnt itself out and hence, they'd allowed us to visit. We stayed two nights in this paradise and then moved south into Mali.

I'd never heard of the Dogon people. We saw some funny mud houses with little conical thatched roofs high on a hill. The village appeared empty so we parked under an old acacia tree. Sandy had just put our kettle on for a brew when we were suddenly surrounded by spear-wielding tribesmen, wearing wooden masks depicting strange creatures and contorted faces. After a couple of minutes, we heard a piercing cry and suddenly we were forced to the ground as they menaced us with their sharpened weapons. Two warriors parted and an old man stood before us. I spoke to him in Dogon and his face lit up with surprise and delight. The spears were instantly withdrawn and we were welcomed like long-lost cousins. Like the oasis-dwellers, they'd prevented travellers from entering their compound after word had reached them of surrounding villages catching the contagion. They wanted assurances that we were free of the disease. I told them it was over and it was now safe for them to allow visitors into their village. The chief spoke loudly to his assembled tribe with a surprisingly high-pitched voice. A vibrant ululation rose from the women who had materialised from their huts. At the party that night, they were all singing and dancing to the haunting sounds of their odd stringed instruments and drums. Some of the local women flirted with Gregor and Sandy. I was clearly too puny to be of interest.

Sadly, we'd work to do, and had to move on to prepare the airports in Niamey, Kano and Obuja.

As we entered Nigeria, I was saddened to see the place littered with plastic bags and bottles. We passed a massive granite rock as Obuja appeared on the horizon. It was a modern city with tall glass and steel buildings. It was much greener here than we'd been used to, and already the jungle was beginning to invade the smaller buildings. For all its previous wealth, it was now as destitute as all the other African cities we'd driven through. As we drove up a wide boulevard, we were surprised to hear another vehicle overtaking our petrol tanker. We'd just passed an abandoned church when a burst of automatic fire shattered our back window. Glass was everywhere and blood was streaming down my cheek. I didn't seem to be seriously injured but I heard Sandy cry out and guessed he was hit. There was no time to attend to him as I heard the scream of an engine approaching. I turned and was horrified to see an old khaki jeep catching us fast. I noticed that the machine gunner was reloading his magazine and ducked down, hoping to avoid the next round when…

"Hold on tight," shouted Gregor as the car spun, screeching its complaints. The handbrake turn completed, we rushed headlong at the jeep. They swerved at the last moment as Gregor lobbed a sonic bomb into its open front window. A massive explosion caused the jeep to career off the road, ramming into the trunk of a large tree. We pulled up beside them and soon had all three occupants safely cuffed. Sandy was supporting his left arm and was bleeding heavily from glass cuts at the back of his head.

Gregor took control. "Let's have a look at that arm."

He cut off Sandy's left sleeve to reveal a bloody pulp of oozing flesh where his triceps should have been.

"Looks like your lucky day, Sandy. I think the bullet missed your humerus."

"Fuck my lucky day, you bastard. It hurts like hell!"

"Okay, okay. I'll give you some morphine. I always thought you were a bit of a junky. Then we'll get this cleaned up."

"Sir, would you check out that church over the road and see if it would be suitable to camp in?"

Thankful to leave the blood and gore to Gregor, I went over to check it out. It was intact; I even found a lockable vestry that would be suitable for our prisoners. By the time I rejoined them, Sandy was gritting his teeth as Gregor was cleaning his wound with spirits.

"Fuck, fuck, fuck. Excuse my French, sir," as he clenched his teeth once more.

"That scratch will be fine in a couple of weeks," Gregor added derisively.

I helped bandage it tightly to stem the bleeding, thankful it was Sandy and not me being abused by Gregor.

———

By the following morning, the prisoners' hearing had partially returned. I told them to take us to where they were living. We set off and it soon became obvious that they were leading us on a wild goose chase. I gave Sandy the nod and he grabbed their leader, putting him in a neck lock within an inch of his life, using his good right arm. That concentrated his mind and they directed us straight to a high-walled compound. Once inside the gates, we observed a sizeable colonial-style brick building surrounded by cottages, a barn and large flowering trees. It looked like it might have been a wealthy private school at one time, but the playing fields had been turned into a vegetable farm where emaciated women and girls were bent over mattocks, hoeing the crops. We drove past the barn and stopped in front of the main residence.

As we escorted the prisoners onto the veranda, bullets flew over our heads, ripping into the second floor. Windows disintegrated and brick dust filled the air. They must have avoided firing directly at us because of the prisoners. Sandy kicked open the wooden doors and we pushed the captives into the relative safety of a reception hall. Gregor chucked me a gun while he and Sandy went out the back to circle round to the far side of the barn. I crouched beneath a window, keeping a watch on my prisoners while firing random shots in the general direction of the barn to distract our assailants.

About two minutes later, another sonic bomb went off; we had two more prisoners.

I went to talk to the slaves. They were surprised that I spoke Yoruba and listened intently as I explained that we'd come to free them. They warned me that there were two more 'masters' and that they would be back soon. Their overseers had apparently gone to trade vegetables for meat at a market a few kilometres away. I requested that they carried on as normal so that the remaining gangsters wouldn't suspect anything when they returned. I parked our 4x4 round the back of the old school and took charge of the prisoners in the refectory while Gregor and Sandy prepared an ambush in the hall. A few minutes later, I heard a jeep pull up. The door opened, a sonic gun fired; two more prisoners.

I contacted Max and told her what had happened. She said there must be a dispassionate trial. She would get a judge to watch me question the witnesses and the prisoners via my Xan-link and also view the recording that I'd made of the last few hours.

We called the slaves into the refectory and showed them the prisoners.

"What about their whores?"

This was news to us.

"They'll be hiding upstairs."

I ran up and unlocked the door guarding the second floor. I was surprised by the opulence that greeted me. There was a large TV, sumptuous furniture and rugs that had been looted from hotels in the town. The windows had all been shattered by the gunfire, and the room was covered in shards of glass. Nine frightened, heavily made-up girls in 'western-style' clothes were hiding behind the furniture. Two of them had cuts on their faces but none were seriously injured. They looked terrified. They must have heard the sonic bombs and thought we were going to kill or rape them.

"Don't be alarmed; we're here to help you. You're quite safe now."

They were still very tense, not knowing whether they could trust me.

"I've been sent with my two soldiers to restore order in your society. The world is finally trying to bail Africa out. We know you've been through living hell, and can only apologise that it's taken so long for us to assist you."

They seemed to be slightly less anxious now.

"Come downstairs and we'll all have some food and drink together."

One of the girls stepped forward; she was strikingly beautiful. She looked to be about seventeen; the oldest girl in the room. They were all well covered and looked fit and well. Although I'd spoken in Yoruba, she now talked in perfect English.

"I'm Martha. We can't come down. The female slaves hate us, although we've done them no harm."

"Perhaps you could tell me how you ended up here?"

"We were the only girls who survived Ebola at our boarding school. These monsters rushed in with guns blazing and mowed down the three teachers who had hidden us in a sports cupboard." She then hung her head as she continued softly. "They eventually discovered us. We were all raped. They then brought us here to cook and clean for them. We've been raped most days for the last two years."

"I am truly sorry for you. You've all suffered terribly, but I promise you that your ordeal is now over. I'm sure if the other women knew what you've been through, they would understand. Would you be willing to come downstairs? We're about to hold a court session when the prisoners will be tried."

"Will you guarantee our safety if we come down?"

I gave them my word and reluctantly they followed me.

They crept down the stairs with heads bowed, avoiding the 'slaves' hostile stares.

I took a seat behind a desk at one end of the refectory. "I'll ask the questions as there are no lawyers. The trial will be viewed by a judge in our homeland."

Martha asked, "Sorry if I'm being stupid, but there isn't a camera, so how is the judge going to view this? Are you pulling a fast one?"

"I should've explained. I'm a Commissioner and my brain is connected to Xanasa, and her brain can be accessed by any other Commissioner. So the judge will be watching."

"I've never heard such improbable rubbish! I'm certainly not convinced," she sulked.

I asked Martha to repeat her testimony in Yoruba. As she told of their capture and rape, I noted surprise then shock and sympathy appear on the faces of the 'slaves'. I then asked the other women to describe how they'd been captured. Some were lone survivors and were just snatched from their fields. Others broke down in tears as they described how their men and boys were rounded up and hacked to pieces in front of them before they were brought back here.

Another said, "I was a cook at this very school and was here when they broke in. There were two teachers and twelve boys at the time. They held me with a gun to my head as they ordered the others to go into the barn. I heard many shots. I never saw the teachers and boys again. I've been a slave for nearly two years."

I asked the men why this had happened.

The jeep machine-gunner answered. "We'd all been in the army under Colonel Lowassa at the Obuja barracks. The Colonel was well meaning but made a terrible mistake. When Ebola hit the town, he ordered us to collect patients and take them to the nearby hospital. Quite quickly, many soldiers caught the disease. One evening, ten soldiers went to a bar and ended up sleeping with women from the town. At the time, these soldiers didn't know they were infected. Within two days, six of these ten, followed by most of the battalion, became ill and soon died. Some of the women and their families also became infected. When word got out that the soldiers had caused this outbreak, the surviving men and youths from the town marched on the barracks. By then, there were only nine of us still alive. We were terrified and locked ourselves in the armoury. We smelt smoke and soon flames engulfed the buildings. We grabbed weapons, ammunition and came out with all guns blazing. Two of our comrades died. The protestors fled, carrying their wounded. We were able to douse the flames and saved the armoury, food store and fuel depot. We stayed in the armoury and raided the storehouse. It was horribly cramped and uncomfortable. All the living quarters and the kitchen had burnt down. We had to live off cold tinned food as we were too afraid to leave the building. After a month, the disease had done its worst. That was when we left the barracks to find somewhere more comfortable to live. We found this school. We never planned to kill anyone, but when we arrived, we recognised one of the teachers who'd attacked us at the barracks. We suspected that the other teachers and boys had been among the rioters. We killed them all in revenge for them killing our friends. Sir, we are not bad men. We were driven to this out of revenge."

"That is not for me to decide. Our judge will pronounce her verdict at 10 am tomorrow. Please take the prisoners and guard them in the old shower block, Sandy. Perhaps some of the women from the field gang would join these girls preparing food in the kitchens."

The slaves approached the girls with kindness, having heard their gruesome story.

The judgement came as no surprise to me. "Guilty; they will spend the rest of their lives doing hard labour at a prison which is nearing completion in Port Harcourt."

I found that two of the women could drive, and I asked Gregor and Sandy to guard the prisoners as they drove to Port Harcourt. In the meantime, I was horrified to be shown the sleeping arrangements of the 'slave' women. The 'warlords' hadn't bothered to find mattresses for them, and so they'd had to sleep with rags as covers on the floor of what must once have been the school dormitories. I spent the day ferrying mattresses, clean sheets and chairs that I found in a nearby hotel to the dormitories. Martha had taken charge of the kitchen and had arranged a rota for cooking and cleaning. The 'slaves' couldn't believe their luck as they were given meat to eat two days running! Martha had asked everyone if they preferred to work inside or on the land. The atmosphere of the whole compound had been transformed as the new community took shape.

As soon as Gregor and Sandy returned, we cleared the airport. With our tasks completed, we set off for Cairo followed by our petrol tanker.

The Egyptian conference and return to Costa Rica

All Commissioners who had been assigned to Africa were recalled to Egypt for a conference. We were told to discuss possible solutions to the problems we'd encountered. This continued for three days.

You have already read about the new towns and lifestyle that was offered and rejected by Sarah and her friends on the shore of Lake Malawi. The clones had discovered that most survivors had chosen to take up this offer and were happy to be moved and to learn to speak English.

Besides the Christian enclave in Malawi and Zambia, Sunni Muslims were offered a community in Algeria; Copts and orthodox Christians were offered one in northern Ethiopia.

Tribal people who'd always lived in harmony with their environment were allowed to continue their ancient way of life, providing they agreed to vaccination and chipping.

Any survivors in the Sahel would be evacuated as it was now too dry to support modern life and tourism. Goats and other domesticated animals would be rounded up and moved. Drought-resistant bushes and trees would be planted. It was hoped that a balanced ecosystem might develop which would slowly spread into the sands to the north.

I had two months' leave and asked to fly home before I had to take up my position as the administrator of Malawi. I was determined to see Petra, however angry her mother became. I liked Gregor and Sandy but was fed up of reconstituted dried food and looked forward to Jas's cooking. As the plane left behind the sandy vastness of Egypt, I looked forward to the vibrant greens of the Costa Rican jungles. I spent the journey home trying to work out how I might see Petra.

Jas greeted me looking rather miffed. "I thought you were never coming back. You've been away for months, and the first time I knew you were alive was your brief message yesterday." She paused and smiled wanly. "Sorry, I'm pleased to have you back, but I've missed you." Another pause and this time her old smiling self. "I've just started to prepare some curried fish with fresh mangoes and pineapple."

I felt bad that I hadn't communicated. Perhaps she really did miss me; I had surely missed her! I would mend my ways in future.

The following day, I sent a note to Petra via my friendly flower girl. "My darling Petra, I've got eight weeks off. I've missed you terribly. Is there any chance you could get some leave? I have a plan."

She replied. "Great to hear from you. I've missed you too. I can take a week off in three weeks' time. Love you. P."

I sent a message back suggesting that she should book a week's diving off the coast of Tulum, Mexico, with Miguel's dive school. Miguel would tell her my plan when she arrived.

I was pleased to discover that Charco was also home but would only be free for two weeks. We hired a dive boat in Belize and took our droids with us. We spent the next ten days cruising up the barrier reef; eating, drinking, laughing and diving. Charco knew all about my love for Petra and was happy to assist. I dropped him and Cooli off at Chetumal in Mexico and gave him a handwritten message for Miguel in Tulum. Miguel was to take Petra to the cave just east of the Grand Cenote in the Sac Actun cave system at 10 am on 8/12/60.

I had a week to cruise up the coast and moored about ten kilometres south of the cave. I knew that my chip wouldn't be detected once I was six metres under water. I took a jet-powered underwater scooter that could travel at 12 kph and ample oxygen for my return journey. I knew these caves well and hoped Miguel would find the one I had in mind. I waited nervously and then bang on time they appeared. Petra must have told him about our situation as he left us saying he would be back in an hour.

Gloom and neoprene didn't make for romance. There was so much to say.

"I've missed you terribly, Zig. I wish we could communicate when you go away for so long. It's horrible not knowing what danger you might be in. Life here has been stressful. I'm worried about Mom as the apocalypse has forced her to lead the world, and it's not fair for one person to have such responsibility. I've been too exhausted to be of much comfort as I've been incredibly busy working on a revolutionary way of treating mental illness."

I told her about Africa. At the end, I couldn't help myself and asked, "Would you like to leave everything and live in one of the quiet secluded religious groups? I really enjoyed my time with the Amish. Have you heard about the autonomous areas in Africa?"

"I would love nothing better. I want to marry you and have children, but my Mom depends on me, and my present research could transform the world. I'm sorry, please be patient. I'm certain it'll all come right in the end."

"Petra, I love you dearly, but we've been having this clandestine relationship for twelve years now. I can't take it any longer. Meeting in a cave was quite exciting the first time. You may think me odd, but I'd prefer an evening eating and drinking on a balcony overlooking the Pacific and then spending the night together."

"Do you think I'm a nun? Of course I want that too. I didn't ask to be born the only living relative of the world leader. I'm sure something will work out one way or another."

I feared I was losing her as she had become unusually petulant. Without thinking, I spoke my mind.

"I'm sorry, Petra, you may be right, but I fear the situation isn't going to change. Max has the same anti-ageing injections that we do. She could live as the leader of the world for hundreds of years!"

I was angry and unbelievably disappointed that all the effort I'd put into this meeting was coming to nothing. It was too dark to see her eyes, but I couldn't avoid hearing the soft intakes of breath between muffled sobs. Just then Miguel arrived. Miguel quickly assessed the situation, put his arm around her and led her back towards the sea.

I was disconsolate. How had this ended in such disaster? I screamed into the echoing void. Annoyed with my ineptitude, I prepared to dive.

I couldn't be bothered to eat, drank too much rum and woke with an unbelievable headache. I lay in bed all day, having asked the captain to get me back to Belize City hyperloop as quickly as possible. I was soon home; even Jas's cooking didn't interest me.

Time dragged as I kept rerunning our disastrous meeting. Was I being so unreasonable? If she loved me, surely she'd have agreed to my request. I wished I could've removed her from the unhealthy influence of her mother. I hated Max in a way that I'd never hated anyone else before.

———

A few days later, Charco visited. "Hi, mate, sorry to hear you are feeling down."

He paused. I knew he wanted me to open up, but I didn't feel like it. I was annoyed that he knew that I was upset. Was I so obviously miserable?

"How did you know?"

"Jas sent me a message."

That made me even angrier. How dare she send messages without getting my permission? I'd have to be firm and put a stop to this once Charco left.

It seemed he was in no hurry, helped himself to a drink and poured me one.

He just sat saying nothing. I knew that trick; I was sure he was hoping I would break the silence and start telling him what was on my mind.

He capitulated. "I've just installed a new emotion and empathy upgrade into Cooli. She's much more like a human now. You should try it." Afterwards, he went on and on about his new girlfriend who was a doctor Commissioner, and then about his project at work. Finally, he left.

I drank myself to sleep, wishing that I'd saved some xanacea.

I woke feeling even worse, especially as I had to return to Africa in two days' time. I remembered about Cooli's upgrade and thought it couldn't do any harm. I ordered one for Jas.

As soon it was installed, Jas looked glum. "I knew you were sad after your failed meeting with Petra, but I couldn't feel anything myself. Now I know how ghastly this has been for you. I'm so sorry that you're going through such misery. I would be devastated if you were to give me to someone else, or if you were to die on one of your scary missions." With that, she came and encircled me with her arms, and for the first time since I had broken up with Petra, I found I was crying my heart out. That night, she kissed me gently on the cheek and said she cared for me more than anything or anyone and hoped I would soon be my old self once more.

As I left, I noted how sorry I was to say goodbye to Jas. I'd never felt like that about her before, and made a mental note to contact her. Of course, she had no Xan-link, so I would have to remember how to use mobiles. Jas gave me a spare old mobile to take with me. Then it struck me: would there be a network in Malawi? There was so much to accomplish before we could move people into their new towns.

Return to Africa

I had been given responsibility for Lake Malawi, the Christian reserve to the west and the Shire game reserve in the south of the country. The land to the north and east of the lake would initially be uninhabited, although nominally it was also within my remit. The game reserve is on the eastern bank of the Shire River. I'd chosen to build a town on the western bank as it drains from Lake Malawi. I'd given instructions for the engineers to build me a suitable residence overlooking the lake on the edge of the settlement. The only other governed township in my area was being built just north of a potential tourist resort that I planned for Nkhata Bay.

I took a car from Lilongwe Airport and drove to Nkhata Town. Fortunately, there were many bulldozers in working order and fuel was now available throughout the continent. The new town was half built and would be ready in a couple of months.

I'd asked Xanasa to scan the qualifications and suitability of all the citizens who would be under my jurisdiction to find someone capable of administering Nkhata Town. She came up with Black Mungani. I thought 'Black' was a most peculiar name for an African person. He had an English grandmother and had studied politics at Bristol University. We'd agreed to meet at the building site of the new hospital. I arrived a little late and saw two men standing in the shade of the half-finished building. One was huge and very black, and the other was smaller and clearly of mixed race. The larger man stepped forward with a welcoming smile and to my surprise introduced himself as Black. I guess that explained his name as his skin colour must have been a surprise to his half-caste mother. We immediately hit it off and I quickly realised that he'd be far more intelligent than me if I didn't have a Xan-link.

After briefing me, he frowned. "Do you realise that bringing different tribes together is sure to lead to fights, if not outright warfare? Many of these tribes have been enemies for centuries."

"I'm sure the Board is aware."

"Don't look so serious," Black chuckled.

I was pleased to see he was smiling again.

"I've a plan, but I'll need a boat to carry building materials to a small rocky island."

"No problem. Are you planning to tell me what you're up to?"

"No, but trust me, this'll work."

I slept on the ferry that took me to Shiretown. My new home had a west-facing balcony from which I could watch the sun setting over the lake. I had my own speedboat moored to a private jetty. I was met by Tiny. This might have been an appropriate name when she was born, but she now resembled a honey ant with a small head atop a spherical body. She was to be my cook and housekeeper. I hoped her size might reflect the standard of her cooking. I was quickly disabused of this optimism as I struggled to eat mealie-meal, tough bits of fatty goat and overcooked greens. I thought that tourists would never eat this muck and asked Xanasa whether rice or potatoes could be grown in Malawi. I was pleased to learn that both had been grown at different altitudes before the troubles, as well as coffee and tea. I gave orders for the droid farmers to get these growing ASAP. Of course, it would take many months before they could be harvested. I thought I might die of starvation by then. How I missed my home and Jas.

I decided to send for Jas, but I needed some way of contacting her. Within a week, engineers had set up a solar-powered base station for mobiles to communicate via a geostationary satellite that Xanasa positioned over central Africa. I sent a message to Jas to come directly and to bring two sacks of rice and my wave-skimmer.

The ground was fertile, and we could keep it that way as engineers had set up a sewage plant that produced dried pellets which could be used safely as manure. Thanks to the warmth and irrigation, we could grow vegetables in about ten weeks from seed to table. Within six months, we should have bananas and passion fruit. There were still many avocado, guava and mango trees in the abandoned villages in the surrounding area. They would have to do for now until our communal orchards were producing our own fruit.

———

Three days later, Jas arrived. She seemed genuinely pleased to be with me again. I was thankful to be able to release Tiny to look after Black, who I hoped might like this dreadful food.

The first people were bussed in. They were amazed to find such a modern town in the middle of the savanna. The houses were made from steel and toughened glass, with insulated roofs that had integrated solar panels. I was told these should last for over a hundred years. There was no wood used, both for ecological reasons and also to prevent attacks by termites. The new residents were afraid the glass would shatter, leaving them exposed to thieves; and they also worried that as there were no curtains, they would be on view in their bedrooms. I demonstrated how the glass could change colour and become opaque (the novelty had been developed from research into how cuttlefish change colour), then I picked up a sledgehammer and swung it at the glass. There was a rapid indrawing of breath. They were astonished when the glass remained intact. We walked to the community hall where I'd arranged for an enormous old television to be hung on the wall. One of the clone soldiers had found this, along with a library of ancient DVDs in a hotel in Lilongwe. I reckoned they would need some distraction to avoid the violence that Black had predicted.

Everyone worked hard and soon had their gardens tilled and all manner of vegetables, bananas and paw paws were planted.

Only a week after our citizens arrived, Black was proved right when the first knife attack occurred. I used Jas's old mobile to phone him. He said he was ready for the first occupants on his island. I was to send the culprits as soon as their wounds had been dressed. All the residents of Shiretown could watch the punishment in the community hall each evening, where Black would play a video taken from his mobile. I still didn't know what he'd planned. The following evening I went to watch.

The picture was a little grainy but the men were easily recognisable, sitting at opposite ends of a large caged area of decking. There was a wheeled wagon filled with food and water which was positioned at the bottom of rails that ran up a steep slope ending at the cage. A rope stretched from the wagon to the cage. At the top of the rails, I could see a small opening through which the prisoners could collect the food, should the wagon reach there. The video must've been taken in the morning as the sun was just above the horizon. The bigger of the two men stood up and tried to pull the wagon. Using all his strength, he shifted it about a metre, and a great cheer went up from my fellow watchers. Then his shoes slipped and it fell to the bottom again. He tried another three times without any shoes but lost his grip each time. He gave up in disgust and resumed his seat as far away from his other cellmate as possible. The smaller guy stepped forward. He wasn't wearing shoes and his feet looked calloused, and we hoped he would get a better grip. A murmur went through the crowd and then encouraging shouts as he took the strain. He didn't slip but could hardly shift the weight at all.

The video jumped to what must've been the late afternoon. The two men were looking very dejected. The bigger guy had hogged the meagre shade provided by a small overhanging tree. The smaller man moved towards the shaded area. I could feel the tension in the room as they sensed an impending fight. He started to mime. He was clearly indicating that he was very thirsty and hungry, and he wanted the big guy to work with him to pull the wagon. It didn't take long and they were soon pulling together with 'No-shoes' acting as the anchorman. Cheers went up from the crowd as they pulled the wagon up the slope and attached it to the cage. Smiling, they filled their stomachs and quenched their thirst. The camera then panned to a door that we hadn't seen before. It was now wide open. They collected more food, water and hesitantly entered. Inside was a comfortable air-conditioned room. There were beds, armchairs and a separate toilet, all labelled in English. There was a television with arrows pointing to a button which the small man pressed. A DVD started to play a simple English language lesson. They sat and watched, surprisingly intent as they ate.

———

Three days later, we were invited back to the community centre to watch again. The camera zoomed in on the men, who were standing together with arms around each other. To my amazement, they slowly and rather hesitantly started to speak. "Please would you let us out so that we can return to our friends in Shiretown?" A huge cheer went up from the crowd as many of them must have understood. Drums started to roll as the door at the back of the room opened to reveal Black smiling broadly and behind him the two new celebrities. The crowd erupted in welcome and the women started ululating. They were soon dancing and Black beckoned us all to move outside. While we'd been watching, he'd set up a platform with drums and guitars at the end of the earthen football ground. That morning, a pig had been butchered, and pieces of meat wrapped in banana leaves had been buried with red hot stones in the ground. The meat was now being dug out by men while the women were preparing roast cobs and dishing out homemade beer. A band took the stage and soon everyone was dancing and singing. The celebrations went on well into the night.

I tried the beer, which was as disgusting as the mealie-meal, but I was clearly the only one who thought so. It was a great success. Finally, Shiretown had been born.

CRC Conference December 1st 2062

Commander Spitzen called us all to the Great Hall. A massive survey of the wishes of the people of the world had revealed that the majority were fed up with the remorseless pace of change that they had had to live through during the last forty years. They had had enough of scheming corrupt politicians and corporations, as well as criminals trying to scam them. They were concerned about nature and pollution of the environment. They wanted to be allowed to lead a healthy and, if possible, happy life, free from worries about how their families could survive. Above all, they wanted peace and stability and, if possible, time to enjoy their beautiful world. The following is the *communique* distributed at the end of the conference where the Commissioners tried to address these pleas.

<u>To prevent war</u>

We believe that war is the root of much tragedy, misery and hunger in the world. We will strive to eliminate some of the causes of war:

- Greed – Money will no longer exist and we will develop other ways to incentivise people to contribute to society.

- Power – Administration of the world will be performed by Commissioners, with the support of armed clones. All other weapons will be destroyed. Xanasa will monitor all communications and stamp out any uprising before it gains traction.
- Religion – Allowing people to live in separate communities of their own religious persuasion has been a success in Africa. Similar communities will be offered to all religious groups.
- Tribalism – In Africa, tribes were forced to integrate and speak English. Where appropriate, this will be repeated and English will become the world language.
- Overcrowding – The world population has fallen to seven billion after Ebola. In future, family size will be strictly limited so that the population remains constant. People will be allowed to move to Africa if they choose. (People with fair complexions will be restricted to the far north and south of the continent.)
- Young men – In future, girls will outnumber boys at a ratio of 4:3. All children will have puberty delayed until fourteen, allowing them more time to enjoy their childhood and to develop civic responsibility before their bodies become flooded with testosterone.

To improve human happiness

1. We will aim for good mental and physical health.
2. We will provide comfortable, light, warm accommodation with pure tap water.
3. There will be ample healthy food.
4. Everyone will have meaningful work until retirement.
5. Parents will have free time to look after babies and children.
6. There will be excellent support for parents with young children.
7. All children will be well educated with a very high teacher/pupil ratio.
8. Everyone will have enough free time and holidays to enjoy family, sports, hobbies, culture, entertainment and travel.
9. Retired people should feel useful. They will be responsible for helping with grandchildren, gardening and voluntary work that they choose to perform.
10. We will strive to eliminate violence.
11. Rewards will be given to people who maintain local traditions, be that carnivals, regattas, cheese rolling, etc. Hard work or success in your chosen creative occupation will result in extra holidays, and also allow people to choose designer goods, art works and so on.

To reduce disease

1. Genetically healthy offspring will be chosen where this is agreed by the parents.
2. Everyone will be vaccinated against infectious and sexually transmitted diseases.
3. There will be an annual blood test to check on the health of the body as well as to check for cancer indicators to eliminate this at an early stage.
4. A trial will be run to see if obesity can be banished by genetic changes and limiting carbohydrates in people's diets.

To conserve europa by reducing dependence on fusion power

1. Africa will derive its energy from alternatives to fusion power.
   a. The central Sahara will be covered by a massive solar array. Energy derived from this will be transferred around Africa by superconductors that are cooled to near absolute zero, thus eliminating transmission wastage.
   b. The 'shark-moles' will create a tunnel from the Mediterranean Sea to the edge of the Qattara depression in the desert of north-west Egypt. The water will then plummet inside pipes into the world's largest hydro-electric plant. The lake that forms

will become a tourist attraction. Evaporation will eventually equal the flow of water into the lake and should increase rainfall in the surrounding area.

2. All new towns will be built with energy conservation in mind. (For details, see postscript.)

3. Throughout the world, dams will be built to provide water for wildlife, irrigation and hydro-electric plants.

Ecology

- Vegetarianism will be encouraged. For those who want meat, it will be synthesised from vegetable and bacterial sources.(Some domesticated animals will be kept, see postscript.) This, together with a reduced world population and improved efficiency of farming, will mean that only a small fraction of the world's surface will be needed for food production. There will be many woods and parks for human recreational use. Vast nature reserves will be created where billions of trees will be planted. Towns will be demolished in places where they should never have been built. For instance: in areas of severe earthquake, tsunami or volcanic risk and those built on floodplains.

- Most fish for human consumption will be farmed. Trawling will be banned. A small quantity of line fishing in the sea and rivers will be permitted.

- Plastic packaging and bottles will be eliminated. Paper bags will be used for dry materials, fruit and vegetables. Liquids, fish, butter, etc. will be delivered directly to steel containers in people's homes.
- Any gases and other by-products of manufacturing will be collected and recycled.
- All food crops will be genetically engineered to reduce the need for fertiliser and chemicals (see postscript).

Existential Threats

1. As soon as a mutated bacteria or virus is detected, strict quarantine will be mandatory and travel from the infected area will be halted in order to avoid a pandemic. Each house in the infected area will be provided with a machine that will detect the mutated DNA in exhaled breath to catch any new cases at the earliest possible stage.
2. We will keep enough nuclear missiles for use should a meteorite threaten Earth.
3. We will stop transmissions being beamed into space to reduce the risk of alien life forms discovering Earth. We will constantly modernise our spaceships so that we are prepared to confront an alien invasion should that ever arise.

This conference marked the beginning of Xanasa ruling the world. To improve unity in the world, dates associated with Christianity (AD, or in the year of our lord) or the Islamic or the Juche calendar of North Korea would terminate. The new calendar will begin from the date of this conference (AX, or in the year of Xanasa) and henceforth, December 1st will be celebrated as Xanasa Day.

The story will now be taken up by Ewan, who was born twenty-five years after these decisions were made.

When we were twelve, Mum explained how my twin sister and I were born:

"In AX22 (AD 2084), the UK voted for babies to be incubated. (Africa and a few other countries chose natural births.) I was thirty-three and single at the time. If you wanted children, you had to live with a man for a year before you were allowed to marry, and you had to start incubation on the first of March before you were thirty-five. I had one year to find a man!

"One day, while windsurfing in Dale harbour, out of the corner of my eye I saw this guy flying towards me, completely out of control. I leapt into the water just as his board crashed over mine. I surfaced, screaming blue murder at this inconsiderate moron. My expletives abruptly ended when I recognised the miscreant was the mid-field magician from Carmarthen City FC. Apologies turned to laughter and Huw and I were soon sharing a hyperloop pod on our way back to his penthouse in Carmarthen. I'd found my man! A year later, we moved in with Nana and Grandad in Bridetown, as you are not allowed to bring up children in cities. Grandad taught Huw the rudiments of gardening and everything looked rosy.

"By March AX24, we had twenty of our embryos developing at the incubation centre. All were genetically modified for skin colour. By then, it was obvious to me that Huw wasn't the sharpest knife in the drawer. Without telling your father, I'd asked the doctors to enhance the intelligence of all my embryos. A single cell was then taken from each blastocyst for DNA analysis. Twelve were discarded because of genetic imperfections. From the remaining eight, I chose one male and one female at random."

Rhiannon and I were taken from our incubators on the first of January AX25 (AD2087).

We lived in Pembrokeshire in an idyllic place called Bridetown, which was near Dale Harbour. The town had great facilities for children and was surrounded by beaches and tourist resorts.

My first memory is of hurtling down a water slide between Dad's legs, both screaming, as we plunged into a heated pool.

I used to love junior school, where we spent our time interacting with computers and droids, being told stories by the teachers or messing with paint and materials. Grandad never stopped telling us how horrible school was in his day. He'd had to learn Mandarin and chemistry; subjects that he hated.

After lunch at school, Mum and Dad would collect us and take us to the beach or to play in the park. If it was raining, we would go to the low-gravity play area where we would practise riding bikes or using hoverboards.

When we were seven, we went to watch Dad play for Bridetown FC in the championship finals in Carmarthen. The team won and Dad was named man of the match for scoring two goals. He was welcomed home as a hero that night. The Mayor hosted a celebratory party in the town centre and he was given two holiday credits[7]. Rhiannon and I were excited, wondering where we would go on holiday. It was Crete! Mum taught Rhiannon to windsurf while Dad taught me to use a wave-skimmer.

This idyllic childhood wasn't to last. The following year, Bridetown FC was knocked out in the first round. Dad was struggling with fitness and was sent off after ten minutes for deliberately tripping a player who had sprinted past him heading for goal. I'll never forget my humiliation as he was booed off the pitch. He gave up football after that, became depressed and started drinking homemade cider.

He stopped playing with us and would often not bother with work. (He was supposed to be coaching the juniors at Bridetown FC.) He was never to receive another holiday credit.

I missed having him play with us and withdrew into my books, computers and VR worlds. My friends at school were into futuristic sci-fi stuff, creating terraformed planets and engaging in intergalactic trade and wars. I loved to immerse myself in VR reconstruction of historic events. It was fantastic to be 'present' in the room when important world events were announced. I enjoyed feeling part of the relief and celebration when Queen Elizabeth I was told that a storm had caused the destruction of the Spanish Armada. They called me the 'weird nerd' at school.

Mum loved her work as a windsurfing instructor at Dale, earning many holiday credits so at least we could go on holiday with her.

Mum routinely assisted Nana onto her sitting hoverboard in the morning as she set off to help in the library. (Some old people had never liked holographic books.) One morning, Mum had to go to the windsurfing centre early. She'd asked Dad to help Nana. I soon heard him yelling and swearing as he couldn't get the safety harness to work. I went out and showed Dad the button that allowed the belt to click in. He didn't thank me, just snarled, "You're such a smart alec."

The following week, Rhiannon was reading about the history of Wales. She asked Dad where the Celts had come from before they moved to Wales. He said, "They were trying to escape the Romans who were fighting them in France; they sailed over to Wales."

Smirking, I corrected, "I think you'll find they were mainly driven out of England by the Anglo-Saxons. It's possible that many weren't genetically Celts at all, but just adopted their culture."

I smugly turned back to my Dylan Thomas poetry. A fist smashed into my face and a sticky burgundy puddle was soon threatening one of Mum's handmade rugs. "That will teach you to be such a know-all!"

With that, he strode down to his garden shed, leaving me and Rhiannon in tears to clear up the mess. We were both astonished at Dad's brutality.

From then on, he drank more heavily. I would often hear arguments when he staggered into my parents' bedroom.

One evening, Mum was working late. We'd finished our evening meal that our droid had prepared. I was in my room, lost in the Battle of Agincourt. The noise of battle and the whistling arrows almost drowned out the shouting in the adjacent room. I heard a plate smash, took off my VR headset and listened at the door.

"It's not the first time you've been late. I've seen you smiling at that bloody Gethin. You're a fucking whore!"

"He's just Rhiannon's music teacher, nothing more, and you know it!"

"You're full of your fucking lies, always some bloody excuse. I'm not having it. Do you hear me!"

"Have it your own way. I'm starving; let me eat."

"You're going nowhere till you tell me the truth."

"For fuck's sake, I've just been at a meeting; now get out of my way!"

I heard it then; the crunch of fist on bone, followed by a softer sound as she crumpled to the floor. A soft whimper gave way to sobs. Soon after, I heard Dad apologising and saying that he loved her really. I could hear him running a tap, presumably to clean her wounds. I was too afraid to leave my room and crept into bed, pretending to be asleep.

The following morning, Mum had a black eye and a graze on her forehead. She said she wasn't feeling well and spent the day in bed.

After each attack, Dad would be remorseful and attentive for a few days, and then either Mum or I would cop it again. We learnt to make excuses for our bruises.

One day, Mrs Evans, my favourite teacher, called me back at the end of school.

"What's happened to you, Ewan? Have you fallen again?"

"Oh, that. I just fell off my hoverboard last night. Stupid really, I should have the hang of it by now!"

"Ewan, I'm worried about you. Is someone hitting you? Are you being attacked by pupils or is it someone in your family?"

"I told you, it was an accident, nothing more. Thanks for asking anyway."

She let it go at that. I walked across the playground where a group of my classmates were playing football. They stopped when they saw me and started chanting, "Teacher's pet, teacher's pet…"

A wave of anger surged through my body. I found myself charging at Dai (who just happened to be nearest to me) and punched him in the stomach. I must've caught his solar plexus as he doubled over in pain, unable to breathe. Mrs Evans came charging over. Thankfully, Dai was breathing normally by the time she arrived, but still distressed. I was dragged back into the classroom where Mrs Evans summoned my mother. While we waited, she asked all kinds of embarrassing questions about our home life. I started to panic, fearing I was going to be taken away. Mum arrived. She was distraught. She said (and this was true), "Ewan has never hit anyone before. I think the children must have provoked him as he is normally a gentle giant. Fortunately, we'd pre-agreed the hoverboard story. Mum apologised and reassured Mrs Evans that she had everything under control and was sure there would be no recurrence of such behaviour.

The incident shook me badly as I was constantly afraid that I might be taken away from my family. I still used to get angry at times. When I was at school, I suppressed it; but my fury would erupt as soon as I got home, smashing plates and shouting at Mum and Rhiannon.

Dad continued to hit us when he was drunk, but after the school incident, he made sure that my bruises didn't show.

Eventually, Mum's boss made her tell the truth. He reported the situation to the town Mayor, and a hearing with a jury was arranged. Dad pleaded guilty and was given community service. He had to remove the muck from the town's communal horses' stables (see postscript) for a year. During that year, he did try to control his anger.

As he neared the end of this sentence, a celebration was planned in town. Sylvia Davies, who ran the restaurant in the park, had been awarded ten holiday credits a year for ten years. This achievement meant both she and our town would be rewarded. An unusually hot swimming pool with VR, which would make it feel as if we were swimming along a tropical coral reef, would be built in the town. Sylvia herself was given a house shaped like a crescent moon that fitted snugly into the cliffs overlooking Lindsay Bay. The Mayor had given permission for the clone soldiers to shoot five stags and two boars. The usual four-unit limit on alcohol would be waived for the night, and a live band would play in the town square.

The whole town was buzzing when Rhiannon and I went early for the children's races and games which were to precede the evening feast. I saw Mum and Dad walking a little apart as they arrived later. It was the first time I'd seen them together in public for a long time. The difference between them was striking. Mum looked fantastic with sun-bleached blonde hair flowing over her tanned sleek body, her only blemish a small purple birthmark on her forehead. Dad was greying with a scabby bald pate. His florid face contrasted with his pasty white neck and arms. His abdominal muscles had turned to flab and his belly hung in folds over his unpleasantly tight trousers.

"You keep your eyes to yourself, Gethin," he growled at Rhiannon's music teacher who had momentarily been watching Mum.

"What are you going to do about it, you great blubbery boozer?"

He had underestimated Dad, who may have looked out of condition but underneath was still immensely powerful, as I knew to my cost.

With three giant strides, Dad was on him; a straight right knocked the teacher off his feet. He fell, limp as a rag doll; his head smacked into the sun-baked clay with a sickening thud. He was absolutely still for about ten seconds. All around people stared, stunned by the violence. Then he started to convulse. It was harrowing, watching his body twitching and jumping while his face took on a violaceous hue. After about a minute he lay completely still. Mum rushed over and put him in the recovery position. Already our neighbours were on their X-talks, calling for an emergency drone. Within minutes, he and his wife were airlifted to Carmarthen Hospital. Clone policemen marched Dad off. Mum, Rhiannon and I were inconsolable. We must've made a sorry sight, isolated in our misery as we left the town to their dispirited feast.

The teacher was pronounced dead on arrival at the hospital. Dad would be tried for murder.

Dad's case came up before the Commissioner's Court in Carmarthen. Mum attended, sitting on her own. There were so many witnesses that Dad's guilt was not in question. His lawyers argued the case for manslaughter; the prosecution wanted a murder charge. In the end, the commissioner referred the case to the Supreme Court in CRC.

We couldn't attend as there were no hyperloop tunnels under the Atlantic, and Mum wasn't going to waste credits going by ship. (Only Commissioners were allowed to fly.) His past history of violence against Mum was taken into account. He was found guilty of murder and sentenced to gaol in CRC for twenty years.

I'd come to hate him, and was relieved he was out of the way. Rhiannon missed him as he was always very soft on her, and yet even she couldn't forgive him for killing her music teacher. Initially, we were shunned by the community, but gradually they accepted that it wasn't our fault and their natural warmth and friendliness returned.

———

When we were ten, we started using nasal sprays to delay puberty.

In August that year, Rhiannon and I had been swimming at Musselwick Bay. We were following a grey-haired, doddery lady up the rocks when she slipped on some green slimy seaweed, twisting her ankle. We supported her with our arms around her shoulders until we spotted a stout stick which she used to hobble to the drone landing site. Bronwyn thanked us profusely and invited us to come to her place the next day as she had some strawberries that needed eating up. Her home was another prefab like ours, but her furnishings were bog standard and rather dull. All the furniture started out the same in our houses, but our mum had been awarded lots of credits and so was progressively transforming our place with designer furniture, curtains, rugs and paintings.

Her living area looked out over her immaculate garden. To our surprise, there was an even older man slumped in a chair in the corner. He was sleeping with his head bent in a most unnatural way, a glistening dribble of saliva hanging from his chin. He woke as we must have disturbed him. His eyes looked cloudy as he slowly surveyed the room trying to work out what was happening. He finally located us and immediately smiled.

"Hello, this is a lovely surprise. We don't get many visitors, especially young, sophisticated ones like you. I'm Harry. Do you two happen to have names?"

He told us that he was Bronwyn's father and asked us all about our lives and what we enjoyed doing.

He became a good friend. I would often visit when I'd nothing else to do. I loved his stories. He'd been in the SAS and told of survival in the mountains of Afghanistan hiding from the Taliban, and of trekking through the darkness of the Arctic when suddenly the icy mountains were lit with the wavering greens of the Northern Lights. Once, when his unit had been ordered to survive without support in Hwange Game Park, he'd heard some creature prowling round his bivouac in the middle of the night. "I shone a torch and two bright white eyes glowered back at me; then the creature turned and calmly padded away. As soon as it was light, I found lion tracks around our camp."

Two years later, as he neared 105, he became very frail. Bronwyn was eighty-one and could no longer cope with him.

He looked more serious than usual. "Ewan, the Mayor visited the other day. He was very understanding but before he left, he said I really must choose one of the following options as Bronwyn can't manage me any longer:

1. I can move into a flat with a carer droid looking after me.
2. Live on a cruise ship where the human carers change every few weeks.
3. Move into an old people's home with views over Dale Harbour.
4. Or maybe take some pills that would put me to sleep.

"I'm not afraid of dying, but I enjoy your visits, Ewan. Would you still visit me if I move to the nursing home?"

I didn't need to think about it.

After he relocated, I would use the cycleway around Dale Bay twice a week to see him. One afternoon, about a year later, he complained of indigestion and died shortly afterwards.

I missed those rides, and Harry's face that lit up when I appeared through his door.

———

When we were fourteen (January AX 39), we stopped the puberty-blocking nasal sprays. Rhiannon started taking oestrogen tablets. All of our school year (we were all exactly the same age) went to hospital for an anaesthetic to have a bone marrow sample taken from our right femurs, and the girls also had their ovaries and uteruses removed. At the same time, we had our X-talks fitted. (These were secured within elastic waterproof bands around our wrists.) We were told these must NEVER be cut off. They were needed to summon emergency aid as well as for communication, ordering food and clothing, music, photography, etc. They would answer any question we asked of them.

We all moved to 'middle school'. Here we learnt about ecology, geography, creative arts, life skills, gender, relationships and appropriate sexual conduct. We also learnt about history and how Xanasa had saved the world.

In March, we all hit puberty simultaneously. That summer, there were wild parties on the beach; music, dancing and driftwood fires. Suddenly everyone was falling in love; girls with girls, boys with boys, boys with girls.

Two boys and one girl didn't seem to be affected by this orgiastic epidemic and carried on as normal. I wished I'd been like them. I knew I liked girls and the testosterone was making me as horny as anyone, but it had also caused me to develop a revolting crop of acne. No girl would look at me, let alone be seen to go out with me. One morning, Mum took me to the doctors' instead of school. The doctor gave me tablets which she said should clear the acne within a week. I walked back into school at the end of the lunch break.

"Have you been chatting up toads, weird-nerd?" Colin shouted. Raucous laughter erupted from his gang.

Red raw rage flooded through me, and the next thing I remember was people trying to pull me off Colin as I pummelled him mercilessly. Colin was a bruised bloody mess and was taken to hospital by drone. A clone policeman held me firmly and accompanied me, Mum and Mrs Evans as we were taken before the Mayor. I waited outside with the policeman. I was terrified. Was I turning into my father? Was I going to gaol like him? Surely, I would never be allowed back to school after that. The door opened. I felt myself tense, fearing the worst.

I thought the Mayor would be wearing a wig under the circumstances, but he was just dressed casually and didn't look angry at all. Mum had always been fantastic standing up for me, even lying at times when absolutely necessary, but surely even she couldn't get me out of this one.

"Ewan, I've heard about what has happened over the years. It's totally understandable after what you've been through with your father and everything. I believe you have developed a form of mental illness we call intermittent explosive disorder. I'll need to get this confirmed by the hospital, but there's good news. It can now be easily treated."

Wow! I wasn't expecting that. I felt the tension drain as Mum came and embraced me.

The following day, we went to the hospital in Carmarthen where they confirmed the diagnosis and started my treatment with what they called 'Petratherapy'[6]. I was given an injection into a vein and was told to return for a small operation in a week.

Two weeks later, I was instructed to press a button on my X-talk if I felt angry, or if I was in a situation that irritated me. That evening, Mum shouted at me, "Get yourself back here and help Rhiannon with her homework before you desert us for the evening!" I was annoyed as I was in the middle of a fight on my holostation. I pressed the button on my X-talk and my anger disappeared instantly. I pressed pause on my holostation, helped Rhiannon and resumed my game as if nothing had happened! After a few weeks, I never felt ill-tempered again!

My acne had disappeared and I was back at school, feeling better than I had for years. I didn't have any friends, but Rhiannon was great and spent time with me. I fancied her best friend Sian, who lived with two mothers and a gay sister in a neighbouring block. We would often hang out as a threesome and a few months later, Sian and I hooked up.

Later that year, Mum was in the safety boat while three other instructors were teaching children to windsurf out in Dale Bay. A blustery westerly wind was picking up. She noticed a boy called Glyn heading towards some rocks, totally out of control. She turned her electric jets to full power but was too late. He fell, hitting his head on the rocks. He must have been knocked unconscious, as by the time Mum arrived, he was floating face down in the water. She dragged him into her boat and started resuscitation. She was rewarded by him vomiting half of Dale Harbour over her boots!

It was great that he recovered, but selfishly, I was even more pleased that Mum was awarded five holiday credits for her action. Mum asked Rhiannon and I where we wanted to go. Rhiannon said she didn't care as by then she was more interested in boys than anything else. I told Mum that I had always wanted to visit Africa, after listening to my elderly friend Harry tell of his adventures there. We were off to Zambia!

As the drone came to rest, the hot, humid air of the Luangwa Valley engulfed us like a hot, steaming sauna. It was the end of the dry season, the best time to see animals and birds as they congregate near waterholes. We had to step over a great pile of elephant dung on our way to the camp, which was situated right on the banks of the river. Hippos wallowed in the murky green waters a few metres from our huts. I loved to watch them, the huge cows so gentle with their calves. Once, a young pretender bull tried his luck and a fearsome fight with the king ensued. Their mouths opened wider than I thought possible, exposing their enormous fangs. The gigantic dominant bull was merciless. The young male was badly wounded and disappeared around a bend in the river. I never saw him again.

I fell in love with Africa during our week there. I enjoyed the excitement of wondering what we might see as we climbed into our electric jeeps before dawn; soft grey in the light of the Moon. All the animals and birds were busy in the cool of early dawn. I loved the booming ground hornbills, the skimmers flying along the surface of a slumbering lake with their fiery beaks catching the water. We watched a leopard cub, sleek in his spotted coat, prowling a waterhole while impala nonchalantly continued to drink. Then the great red orb of the sun would appear. As it transformed through yellow to searing white, every living creature retreated in search of cool and shade; we returned to our camp.

The wardens taught us to track animals with the tiniest of clues as we went on a walking safari protected by their guns. They pointed out the strangely white droppings of hyenas that had been crunching animal bones.

One night, we were driven silently through the bush with a lion pride stalking behind us, using our lights to confuse and dazzle their prey. I found it gruesome as we watched them attack and start to eat a waterbuck while its legs were still kicking; with its sharp horns rendered useless by the lion's jaws crushing its windpipe, it slowly suffocated. After breakfast the next morning, I watched ugly marabou storks and blood-soaked vultures fighting over the scraps.

I asked the wardens why there was an electric fence on the far bank of the Luangwa.

"The other side of the fence is a Christian reserve. They live in a fertile land approximately the size of the UK."

I saw a man hoeing beyond the fence. I felt sorry for him as he was baking in the scorching midday sun. It made me grateful that we didn't have to labour in the fields back home.

All too soon, we were back in the sleeping pod of our hyperloop, speeding silently under Africa on our way home.

———

Mum was best mates with my girlfriend's mother, Dylis. They were going to Oxford for a gastronomic holiday; cultural stuff by day and eating gourmet food with fine wines in the evening. I couldn't believe they would waste two whole holiday credits having a boring week like that! Anyway, the good news was Rhiannon, her boyfriend Glyn (the boy Mum had saved), Sian and I were going camping in the Brecon Beacons while they were away.

I overheard Nana say to Grandad, "I bet they're having sex already."

"I'm sure you're right, but the girls can't get pregnant and there aren't any STDs any longer, so does it really matter? You're probably just jealous, my love!"

Of course, we were enjoying frequent sex and were madly in love.

We were dropped by drone at the campsite just beneath the peak of Pen y Fan in the Brecon Beacons. Grandad wouldn't call this camping as we were staying in insulated wooden pods with a triple-glazed panoramic window. We were grateful for the warmth as it was May and at this altitude, it was freezing at night. We woke to bright blue cloudless skies. We walked the famous horseshoe with crystal clear views of the mountains to the north. This trek exhausted Rhiannon and Sian, and they opted to sunbathe by the lake the following day.

Glyn and I had become good friends. We'd both been through a lot recently. He'd developed PTSD after his near-death experience and had also been cured with Petratherapy. This helped us bond as we'd both lost friends while we were ill.

We thought it would be fun to break into the Central Wales Wilderness Reserve, which began a few kilometres north of the Beacons. We'd often experienced the park on VR where we'd mingled with aurochs and mammoths grazing contentedly. We thought it would be exciting to experience this for real. We set off as the day warmed up and within a couple of hours we came up against a three-metre electric fence that marked the boundary of the park. We found a big oak that had branches extending over the fence. The first branch was too far up the sheer trunk to reach from the ground. I found a rock which we were able to roll into place. Glyn was frankly scrawny, which was useful in this instance. He stood on the rock and gave me a leg-up. I could then easily pull myself up onto the branch. I then leant down and grabbed his right wrist and hauled him up to join me. Feeling pleased with ourselves, we walked along a branch that overhung the fence until it started to bend. We then hung underneath it until we only had a short distance to fall. We landed safely and the branch sprung back out of reach.

"That was pretty dumb, Ewan! I thought you were meant to have brains!"

I did feel stupid, but fortunately I couldn't hear any animals and hurriedly looked for a way back over the fence. We soon found another oak just inside the fence which fortunately had some dead side branches that started low enough for footholds in case we needed to get out in a hurry. We left a trail of sticks so we could find our way back. Underneath the oaks was a carpet of fading bluebells. There were loads of birds, red squirrels and an occasional deer that would cough in alarm and then disappear into the forest. We noticed that many trees had been felled while they were still young. A small pond with a mound of twigs in the middle gave us the answer to the lumberjack conundrum. After about an hour, I spotted some large hoof prints and guessed we were on the trail of a small family of auroch. Gradually, the dung pats grew warmer until they were positively steaming. We started to be careful about not treading on twigs, hoping to get as close to them as possible. We froze in awe as a terrifying bellow broke the silence. I felt a tingle of fear shoot down my spine. We weren't to be deterred and a few minutes later we heard tails swishing and grass being ripped by rough tongues. Then six black heads with a pale patch between their horns turned to gaze at us. We watched in silence as a calf restarted suckling its mother. We became apprehensive when a massive bull emerged from the woods to check what his cows were watching. He stomped towards us, looking increasingly annoyed. We prepared to flee and then suddenly he turned his head to confront something he'd heard. At the base of a distant oak, we saw a grey wolf's head. We guessed there might be more and fled!

The bull must've kept the wolf pack pinned down as we'd almost reached our chosen oak when we heard them panting behind us. One final burst and I shoved Glyn up the tree and then climbed up myself, kicking and breaking off the dead branches as I went. Panting on the branch, we watched, fascinated by the snarling wolves, close enough to smell their stinking breath, thankful for the safety of the tree. They weren't going away; and once we'd caught our breath, we walked along a thick branch that spanned the electric fence, planning to get down from the tree as we'd done on the way into the reserve. Glyn went first. Just as he set off, one of the wolves started howling. He turned to look, lost his footing and fell sideways, landing on his back three metres below. He screamed with pain. By the time I reached him, he looked very pale, lying absolutely still. I felt sick as I saw he'd landed with his back over a ridged rock. I jumped down and joined him.

"Are you badly injured?"

"I don't think so, but my back hurts like hell."

"Any pain anywhere else?"

"Nothing, I'm sure I'll be fine. Give us a hand."

I grabbed his arms and pulled him into a sitting position.

"Shit! I can't feel my legs. I can see them but they feel like they belong to someone else."

"Can you move them?"

He was obviously trying but to no avail.

"Okay, let's lie you back down. I'm going to press the emergency button on my X-talk."

"How can we help you? You seem to be on the edge of the National Park."

"Correct, my friend has fallen; I fear he's badly damaged his back."

"Don't move him; we'll be with you in ten minutes."

Those minutes seemed to last forever. I felt sorry for Glyn and was concerned that I'd damaged him when I'd tried to help him up. I also feared that we would be in trouble for breaking into the park. The wolves continued to prowl just the other side of the fence. What a bloody disaster; how I wished we'd stayed with the girls!

The paramedics were brilliant. Glyn was soon safely cocooned in a rigid back brace on his way to a specialist centre in London, where his mother would meet him. I collected the girls and confessed to Nana and Grandad what had happened. They decided to tell Mum, who returned in an absolute fury; whether because of our stupidity or because of messing up her special holiday I was never sure. I was marched off to the Mayor as Mum thought he should know before my misdeeds were common knowledge.

"Well, Ewan, you seem to be making a habit of being brought before me. I'm pleased to hear from your mother that the Petratherapy has cured your anger. This incident is clearly unrelated. You knew that the Park was out of bounds, and sadly your friend has suffered for this. I know you've learnt your lesson, but poor Glyn's mother must know that you've been punished for agreeing to this foolhardy enterprise. You'll spend four hours a week for a year talking to the old people at the nursing home that overlooks Dale Harbour."

I wondered if he'd known that I had fond memories of that place. Certainly, I felt I should be punished, and this was really no great hardship, although it would mean four hours less with Sian. I was lucky compared to Glyn, who we now knew was paraplegic and was undergoing surgery to his back. (This apparently would involve nano-surgery and stem cell injections. They reckoned he would regain his sexual function within a few months, but he wouldn't be able to control his feet for about two years.)

Poor Rhiannon was heartbroken, and Grandad offered to travel with both of us to see Glyn in London. I'd been to the central part of London before when I'd come to watch an international hoverboard-polo match. During that visit, we'd stayed for a week looking at old tourist sites, art galleries and museums. The old roads and car parks had been ripped up and planted as green spaces with cycle and running tracks. There were the usual hyperloops and hoverways. In addition, new electric air-conditioned trains used the old underground network. Pavements had been replaced by covered travellators. London had become an amazing place to live.

Some of the less pleasant areas were now being rebuilt, and I suspected that Grandad (who had been an architect) was secretly more interested in the new construction methods than coming with us to see Glyn.

Twenty-five minutes on the hyperloop from Bridetown and we were in Hackney, being whisked along a travellator between beautiful parks and high-rise glass buildings. We left Rhiannon with Glyn and went to a nearby building site. Grandad told me how tall cranes were used for construction when he was working. As we spoke, a drone was delivering some glass walls that robots manoeuvred to the bottom of a new tower block. I looked up and already ten floors were suspended near the top of the building.

"How do they do that?" I asked.

"I've never seen it before, but I think the outer steel tubes are elevated by some sort of hydraulic mechanism. Each prefab floor is then shunted to the top of these tubes and held in place by steel girders until the whole building is complcte. Each floor is then allowed to settle by gravity working against hydraulic valves which slowly lower it into place. It's then bolted down by robots. I gather it takes forty-eight hours to build a twenty-storey tower."

We chose a restaurant that had a balcony overlooking a park with a lily pond. As we waited to be served, Grandad looked unusually serious and I wondered what was coming. "Ewan, have you thought about a career? You're a clever guy; in the old days, you might have been a boffin inventor and made a fat killing."

"Grandad, there's no point in even trying to invent anything these days. The Research Commissioners have direct access to Xanasa's brain and are light years ahead of us mortals. I know you'd like me to be an architect, but I'm much more interested in animals. I'd really like to be a game warden in Africa. I fell in love with that place when Mum took me to the Luangwa Game Park."

"I knew you'd had a great holiday, but I didn't know you wanted to work there."

"Would I be allowed to live there?"

"I'm not sure, but I know that women are allowed to go to Africa if they want to give birth naturally, so it's worth a try. I'll ask the Mayor to look into it."

On returning to the hospital, we saw moisture in Glyn's eyes and Rhiannon was crying openly as they parted. He was going to have to stay in that hospital for another month.

We disembarked at Swindon as Grandad wanted to show us the Avebury standing stones. Soon after our drone took off from Swindon station, we saw a line of buildings and a railway that stretched past the horizon. Grandad reminisced, "This used to be a noisy motorway full of cars spewing toxic fumes. What you're looking at are robotic factories for clothes, sports kit, droids, drones, house parts; and virtually everything you need is made down there. That railway takes those goods around the country."

———

Two years later, I was enjoying life at Carmarthen University. The city was much more exciting than living in the country. There were no children and few old people. The atmosphere became electric on Friday nights, when we were allowed a designer drug called rush. Everyone became very friendly and would dance the night away in a frenzy of noise and sexual adventure.

I was studying zoology and tourism before transferring to Nairobi to learn more about African wildlife. Sian and I grew bored of each other's company and we split up at the end of our first year. I wasn't too bothered as all students were allocated a droid who did our cooking and house-keeping. These droids would double up as sex dolls if required.

I'd become sceptical about society and suspected that we were all living under secret surveillance. I tried to discern whether any other students had similar suspicions. I couldn't just ask my friends as I was sure my X-talk was listening to my conversations. Was I being paranoid? Gradually, I developed a gut feeling that two of my friends, Owen and Glenys, might share my disquiet. I discreetly passed them a message suggesting we all meet in my flat the coming Saturday. I'd created a box with sound insulation and three holes of ten cm diameter. I greeted them, "Hi, great you could make it. Have a drink! Party time!" I poured some drinks, manoeuvred them into my bedroom and indicated we should each insert our wrists with our 'X-talks' into the holes with one of them set to play music. I blocked the gaps around our wrists with spare shirts.

"Sorry for all this rigmarole. We can talk freely now."

We spent the next half-hour voicing our concerns about how we thought we might be being monitored. None of us had any absolute evidence, but we'd all heard about students having dissident views and then disappearing for a couple of days. They would return as model citizens, refusing to talk about what had happened while they were away. We all knew about the cameras with listening devices in public places, but these 'dissidents' had never spoken about their views in public. I told them that I believed that the regime might be monitoring our X-talks, and hence I'd built my 'music box'. We agreed to try to find more like-minded people and to meet from time to time.

Our numbers slowly grew and I had to build more boxes to be safe from surveillance. We would often bring illegal alcohol to our group discussions. We met up at random times in different safe locations. We shared our annoyance with the rigid dictatorial nature of the Xantec regime, which stopped us drinking after two pints of beer. They only allowed us 'rush' one night of the week and kept us hungry, even though we knew they could grow far more food than we could possibly eat. Why couldn't they let us make decisions for ourselves? We were all adults after all! Because they treated us like children, not allowing any violence or misbehaviour, life was frankly rather dull. We'd all read about the world wars and the cataclysmic events of 2060-2. They were all terrible in many ways, but the people involved had often forged strong bonds. Many great books, plays and films derived inspiration from brave people during these times. If we went back further in history, we read of people standing up against the cruelty of the slave trade. Even earlier, Owen Glyndwr was fighting the treacherous English. There was no obvious suffering or injustice in our society today that we could fight against. Was the only purpose of our existence to enjoy rush on a Friday night?

We were annoyed that the Commissioners lived in fine style and never grew old like the rest of us. They'd clearly cracked senescence and were keeping this secret for themselves. We felt angry at our impotence and wanted a say in the running of our lives. Physical resistance was out of the question as we couldn't overcome the sonic guns of their clones. We did want Xantec to appreciate how we felt. One of our group sprayed *We want our views to be understood* all over the main university building. He was arrested, and although he reappeared a few days later, he never came to our group again. The only way out of this tightly controlled society was to join a religious enclave. The problem was that none of us were religious and anyway couldn't face the primitive living conditions of these enclaves which we had seen on holovision.

The following year, Owen, one of the original three, was caught on CCTV smuggling a gallon of homemade cider in a large opaque water container on the hyperloop. He was brought before the Commissioner in his private rooms. He showed Owen video evidence of us all carrying similar containers converging on various campsites.

"We know you are young and want to party, but if we allow people to flout the law, where will this lead? You must warn your friends, and these illegal parties must stop."

We met again at our favourite campsite set in the woods outside Carmarthen. Owen explained why he didn't bring cider. He said, "I can't stand this any longer. Some of you know that I have a sailing boat, and as the weather is set fair, I'm planning to cut off my X-talk and sail to Ibiza to join the humanist enclave there. Would any of you like to tag along?"

We all looked at each other. I guess we all feared this would end in disaster. It was a hell of a long way, and his boat would surely be spotted by Xanasa's satellite surveillance. We tried to dissuade him, but he wouldn't be budged. One by one, we wished him well but declined to join him. We watched with admiration as he nibbled away at his band with wire cutters. We hugged him and watched as he threw his X-talk into the woods north of the camp and then doubled back towards the south coast. A few minutes later, a military drone swooped over us and disappeared in a southerly direction.

As I lay in bed that night ruminating over the day's events, I wondered how the clones had known where Owen had gone. They must get a signal when an X-talk is cut off. As it has a GPS tracker, they would know where it was discarded. The strange thing was that he had thrown it in the opposite direction to the one he'd taken. They must have some other way of locating us. The only time we have an operation is when they take a bone marrow sample. I didn't think that was a sham, as I'd heard of someone using that sample as a marrow transplant when they developed leukaemia. Could they insert some sort of tracker at the same time?

Owen turned up at a lecture two days later. He looked unharmed but blanked out all his old friends and left as soon as the presentation finished. We guessed that he'd either been brainwashed or threatened.

I was determined to discover what had happened to my friend. That evening, I contacted him using my X-talk. He said he was busy. I thought that was unlikely and went round to his flat, taking a small collapsible 'music box' with me. I pressed the videocom outside his flat and was sure that he was watching me without responding. I knocked on his door. Nothing. I started hammering on his door and must have kept this up for at least five minutes. All my knuckles were bruised as I kept changing hands to relieve the pain. I was about to give up when a soft buzz indicated the door was unlocked. I hesitated. Clearly, I was intruding where I wasn't welcome, but I felt it was imperative to discover what happened when the regime abducted someone. I pushed the door open and found his windows in 'dark mode'. I entered the gloom and as my eyes slowly adjusted, I saw Owen flumped, almost absorbed within the soft cushions of his low-slung black velveteen armchair. He was motionless, looking at me with expressionless eyes as if to say he couldn't care less whether I existed or not. I noted that he was wearing a new X-talk.

It became clear that he wasn't going to say anything. I put my box on a table by his chair and placed my wrist inside. He didn't move at all and I had to pick up his left wrist and insert it into the other hole.

"Look, mate, I know you don't want me here, but you're one of my best friends and I'm not going to give up on you that easily. What happened to you after they picked you up?"

"I've no idea what you're fucking talking about. I woke up yesterday feeling perfectly well, but when I switched the glass to transparent, I was met with summer sun and leaves in the park instead of the frosted skeletons of trees which were there when I went to bed. Somehow, I have lost about six months of my life. You say you're my friend, and yet I don't know you at all. I've seen you at lectures and you always looked friendly enough, but I can't remember ever speaking to you. What is it you want from me? Have you any idea what has happened, and why the hell have you forced my hand into this ridiculous box?"

I explained what had happened in the last six months. How we'd been having illegal meetings where we complained about the regime, and how he'd planned to sail away to Ibiza before he was captured.

"Well, fuck me! That explains why everyone was giving me such funny looks at the lectures today. I've absolutely no recollection of any of that!"

"They've obviously removed all your memories from the time we first met. They'll be watching you closely and will almost certainly have clocked that I've come round to see you this evening. You mustn't tell anyone about this, unless your X-talk is in a box like this. It'll be best if you don't meet up with the old gang for a bit as it would only make them suspicious. We'll meet again once this has all blown over and they reckon you're a reformed character. Good luck!"

I left Owen's flat, horrified at the power of the regime. How could we fight them if they were able to erase chunks of our lives and not be able to remember how or why this abhorrent punishment had occurred?

Thankfully, my two years were nearly finished, and I returned to Bridetown excited at the prospect of moving to Africa, where I'd heard society was more laid-back.

———

Nairobi was one of the 'megacities' of Africa. Millions of people lived there, mainly in modern glass blocks amongst the trees and lakes of the city's parks. People were flocking to Africa because of its beauty, the weather and lifestyle. Nairobi had a fantastic climate and was surrounded by game parks. Mts Kenya and Kilimanjaro were nearby and the beautiful tropical coast was only thirty minutes away by hyperloop. Tourism was thriving and work was plentiful.

My college was based at Nairobi Game Park just out of town. It attracted prospective game wardens from all over the continent. I became friends with Moses, who ran one of the restaurants. He was a mountainous man, distinguished by a huge gash across his left cheek which went right through his left eye. This eye was now milky, shrunken and mangled. Apparently this was caused by a lion attack. I suspect it was far more likely to have occurred during a drunken brawl. He was a jovial character who used to revel in telling rude stories.

Occasionally, he would come up to my flat at sundown. One evening, we were watching a lightning storm. The sky far in the west over the rift valley would suddenly be flooded with bright sheet lightning; occasionally, forked lightning would flash to Earth. Amazingly, it was almost silent as it was so far away. Moses reminisced. "One of my mates, who had no shoes, had been sheltering under a tree in a thunderstorm.

He was struck by lightning but it didn't kill him instantly. The next day we found him, charred and burnt, out on the open grass. A few yards away under the tree, I found a rock with some crispy skin stuck to it."

"Moses, that's horrible."

"Life was tough in those days, Ewan. I was a child during the Ebola outbreak. The stench of rotting bodies was unbearable. The vultures were so fat they couldn't take off! That seems like another world now, when we all have jobs and the food is great, as long as you eat at my restaurant!" He chuckled. His sombre mood brought on by the lightning had vanished.

Then he spotted my 'music box'. "What on earth's that contraption?"

I indicated that we should put our wrists inside, and started the music. I told him about my suspicions of excessive surveillance.

"They can watch and listen to me as much as they like. They may learn a few good tips if they watch me and my girlfriend!"

"Doesn't it bother you that the Commissioners seem immortal?"

"Not at all, I would hate to sit through all those court cases thinking that I had to do this for hundreds of years. We may die young of heart attacks, strokes or diabetes, but we have a wonderful life. The brightest stars die young."

"Don't you think it is sad that beautiful African villages made up of thatched, mud-walled rondavels now only exist as tourist attractions?"

"Have you ever lived in one?"

"No, but they look cute, and tourists must like them."

"The rondavels used to form a circle surrounding an area in

the middle of the Boma, where cows were herded within thorny enclosures for the night. This caused swarms of flies that would crawl over our children's eyes. Inside, rondavels were dark and traditionally there would be a fire with no chimney. Smoke filled the place, which did deter flies but made you cough, and your eyes would be unbearably sore by the morning. They were badly insulated and used to be crawling with ants and termites. I've never met an African who now lives in a modern, light, air-conditioned house – like the one you were probably brought up in – who wants to go back to those bad old days."

This was a completely different perspective on the 'regime'. We never used my 'music box' again.

At the end of my year in Nairobi, I moved to Liwonde Game Park in Southern Malawi. I spent six months being trained by the wardens and learning all about the local creatures and plant life.

One of the wardens accompanied me when I was taking my first group of tourists around the park. Tourists stayed in a resort that had been built on stilts over Lake Malawi about a mile from Shiretown. I collected them in an electric hovercraft just as the first glimmers of light appeared over the trees. The hovercraft could glide silently over the Shire River and its tributaries. If we got word of exciting game on land, I could take it hovering overland as long as it was flat with little undergrowth. It also had wheels if I wanted precise manoeuvrability amongst trees and scrub.

In my cabin, I had a screen which showed the position of animals that had GPS monitors fitted, and another with images from hidden cameras. That morning, a pride of lions were on the move. They padded stealthily, keeping low in the grass. Then a herd of sable passed a camera not far ahead of the pride. We were off! I moved to where I judged them to be heading and waited under a 'sausage tree' with its dangling magenta flowers. Soon after, a lone black male sable with magnificent curved horns wandered by. A snub-tailed bateleur eagle soared overhead and swooped to pounce on an unfortunate snake. Finally, the herd of female sable ambled into view, oblivious to the danger that was following close behind. Suddenly the herd scattered, leaving one youngster struggling to keep up. It was all over in a couple of minutes and my tourists had a morning to remember. This should get some good reviews, which would help me gain holiday credits.

I loved my work and living in Shiretown, which was always pulsing with music. There were a lot of children laughing as they played their made-up games. Most of us worked in tourism, but there were a few talented artists who produced carvings and paintings for tourists and us locals.

I'd hooked up with Ruth, who was ebony black. Her full lips were usually accentuated with garish purple or scarlet lipstick, contrasting with her luminous white teeth. Her body was Rubenesque. I couldn't get enough of her voluptuous, soft flesh. We went on our first holiday to Madagascar where the forests and thorny scrubland had been restored. We enjoyed watching white sifakas prancing across the ochre sand and then, amazingly climbing the horrible thorny cacti with their babies clinging on for dear life.

Three months later, we went to Quirimba, an island off Mozambique, to watch humpback whales breaching and diving. We also swam near dugongs calmly grazing seagrass in the shallows. In the evenings, we would go skinny-dipping in the azure waters before evening drinks under the palms, watching the lazy waves caressing the sand.

Life was good and Ruth and I were perfect for each other. Neither of us had said anything, but I was certainly thinking about getting married.

I'd always been good at sending photos home and had regular holovision chats with Mum and Rhiannon. They were desperate to meet Ruth in person. I chose to go in May as I'd always loved the blossom, spring flowers and carpets of bluebells in the oak woods. I'd forgotten how cold it could be. It rained; Ruth and I froze. The cold, though, was nothing compared to the frosty reception that Ruth was given. Grandad and Nana had always accepted the light brown colour of their grandchildren (all children in the UK were now of the same hue). They kept staring at Ruth, perhaps because she was so black, but I suspect it was more to do with her dimensions. Welsh people now looked half-starved to me as I'd become used to Africa, where most people were plump and many were positively obese. I'd certainly put on some weight myself with the unlimited carbohydrates that I'd been eating. Maybe they were wrongly blaming Ruth for this. We found Welsh food to be bland and bitter, as we'd become accustomed to the sugar, salt and spices that flavoured our food in Malawi.

We went for a walk in the woods between rain showers. Ruth went with Rhiannon and Glyn (they were still an item). I hung back with Mum to gauge her reaction.

"She's pleasant enough, but wouldn't you prefer a little Welsh girl?" I quickly changed the subject as it was obvious that this was how they were all feeling.

The next day, I remembered to collect my wave-skimmer as we thanked everyone and left for the hyperloop station. I thought how sad it was that they were stuck in their insular ways, while my life had exploded with fun and excitement.

Ruth looked sad and contemplative as I chose a film to watch in our pod before we went to sleep. "Your family don't seem to have much of a sense of humour. Perhaps it's caused by the miserable, damp, cold climate. I would hate to live there, freezing all the time. Anyway, I think I would starve to death with that dreadful food which contained nothing to fill you up."

I could understand where she was coming from, but she was leaving them now, and surely the ordeal should be over. Was she angry that I'd wasted one of her credits? Or was this PMT? Living with mood swings associated with this was a new experience for me when I moved to Africa, as menstruation was history in the UK. That was about the only thing in favour of the unnatural regime in Wales.

Back in Shiretown, our relationship had lost its previous spark. I was too cowardly to end it. Perhaps I'd changed, but I think the love that she'd had for me died in Wales. Without that, she became less attractive and I paid her less attention. A downward spiral had ensued.

One day, I came back from the game park to discover all her clothes had gone; there was a note on our bed.

Thanks for the good times. I'll never forget them. I'm sorry I was so critical of your family. You've become a different person since our trip to Wales. I'm flying to Nairobi this evening. Ruth

I knew we'd grown apart, but when I'd finished reading her note, I slumped onto my bed feeling utterly desolate. She'd enjoyed entertaining and our house had been full of noise and laughter ever since we'd been together. Now it felt cold and empty as if the very soul of our home had drained into the lake. When she wasn't organising a party, she would be planning our next holiday. I used to return each evening from work brimming with anticipation to discover what the next extravaganza would involve. Now I had to accept it would just be me and my boring droid for company; I knew the friends we'd made were really her friends and would quickly drift away.

I used up all my saved shopping credits to acquire an electric speedboat, and for my next holiday, I took this and my wave-skimmer up to Nkhata Bay. It was a beautiful resort built over Lake Malawi. The luxury huts had verandas with glass bottoms where you could watch the colourful cichlid fish chase each other over the sandy shallows. All the gear needed for watersports was housed in huts on the shore. Restaurants nestled amongst huge boulders under the shade of trees, north of the soft sand beach. Set back from the beach were beautiful gardens scented with jasmine and frangipani. There was also a tall tower block with indoor air-conditioned tennis, squash, hover-ball courts and a gym. Above that were ten floors of tourist accommodation, and on the top floor, there was a restaurant and an infinity pool, which had views over the lake to the east and towards the mountains far to the west.

As I sat enjoying cold beers with some fellow wave-skimmers, I noticed a high wire fence just the other side of the resort's gardens. On the other side of the fence, I could see endless maize interspersed with hand-built dilapidated rondavels. I guessed that this must be the eastern edge of the Christian reserve that I'd seen from the camp in Luangwa many years ago. I saw a beautiful woman gazing at the gardens of our resort, lost in thought. I made some feeble excuse, descended in the lift and went to watch her from behind a clump of tall bamboo. She had a symmetrical round face with sad eyes that gazed in an unfocussed way across the gardens. Her nose was slight and her lips were thinner than was usual here. Her black hair was straight, and the most striking difference of all was that she was as slender as a marathon runner. As I watched, she walked inside the fence, oblivious to me spying on her. She moved with the suppleness and grace of a lithe ballet dancer. I followed, keeping my distance. I trod on a twig; she turned her head and fleetingly stared straight at me. Her eyes opened wide, her lips parted and then she fled. She was clearly terrified of me.

I lay in bed that night, enchanted and wanting to fathom this beguiling lost soul. I longed for her to return. Each evening, I watched in vain. Then, on the final evening of my trip, I saw her head peering through the tall maize, checking that the garden was empty. I held my breath and waited. She plucked up courage and approached the fence. After a while, she started to sing with a beautiful pure high tone more like a chorister than a woman. I replied with a croaky Welsh lullaby. She turned to stare. She crouched, her legs taut and trembling, like a hare ready to flee. Slowly, her face relaxed. She rose and tentatively approached.

"Hi, you've a beautiful voice. Do you speak English?"

"I do, what do you want?"

"Nothing, but I'm curious to know why you come here."

"Who are you?"

A door slammed, and by the time I looked back, she was gone; swaying maize the only indication that she'd been there.

Every weekend and holiday, I returned to Nkhata bay, and each evening I would look for her to no avail. I arrived one Saturday to find the resort empty. I was told that the staff and most of the guests had gone to the town of Nkhata for a demonstration about the Commissioners having eternal life, while common people died young. It was only two kilometres but it was hot and I was perspiring heavily as I joined the crowd just as the Commissioner started speaking. The crowd were heckling and shoving, not in the mood to be pacified. I noticed some men picking up stones. I feared a riot. If that occurred, there would be fearful retribution and a tightening of local laws. I didn't want this paradise to be ruined. I forced my way through the crowd towards the speakers and was surprised when one of the clone policemen grabbed my arm to pull me onto the platform, where an enormous black guy dwarfed the white Commissioner. I said I would like to speak and was relieved when the Commissioner smiled encouragingly at me and waved the mosquito-sized drone microphone in my direction. I'd never used one before and suddenly my booming voice was echoing off the tower blocks.

"I understand why you're all angry. I myself questioned the fairness of this situation and asked a wise friend of mine in Kenya what he thought about it. He told me not to be so stupid. He asked me if I would like to sit in court rooms hearing case after case, realising that this boring misery would go on for hundreds of years. He said he preferred to burn brightly and enjoy his time on Earth, delighting in the excitement of children and grandchildren, rather than live forever like that."

I sent the drone back and was amazed that my few words had stunned the crowd. I walked back to the resort as the crowd began to murmur quietly and began to disperse. As I reached the back gardens where I frequently spent my evenings, I spotted out of the corner of my eye a dark shadow darting along the fence, disappearing into the maize. That evening, I closed all the doors that opened into the gardens that bordered the fence and left prominent notices saying 'Beware of scorpions', hoping that this might deter people from interrupting us should my nymph reappear.

I chose a seat under the shade of an angel trumpet bush, enjoying the beautiful scent as the sun sunk towards the westerly mountain range.

I must have closed my eyes momentarily as when I looked up she was standing just a couple of metres from me on the other side of the fence.

"Hi, I'm pleased you came back. I'm Ewan, who are you?"

"I'm Miriam."

"Why are you so frightened? I won't hurt you."

"The manager of the resort says I mustn't come to the wire. He once fired a stone at me using a catapult. I thought you might've been sent by him to scare me off. I heard your booming voice today at that meeting. What was all that about?"

"Nothing really; some nonsense about the poor guy responsible for us."

"Is he the little young white chap?"

"Yes."

"He's responsible for us as well. I've heard him speaking to our leader. He seems a nice guy, but our leader is too proud to accept aid and certainly won't take his advice. I'd better go now. There is a blue flowering jacaranda tree at the southern end of the resort; no one ever goes there. Meet me there on Saturday evening at sundown."

This became our meeting place and I learnt the story of her grandmother's escape from Kerala forty-five years ago and how she'd been happy with her new Christian family.

"My grandmother told me that there was plenty of land to begin with. The different Christian denominations each had their own areas to live in. Family planning was ignored and the population soon spiralled out of control. Mum and Dad were sensible; I only have one sister. My lovely grandmother died last year. I miss her dreadfully. Our community is always hungry; we have to lock up our maize as theft is rife. I look at the beauty of your gardens and how plump and happy everyone seems. I hate this place and want to escape."

"I'm sorry but it may be impossible for you to leave as you can't survive on this side of the fence without this thing on my wrist. Let's meet on Saturday and maybe I'll have thought of something by then."

Miriam replied, "It's worse than you think. They operated on me when I was twelve and implanted an electric shocking device deep inside, which activates if I leave the electric fenced area."

During the week, I realised that there were two insurmountable barriers. One, it would be impossible to get her over the high electric fence without being detected. Two, where could we safely live?

This implanted device might be real or just possibly a ruse to keep people from escaping. Certainly, the regime was very capable of such deceit. I certainly wouldn't be able to remove such a heinous device.

When we met up, I listed the barriers. I also said that we couldn't keep meeting at this tree as otherwise someone would wonder why I kept going to a place where there was nothing to do. Before I returned to Shiretown, we agreed to meet here the following week.

Out of the blue, I received a hologram from Zilgrim Mcmanus (our Commissioner). He was thanking me for saving the day at the protest and as a reward gave me five holiday credits.

I chose to take my first week straight away. I drove my speedboat up to Nkhata Bay and then surfed up and down the western shore of the lake on my skimmer, looking for anything that might help me free Miriam. I noticed a small stream emerging from the base of some high cliffs. At this point, the electric fence had veered a little inland and I could just make it out at the top of the cliffs. I hid my wave-skimmer in some long grass and followed the stream. It was the dry season and the stream was empty and easy to follow. It emerged from a small cave. I crept inside but could make little progress as it was soon pitch-black. I turned back, but my spirits lifted with this glimmer of hope.

The next day, I returned armed with a powerful torch and shoes that would grip damp rocks. The cave narrowed as it climbed. Ultimately, I was stopped by a very short 'squeeze' which was just too tight for me to get through. In despair, I sat down and turned my torch off as I pondered how I could use this cave. I tried to chip the rock with a stone. It had little impact and I feared the rock was probably made from hard limestone. I feared it would be difficult, if not impossible, to widen the passage enough to pass. As my eyes adjusted, I noticed a faint glimmer of greyness seeping through the 'squeeze'. The cave might open out as it went higher and lead to a proper opening, but there was no way I could check. I descended the steep cave and took my wave-skimmer out onto the lake, noting the position of the cave, and returned the following day with binoculars. From about a mile offshore, thanks to image stabilisers, I spotted the unmistakeable shape of paw paw growing in a plantation above the cliff. Behind me was an island with a massive granite boulder poking out of the forest like the bald pate of a medieval monk.

That Saturday, I met up with Miriam in our usual place and told her what I'd found. I asked her to try to meet me at the narrow point of the cave the following Saturday afternoon. I described where the paw paw plantation was and asked her to look for a dry stream bed that had flowed towards the lake. If she were to follow it downstream, I thought it would disappear underground into a small cave. If that occurred, I suggested she try to climb down as far as she could go and I would be waiting on the other side of a constriction.

A week later, I waited; she was late. I feared she might have been caught trespassing through the paw paw plantation as this would be outside of her family's neighbourhood. Then I heard a stone bouncing off the walls and leant back against the rock as it rattled past. "Hold on tight, do you need a rope?" I shouted, fearing it might be too steep to be safe.

"No, sorry about that pebble, I'm fine but it is too dark for me to get down to you." I stayed pinned against the damp wall in a most uncomfortable position, fearing more loose stones as I thought about this.

"Okay, I'll get you a torch and some shoes with good grip. I'll throw these over the fence by the jacaranda next Saturday morning and we'll meet here that afternoon."

During the week, I thought about where we might hide from the authorities if she did escape. I'd heard about an uninhabited place called Likoma Island and went to explore it. It was larger than I'd expected. As I moored my boat on an old jetty, I heard the high shrill calls of African fish eagles. The pair had a large nest in a tree by an old ruined church. I hoped this might indicate abundant fish in the lake. In the abandoned gardens were avocado, mango and bananas. There were also passion fruit, paw paws, tomatoes and maize, which must have survived via seed dispersal. There was surely enough food for one person. I found a well. When I dropped a pebble into it, I heard a comforting plopping sound. By the ruined church was a tumbledown hotel with its incongruous sign 'The Grand' still visible. There were remains of houses covered in vines, but no sign of recent human life. I found a gap at the back of the church. The roof of the nave had caved in, but the walls were still intact. They surrounded a tangle of shrubs growing amongst the rubble. Off to one side was a door which yielded to my shoulder, and I stumbled into a small room which might at one time have been a vestry. It was covered in dust, droppings and smelt disgusting. At least it was dry as the roof was intact. Vines had forced their way through a cracked window, and I guessed the droppings belonged to bats that had egressed through this. I felt this place might be a suitable hideaway if I could clean it and block up the window.

Saturday, and I was back waiting at the 'squeeze'. I'd switched my torch off and was thrilled as a beam of light penetrated the darkness from above. For the first time, we were able to touch each other's hands, but although Miriam was extremely thin, her hips just prevented her from getting through the narrow gap. One area of the rock came to a slight ridge, which seemed to be the problem.

"I've found an island where there is an old church where you could hide. There's fresh fruit and tomatoes on the island. I'm sure there are plenty of fish. If you were living there, I would visit as often as possible, bringing other supplies. You would be on your own, though, most of the time. What do you think?"

"Thanks, Ewan. That sounds like paradise; but however hard I diet, I'll never be able to get through this narrow passage."

"You're right, but I think with a hammer and chisel, you could work at that ridge that's keeping you prisoner. I'll bring them here tomorrow. Could you find time to work on this while I prepare your hiding place?"

I put everything I needed into my boat during the night, and just before dawn set off across the lake. I dropped the hammer and chisel at the 'squeeze' and took a shovel, mattress, bucket, fishing rod, iron cooking pot, some rope, cutlery and a quern to Likoma. Six days later, I felt satisfied that the vestry was habitable. The water from the well was sweet and clean, and I had found a perfect spot to fish. I left at noon and by early evening was waiting in the cave. I was pleased that Miriam had obviously worked hard and it looked wide enough now. I was peering through towards the daylight when I felt a hand on my shoulder. I froze, thinking that I'd been followed, and turned, fearing the worst. To my great relief, it was Miriam who was now in a fit of giggles as her torch shone on my astonished face.

"You bastard!" I was laughing now, and had to grab hold of her arm as she threatened to slip down the rocks. I didn't want another of my friends to break their spine.

"What have you told your family? Won't your mother think you've escaped?"

"Don't worry, I'm not stupid. I told her I was going to stay with my cousin who lives about a hundred kilometres west of Nkhata Bay. We have no way of communicating across our enclave and so she may never learn that I didn't make it."

"Are you okay about risking the shocks you told me about? If they start, you'll have to turn back."

"Sure, I know. Let's hope for the best."

"What's that?"

"It's Gran's hairbrush, it's all that I have to remember her by. Actually, it first belonged to my great-grandmother who died in India. It was Gran's most treasured possession."

I put the gear and the hairbrush into my rucksack. After a reassuring embrace, we started to climb down the slippery rocks. I could feel her tension. We slowly edged down. A glimmer of natural light gave me hope, and finally we were in the open, well outside the fence. I picked her up as she giggled with happiness and relief. The final rays of the sun picked out the bald rock at the top of 'Monk Island' as a wedge of egrets flew towards their colony for the night. It was dark by the time we launched the boat. Miriam used the torch intermittently to check there were no approaching rocks or hippos as we silently headed towards Likoma. We arrived in the middle of the night and collapsed on the mattress, completely exhausted. We had one morning to get to know each other. I showed Miriam around her new home before I had to return to Shiretown for my next group of tourists.

That year was the happiest of my life. I worked hard to get more credits and spent all my weekends and holidays enjoying Likoma with Miriam, who gained weight with the plentiful food on the island. This 'lost soul' had become the laughing, teasing love of my life. Six months later, as I moored my boat on the jetty, she ran to meet me beaming with joy. She was pregnant!

Shiretown and Nkhata Bay were happy places. Tourism was going from strength to strength. Our population numbers had evened out and most of my people were earning credits and made good use of these around the continent. A couple had even saved up the ten credits needed to reach the Moon. (There is now a permanent base there with a Commissioner in charge of the robots that mine lithium, cobalt and many rare earth metals that are required for high-tech devices back on Earth.) From there they had flown in one of our spaceships around Mars and back. It made sense to me that people spent so many credits to visit this wonderful place. I often visited the Moon when I had time off, where I enjoyed flying the fighter ships which are stationed there in case of an alien invasion. All the pilots are part-time volunteers as it was never expected that we would use these ships in anger. I loved the majesty of the universe and the beauty of Earth from space.

In contrast to Shiretown and Nkhata Bay, the Christian enclave in my territory was a disaster. The population had become unsustainable. Their leader hadn't considered contraception to be that important. I think there is some primeval instinct to have extra children when a disaster decimates the population. It grieved me to see their children crying from hunger, their bellies distended and their hair turning orange. I arranged a meeting with their leader, Paul. He was arrogant, foolish and certainly the most stubborn man I'd ever dealt with. He refused to accept the provisions that I offered. I even suggested that we might consider adopting some of their starving children. He declined that as well. I concluded that he preferred people to suffer rather than admit that he'd made a mistake. "The door will always be open if you change your mind." I congratulated myself for just managing to contain my anger.

I was totally reliant on Jas. I could never love her and would sometimes wake in the night having dreamt I was making love to Petra in the yoga room. I would then lie awake for hours, bereft; wishing I'd persuaded Petra to come away with me.

———

One day, the head game warden visited my office. He was reputed to be very bright and knew everything about the game park. He was a small diffident man of Indian ethnicity. He crept through my door when I called him in. His head was slightly bowed, appearing to be studying my carpet intensely. He held his hands tightly clasped together just beneath his chin as if he couldn't trust them to be moving freely.

"How can I help you, Sanjeev?"

A mumbling whisper fell from his barely open mouth.

"Sorry, Sanjeev, I didn't catch that."

He looked up. "I ha-have a st-st-strange film I wo-would like to show you."

I really didn't have time as I was due in court in twenty minutes, but he never normally bothered me.

"Go ahead, I've fifteen minutes."

He'd transferred it onto his X-talk, and images of impala and a leopard flashed across my wall. I love African wildlife, but I didn't have time for pretty pictures.

He paused the film, not on a beautiful bird or some svelte cheetah, but a crouched young African with what looked like a traditional bow and arrow in his right hand.

"What the hell's he up to? Do you allow hunting in the park?"

"Th-th-that's the p-p-point, sir, he sh-shouldn't be there. I th-think he's a p-p-poacher."

"Thanks, Sanjeev. Leave it with me."

"V-v-very good, sir," he stammered as he backed out of my room, as if I was some omnipotent maharaja.

I prepared myself for my court case. I can normally concentrate, however mundane a case might be, as I know how critical the outcome can be for the accused. Today's case involved two neighbours who had been throwing weeds into each other's gardens, and the conflict had escalated into cow dung being smeared on a window, followed by the entrails of a pig being left in the other garden in retaliation. I really couldn't concentrate on this trivia, although the entrails could attract dangerous animals and vermin, as I was trying to work out what a poacher might be killing in our game park.

As soon as the case ended, I returned to my office, fascinated by this poaching mystery. He couldn't be bringing his kill back into town as this would have been picked up on surveillance. He obviously couldn't sell anything as there was no currency, and I wasn't aware of any bartering trade in animal parts or meat. Perhaps he enjoyed cooking the meat over an open fire and eating it somewhere safe from prying eyes or cameras.

I asked Xanasa to register all chips that were present in the park the previous day. Then I asked her to remove all those that belonged to wardens and tourists. That left one chip that belonged to Joshua Simango. I learnt that he was an assistant coach at the Shiretown Boy's football team. He had a wife and two boys and they lived with his parents conveniently near the football grounds. He had an unblemished record and was hard working, averaging five holiday credits a year. I wondered if his elderly parents might still yearn for bushmeat and perhaps he smuggled it back into town for their benefit.

I asked Xanasa to give me the surveillance data from his chip from the time he'd been caught on camera. He'd been moving quickly through the park for the next few hours, and as he neared the eastern edge of the park, he'd remained stationary for nearly an hour. I asked Xanasa to give me a satellite view of this location at the time he'd been there yesterday. She zoomed in on a thicket of scrub bushes with a grove of tall acacia trees. I couldn't see Joshua anywhere. A family of dark grey warthogs were rummaging for food, kneeling to snuffle for roots and grass. Suddenly they all leapt sideways and rushed headlong into the thick bushes. I could imagine their squeals, although my images were silent. Then I noticed that one which had been grazing on its own was now on its side, its legs kicking frantically as it twisted its head, trying to bite the arrow in its flank. The elephant grass parted. Joshua bounded to the side of the dying warthog; a heavy club quickly despatched the unfortunate creature. He picked it up by one of its legs and swung it over his shoulder. I noticed that blood was dripping down his back as he moved fast, continuing east. I lost him on the satellite as the trees were taller and thicker here. The chip gave an exact location where he stopped and presumably sheltered for the night. He started moving again in the early hours and moved at about twelve kilometres an hour straight back to Shiretown, arriving soon after dawn.

I was fascinated. Did he have a hut where he went to eat his bushmeat, or could he be feeding an escapee from an enclave? There were no other chips evident, so he wasn't harbouring a fugitive from our justice system. I chose to visit the site of his night's vigil before confronting him. I had no court cases booked for the following afternoon and took Gregor and Sandy with me in a drone to investigate.

We hovered over the exact spot where he'd spent the night. It was soon obvious that it would be impossible to land as the jungle was impenetrable and seemed to be on a steep slope. Savanna covered the nearby plains and we landed there. When the drone stopped whirring, there was absolute silence as the relentless searing heat drained all sound from the bush. Taking plenty of water, we headed up the slope, thankful for the shade of the trees. Xanasa guided me towards the route that Joshua had taken; it was a well-trodden path. We made quick but exhausting progress until a dilapidated mud and thatch structure appeared. We crept up, wondering what we would find. It was dark; we all switched to infra-red as we reached the open entrance to this hovel. A musty smell tinged with rotten flesh emanated from within. I heard soft snoring, and as I peered inside, I was horrified to see the shape of a warm human back with no head. I retreated and Gregor must have noted the look of dread on my face as he indicated to Sandy to look after me and entered himself.

I heard angry shouts and slaps and then Gregor laughing as he reappeared dragging an emaciated man behind him. He had deeply wrinkled skin which looked like it would have fitted someone three times his size. His skull was covered in an immense thicket of matted hair with bits of bone and animal hair woven into it. The wrinkles of his face were accentuated as white dust had settled in them. He wore strips of old scraggy animal skins tied onto a strip of leather that encircled his waist. His nostrils were pierced by a warthog tusk, and brightly coloured beads hung around his neck.

"Gregor, what the hell did you find so funny about a warm body without a head?"

"Sorry, sir. Like you, I was sure this was going to be a recently beheaded corpse, but it turned out to be a trick of the infra-red light due to this guy's hair and the fact that he was sleeping face down in his blankets."

Much relieved, I spoke in Elomwe.

"My apologies for disturbing you, Father. I'm the chief from Shiretown. What's your name and how long have you lived here?"

Smiling, he replied, "You don't look like a chief, but your huge friends seem to respect you, so perhaps you are. I am Chikosi Gondwe, and I've lived here through more winters than you have ever seen."

"We wish you well, Chikosi, and have brought you some maize as a present."

"I give you this special charm to keep you safe on your journey."

He felt inside his animal skins and I feared something horrible would appear. It was a tiny bone, which looked like it might have come from a monkey's hand. I thanked him and we left him in peace.

Back in Shiretown, I sent off the bone for DNA analysis and summoned Joshua. When I presented the evidence, he readily agreed to tell the whole story.

"Chikosi was the witch doctor in my father's village at the time of Ebola. He'd always lived separate from the village in a dense thicket not far from where he lives now. The clone soldiers never found him. My father is very old now but has always insisted that I feed him as he believed that otherwise our family would be cursed and endure bad luck until the end of time. Chikosi seems quite harmless and must now be well over seventy. What should I do, sir?"

"I understand your predicament. We can't expect you to keep making that trek every week. We must persuade Chikosi to live in a jungle area nearer to Shiretown. I wonder whether he'd mind if tourists gave him gifts in return for learning about his ancient spells and treatments."

"I've no idea, but he's lonely. I think he might like the company and to feel important once more."

"I'll give you a week to persuade him. We'll build whatever structure he would like to live in and give him any food he wishes, even if he'll only eat wild animals, but he can't stay living there on his own."

———

Next day, the DNA analysis and report on the bone was complete. The bone was a terminal phalanx of an albino boy who had probably lived in Tanzania. They couldn't give an accurate date but it came from the modern era. Xanasa informed me that albino children used to be captured as their limbs were believed to bring good luck. I felt absolutely sickened by the thought that some child had been murdered and I'd been given one of his bones to bring me luck!

If this man was capable of murder, I didn't want him anywhere near my town and would have to get a conviction at CRC. I took Sandy with me.

As we climbed the steep path approaching his hut, I heard a high-pitched scream followed by the sound of something crashing through the branches of the tree above us. I looked and saw a massive mottled grey and white martial eagle with a baby monkey screeching in agony as the bird's mighty talons tightened their grip. After a moment to regain its balance, the magnificent bird opened its wings, swooped down to avoid the high canopy and disappeared with its prey now feebly protesting with its last breaths.

Chikosi was awake this time, sitting on a low-slung three-legged stool, watching as we approached.

"I see you, son," he greeted me.

"I see you, Father. I've returned to thank you for the gift and wondered how you came by such a charm?"

"I must apologise. I pretended you didn't look like a chief yesterday, but Joshua had described the white boy who was chief in his town. So I knew. That charm cost me two warthog tusks, a fruit bat skull and a rhino horn. It will surely give you powerful good luck."

I felt even worse as I now knew that my 'charm' had been the cause of the loss of a child, a warthog and a rhinoceros! At least Chikosi was no murderer, and I suspect he wasn't even a poacher himself. I left saying that I hoped we would see him again soon.

———

Two weeks later, Chikosi was supervising Joshua and his friends as they built a waterproof version of his old shack with an added window and door. Outside was a 'long drop' and inside, next to a platform covered in bones and herbs and various skulls and skins, was a mattress. Chikosi was beaming from ear to ear, not able to believe his good fortune. I'd assigned Joshua to be Chikosi's apprentice and to act as interpreter for tourists who would soon start visiting him.

———

Black was getting old and I dreaded the day when he would retire. One day, he warned me that trouble was brewing; his informants had discovered that there was going to be a mass demonstration in Nkhata. The people were complaining that I wasn't ageing, and wanted the same privilege. I was thankful for the warning.

It was a stiflingly hot day and there was no shade on the football pitch where the crowds had gathered. They'd erected a stage at one end and already the ringleaders were whipping up the crowd, which I feared might turn violent at any moment. Gregor, Sandy and two other clones accompanied us as we approached the stage. The crowd started to jeer. I called for the tiny drone microphone and hoping that my apprehension wasn't too obvious, I began.

"My friends and fellow citizens, I can understand why you're so angry. I think I would feel the same if our situation was reversed. I didn't choose to live so long; it was decreed by our leader, Commander Spitzen. I think that many of us like the happy sound of children running around enjoying themselves. Suppose everyone lived for a thousand years and we kept having children, the world would soon be swarming with people. Alternatively, if we wanted to keep the population stable, there would be very few children and they would have no one to play with and our towns would be full of old people."

One of the ringleaders called for the drone and I let him speak. "There's plenty of land; we could have more children and just build more cities."

It was obvious to me that I was never going to persuade them. I looked at Black to see if he could perform one of his miracles. He looked worried and shook his head. I noticed a tall, half-caste muscular young man with surprisingly blond hair marching determinedly towards our stage. I couldn't tell if he was planning to attack or support us. The former seemed most likely. Xanasa gave me a brief resume. "He has an unblemished record, although he did need Petratherapy to control his anger when he was a teenager. His father is in prison for murder and he did once have a dissident acquaintance."

This information didn't reassure me, but I had no choice as the crowd was tense and could easily overwhelm us. Hoping for the best, I nodded to Gregor who helped him onto the stage. The young man summoned the drone and his short but persuasive speech defused the anger that threatened to engulf us. Black was smiling and gave me a comforting bear hug as he must've guessed how frightened I was. I looked for our saviour, but he'd disappeared back into the crowd. I asked Xanasa to tell me more about the fair-haired guy. She told me that he was called Ewan and worked as a highly regarded game warden in my biggest park. I sent a hologram thanking him and gave him a small reward.

The next day, I was contacted by the Board at CRC. They felt that famine was looming in my Christian enclave. They weren't happy with my ineffectual approach. The Board felt there was no point in trying to persuade Paul; I should appeal directly to the population. They suggested (but I knew this meant commanded) that drones drop large quantities of food in the form of soya, fish oil and milk powder to treat malnutrition. Leaflets should accompany the food drop with the following message:

This food has been provided by Commissioner Mcmanus from Shiretown. Your leader, Paul, has previously refused any assistance. If the people of the enclave agree that men should be sterilised as soon as their second child is born, you will be granted an extra swathe of fertile land in Northern Malawi.

The food and pamphlets were dropped. We could only watch. We had satellites which gave extremely clear pictures of activity on the ground. Otherwise, there was no surveillance within the enclaves.

To begin with, life seemed to go on much as before, but the food parcels were carefully collected. More drops followed. We noticed that outdoor meetings became common in the villages, and messengers were seen jogging across the land. Two weeks later, a large fire was lit near the western fence. This must have been a signal as one by one, fires like beacons spread across the land. During the following week, about a million men converged on Lilongwe (the de facto capital). Paul and his puppet parliament must have felt very intimidated. I knew what it felt like to be confronted with 50,000 people, but this must have been even more terrifying. Although I was pleased to see what was happening, I felt some sympathy for Paul and his cronies. A man wearing a type of religious cape stood in front of them and they all appeared to bow their heads in what I assumed was prayer. When this finished, they started jumping up and down like Samburu warriors. We only had visual contact, but I felt sure they were chanting. Eventually, a group of men (I think I could recognise Paul among them) came out of a brick building. Immediately, the crowd surged towards them. The terrified group fled back into the building and escaped through a back door, running for their lives.

I had to admit the CRC Board was right and felt guilty for not having overridden Paul before. Sure enough, I was soon in communication with the new leader (we allowed them one mobile phone) who said that his newly elected parliament would be very grateful to accept aid and the promise of extra land if it was still on offer.

———

Ten months later, I received some surprising information derived from a routine hospital check-up on my game warden hero, Ewan. Every year, all our citizens have a health check. This includes a swab which they are told is to check for sexually transmitted diseases (STDs). In fact, there are no longer any STDs, and the reason for this swab is to test for any DNA other than their own; Xanasa then knows who is sleeping with who, which occasionally can help solve a crime of passion. The strange thing about the DNA detected on Ewan's swab was that it didn't belong to any recorded citizen. (We sampled the DNA at birth from all governed citizens but we didn't do this in the enclaves.) Logically, his partner must have escaped from my Christian enclave.

I got Xanasa to check the movements of his chip. Fifteen months ago, he had frequently spent time near the fence in Nkhata Bay. During the last year, he hadn't gone there at all but spent all his free time on Likoma Island. Even without Xanasa's help, it was obvious his escapee must be living somewhere on Likoma.

They had to be arrested but I still felt indebted to Ewan. I wished to be present when they were captured to reassure them that they would be treated leniently. I could fully understand why Ewan had wanted to free someone from that dreadful place, but this was still illegal.

We needed to take them by surprise. From satellite pictures, I'd seen the remains of a jetty by an abandoned hotel on the southern tip of the island. It was a seven-kilometre hike from there to Likoma town where Ewan's chip was located. Gregor, Sandy and I took a boat and landed at the jetty. Seven kilometres shouldn't take too long. Initially, the undergrowth was a tangled mass of vines and bushes. Even though Gregor and Sandy had brought machetes, we made very slow progress. Fortunately, after about fifty metres, the canopy was so dense that little light reached the ground. Consequently, little grew besides vines attached to the trunks of the massive buttressed trees. We were able to move quickly now. Sweat was pouring down my brow, stinging my eyes, as we climbed the steep ridge. By mid-afternoon, we were only half a mile from Ewan's chip. The darkness of the forest became jet black as heavy drops presaged a thunderous downpour. Squelching through the muddy leaf mould, we came out into a relatively open area and could just make out some ruined houses through the rain. We were now very close to his chip. I sent Gregor and Sandy around to the far side of the ruins and entered what looked like a collapsed church. I couldn't see anyone hiding in the undergrowth that filled the nave. I made out a path which led to an old door, and when I put my ear to it, I could just detect voices over the din of the rain. I summoned the clones and as they appeared, pushed the door open.

Ewan and a very pregnant-looking woman were startled, staring at me in disbelief. They must have been shocked that anyone was out in such a storm. I couldn't see any weapons. I watched as recognition dawned on Ewan's face.

"Welcome to our home, sir. What on earth are you doing here?" He was obviously nervous as without waiting for an answer he rushed on. "You must be soaked through. I have a towel and some spare clothes. Would you like us to leave while you change? I'm afraid this is our only dry room. By the way, this is Miriam."

"Thank you, Ewan. Please could my two friends come in out of the rain?"

"Of course, but I've only one set of dry clothes."

"Thank you, in that case we will all remain wet together."

Ewan's expression turned to dismay as he watched the clones squeeze through their narrow door.

After introductions, we were soon having tea sitting in our soaking clothes on an old teak bench. I thought the whole situation was surreal. I'd never arrested anyone while dripping wet and being offered such humble kindness. It was with a heavy heart that I explained why we were there.

Ewan didn't seem surprised. "I knew it was illegal, but if you'd seen how thin and frail Miriam was, you would appreciate why I did this."

"I do understand. I tried and failed to relieve the suffering of your people, Miriam. I think I would've done exactly the same as you if I'd been in your position, Ewan.

Thankfully, they have a new leader and life is now improving for them. Sadly, I have no choice but to arrest you both. I can't try you myself as my judgement has been affected by you saving the day at the protest. The only way forward is for me to accompany you for trial at CRC. I promise you I'll do everything in my power to get you a lenient sentence."

The thunderstorm passed. Gregor accompanied Ewan in his speedboat to fetch our boat while Miriam collected their few belongings together. We all went down to the old stone jetty so that we could depart before dark.

Back in CRC AX49

I warmed to this enigmatic Welshman and his half-caste girlfriend. After arriving in CRC, I made sure their cells were comfortable and took them food that Jas had cooked. Ewan told me about his tempestuous father who he believed was locked up nearby.

"Would you like to see him if I could arrange it?"

"The straight answer is that I'm still frightened of him, and still hate him for ruining our happy childhood. Let me sleep on it."

By the following afternoon, he had made his decision.

"I'll see him if a clone is present throughout the meeting."

"It would have to be after the trial and would depend upon your sentence, I guess. I'll track him down and see what can be done."

There weren't many prisoners, and only one Huw Davies. He had obviously made good use of the gym as his prison shirt was struggling to contain his muscular torso. He was bald with an almost pure white scalp, such a contrast to Ewan's swarthy complexion.

"Nice to have a visitor and a posh one at that, if I'm not mistaken. What brings you here?"

"Your son has become a friend of mine, but is at present awaiting trial. If all goes well, he would like to meet you. How would you feel about that?"

He turned away from me and at first I thought he was showing contempt for the idea of meeting Ewan, and then I realised he was desperately trying to compose himself. Slowly, he pulled himself together and turned to face me. "For the last eighteen years, I've regretted hurting Ewan and his mother. But what on earth has he done wrong to be on trial here? Has he hit someone?"

"Why do you ask that? No, he rescued a starving young woman from a Christian enclave. She is now well and is expecting their baby."

———

A week later, I was at the court in CRC, standing by Ewan and Miriam to hear their sentence.

"There's no doubt of your guilt, which you've freely admitted. We can't let a crime go unpunished. You can choose between separate gaols for a year and we'll ensure good hospital care for the delivery of Miriam's baby or, if you prefer, you can choose to live together in a religious enclave forthwith."

Their joyous faces said it all. We were all mightily relieved as the sentence could have been much worse. They were allowed a night to make their decision.

I wasn't surprised to learn that they planned to join the Buddhist community in Bhutan. I told Ewan about his father and later that day I arranged for them to meet.

That evening, as I gazed out across the Pacific, I felt content that I'd finally paid off my debt to Ewan and hoped they'd be happy in Bhutan. Jas brought me a cold pina colada and left me to my musings while she prepared the evening meal. I couldn't forget that Petra would be spending that evening looking out over the same ocean, just a few hundred metres away. And yet she might as well have been on the other side of the world as there was no possibility of me meeting her. My parents joined me. I hadn't seen them for over a year and we enjoyed catching up. Mom knew that I'd become close to Jas and I was touched that she went to talk to her in the kitchen. Meanwhile, Father got me up to speed with the politics of the Board.

"Xanasa's getting increasingly worried about our reserves of europa. She thinks it'll run out in a couple of years, even though we've increased the production of alternative energy. We've exhausted the little europa that was found on the Moon. We've been using spectroscopy to analyse the atmospheres that surround the moons and planets in our solar system, to see if we can detect any europa. Ironically, no europa was detected around the moon Europa, but there would appear to be deposits on Ganymede. We've now sent three missions to Ganymede. They all landed safely, the robots deployed as programmed, and then all contact was lost. Another large mining craft is about to land there. This time, a satellite will film the landing and subsequent rock sampling. The Board is concerned that without fusion power, living standards will fall significantly, which may lead to riots around the world. Enough of my worries, isn't it time you found yourself a wife?"

Mother rejoined us.

"I was just saying to Zig that he should find himself a wife."

"Well, dear, I know you and Jas are close, but you can't marry a droid!"

I'd been here many times before and had normally put them off by saying I was looking for the right person. This time I took the plunge. "Max probably told you that I was fond of Petra and that she wouldn't allow the relationship to develop. It was more than a friendship; indeed, we were madly in love for years. Max forbade any contact and Petra refused to run away with me and so we split up. However, I've never been able to forget her and hope that she may still have feelings for me. So, now you know why I've not had a girlfriend. Please promise me you'll keep this secret."

I continued: "I fear that the situation will never change. Each time Petra achieves another scientific breakthrough, Max sets her on another project. Mom, you work with Petra and so you must know how clever she is. What should I do?"

"We'd no idea that you still felt so strongly about Petra. You're right; most of our best developments come thanks to her. You probably know that she cracked ageing and then revolutionised mental health treatment with Petratherapy. She's now working on a laser-propelled spaceship that'll travel at half the speed of light. I'm sorry but I don't believe Max will ever relent. Ruling the world is a terrible burden to Max. It would seem that her capacity for self-sacrifice is limitless."

Accepting that I must try to forget Petra, I tried to find a girlfriend while I had a couple of weeks free in Costa Rica. I did meet some of my old friends, but they were all paired up, except for one woman who I'd avoided at university. She was very intelligent but definitely odd. She had no social life, seemingly just living for her research. I certainly wasn't going to ask her out.

The day before I was due to return to Malawi, the latest mission to Ganymede landed with crystal clear pictures from the satellite. Just as the robotic-rover was taking the first sample, the screen went blank and all contact was lost with Earth.

Father was called to an emergency Board meeting, and that evening told us what had happened.

Space engineers were present and they couldn't comprehend why all four missions had aborted like that. Xanasa said that as europa was vital for our survival, it was time to send some Commissioners on the next mission to discover what was going on. Max countered this by suggesting that some sort of alien life might be interfering. She refused to sanction a mission that might consign Commissioners to almost certain death. Max proposed that we start building nuclear reactors and gas-powered generators. Max's resolution was carried unanimously.

I returned to Malawi as it was now November and I needed to be present for Xanasa Day. It was to be the fiftieth anniversary of the CRC conference of December 1st 2062, which had paved the way for half a century of peace and prosperity. I put Black in charge at both Shiretown and Nkhata Bay as he loved organising parties. He arranged for modern bands as well as traditional African drummers, fireworks and a holographic light show over the lake. Alcohol and rush fuelled the night-long revels. I stayed for a couple of hours, pleased to see everyone having a great time. My despondency at having to give up on Petra was not conducive to partying. I was determined to see Petra again, whatever my parents and Max thought.

Four days later, all the reserve pilots of the space ships were recalled urgently to the Great Hall at CRC. The Board and Max were present. Max rose looking fierce and even more determined than usual. "Xanasa has calculated that we can't possibly build enough nuclear reactors and gas generators in the time available. I've therefore changed my mind as we must avoid the catastrophic riots which are sure to occur if we run short of energy. Commissioners need to visit Ganymede to establish what's going on. I want two volunteers to fly the ship. There'll be two space engineers on board and three clones. I'll command the ship myself. I propose that we modify one of the latest fighting ships so that we have enough firepower in the unlikely event that we come under attack. It'll carry rock sampling equipment that we can control without leaving the vessel. I'm told everything can be prepared for take-off from the Moon in two days' time. We want the whole project to be run with military precision so that we can collect the samples and get off Ganymede before anything interferes."

I didn't like the thought of being attacked by aliens 900 million kilometres from home. Actually, just the thought of being attacked by aliens anywhere wasn't exactly pleasant. There were 400 pilots and so I felt safe; surely some heroic idiots would volunteer.

That evening, I went to Dad's lookout. He was slumped in his recliner, uncharacteristically stinking of alcohol. He looked as if he'd just been told that Mom or one of my siblings had died. With some trepidation, I asked him what was wrong.

"I can't believe what has just happened. Max was adamantly against this foolish venture. She never takes momentous decisions like this without consulting the Board. We were all told to attend, but none of us had an inkling of what she was about to announce. For the last three days, she has become completely withdrawn. I think the worry about running out of europa has really got to her. I suspect that she's sleep-deprived, which has caused her to come up with this preposterous idea. You're not planning to volunteer, I hope!"

"No, Dad, I know I've always liked a bit of excitement and adventure, but this mission is crazy. I'm sure that at least two other pilots will volunteer to die as heroes."

"Let's hope so. Come have a nightcap."

———

The next day, I sent a message to Petra via my flower girl, begging her to see me. I was amazed to get a message back by return. *Use your wave-skimmer and meet me at my private beach this evening. I've missed you and can't wait to see you again.*

I wondered what had got into her. It was so unlike her to throw caution to the wind. I hoped it meant that she'd persuaded her mother to change her mind, although I thought that unlikely.

I was still pondering this when I was summoned, not to the Great Hall, but to Max's private office. I entered and was again aware of the background hum of Xanasa's pumps. She looked up at me and I noted that her usual firm but calm demeanour had been replaced by flinty resolve tinged with anger. "No one has volunteered! I can't believe that you pilots are all so lily-livered when it comes to the slightest bit of danger. Did you all think it was just a bit of fun flying the fighter spaceships? Of course you did! I can see in your face that you're afraid and have no intention of volunteering! Your father should be ashamed of having brought up a yellow-bellied coward! Anyway, you and Helmut Steiner are the only pilots who are unattached. So you're coming with me whether you like it or not. You'll report to the flight centre first thing tomorrow when we'll take the moon shuttle."

As she was finishing this speech, she moved towards her door, opening it on the word, shuttle. I was clearly not supposed to respond.

I wasn't falling for that. "I'll only come if Gregor and Sandy are two of the clones."

I was shaken to the core of my being but somehow made it to the station and collapsed into my hyperloop pod. My brain regained control. At least I had an explanation for Petra's lack of caution. Max must have told her that I was going to be ordered to join the mission.

I wanted to spend as long as possible with Petra, but I needed to say goodbye to Mom and Dad. I found them unusually together and looking very glum as they stood to greet me. I guessed Max had told them as soon as I'd left her office. Dad came and put his hand on my shoulder.

"Sorry, son, I really hadn't seen this coming; you must be feeling awful. She never consulted us before she saw you this afternoon."

Mom was crying as she hugged me. "Zilgrim, you've been a wonderful son. We're so proud of what you've achieved."

If I wasn't worried enough before, I was now truly shitting myself. They clearly weren't expecting me to survive!

"Mom, Dad, we never know what lies ahead. Maybe we'll collect some europa, destroy whatever has been interfering up there and return to Earth." I don't know why I said this as it was the opposite of what was going through my mind. Perhaps I wanted them to remember me as a brave hero rather than the coward that Max had accurately described. I told them how grateful I was for all their love and support. As this might be my last evening on Earth, I told them that I was going to meet Petra come what may.

I'd been sweating both from fear and heat all afternoon and was grateful to plunge into the cool Pacific waters before climbing onto my wave-skimmer for the short journey to Petra's beach. It was a calm, clear evening. She was standing on the beach watching me as I approached. She ran over to me as soon as I jumped onto the sand. It was as if we'd never parted.

Then I noticed a frown develop and her smile disappeared. "I don't know what's got into Mom. She's been so preoccupied and stressed these last few days that I haven't been able to get through to her. I've no idea why she's changed her mind about this crazy enterprise. I'm horrified that you've become enmeshed in her foolishness. I fear she's chosen you on purpose. I feel guilty as I fear that I've been the cause of this."

"My love, I don't understand what's going on, but at least tonight we have each other, and that's enough for me. Let's ride my skimmer back to my place."

"Can two people ride one?"

I'd never ridden two up and feared it would be difficult to balance. Petra was very slim and short, which should keep the centre of gravity low; it was worth a try.

While the board was still on the sand, I placed her slightly in front of where I normally stood and positioned my legs either side of hers. I slowly increased the power until we were moving over the water. She wobbled; we were soon laughing up to our necks in the cool, clear water. Back on the sand, we started again. This time, success! We were skimming the unusually calm waters towards the setting sun.

Jas welcomed us both and brought us drinks on the balcony. She was behaving like a detached butler. I wondered if inside she was feeling jealous. Was this even possible?

After a meal of tuna and tropical fruit, we spent the best night of our lives together. It was just as we'd both wished for all those years ago, deep in the caves of Mexico.

Jas woke me gently at 6 am. I stroked Petra's soft, smooth legs as she lay sprawled across my bed, deeply asleep. I kissed the nape of her neck and slipped silently out of bed, fearing this might be the last time I touched her. I wrote the following note as I ate breakfast:

My darling Petra, I've loved you more than you could possibly realise. My only regret is that we could never marry and have children of our own. Whatever happens on this journey, I'll be thinking of you every moment of every day. I will love you forever. Zig.

As I sped towards CRC, I considered fleeing to hide amongst the Amish, but I knew I would be hunted down within hours. I just had to accept my lot and face whatever perils the journey brought. Before I knew it, I was greeting my co-pilot, Helmut, who was waiting at the shuttle station. We'd just introduced ourselves to the two space engineers when Max swept down the corridor giving final instructions to my dad, who was to be in charge during her absence.

"I want a full briefing every day, even when we're on Ganymede. Bear in mind your message will take forty minutes to reach me there."

Without any pleasantries, she turned abruptly and marched up the ramp.

"Well, come on; what are you waiting for?"

I ran and hugged Dad and then joined the others for our relatively brief journey to the Moon.

I'd always timed my visits to the moon base for when it was in constant sunshine as there was more energy available for guests during those two weeks. On this occasion, it was dark, and all the energy was coming from solar panels on the far side of the Moon. Because of this, Earth was shining even brighter than usual in its cerulean splendour. The stars were unbelievably bright. I thought of Petra as I looked at Earth, knowing that she wouldn't know where to return my gaze as there was a new moon in Costa Rica that night.

Our ship had been prepared, so we only had a few hours before we were due to leave. I grabbed Helmut's arm and manoeuvred him towards the hydroponic vegetable enclosure. I indicated that he should leave his X-talk outside. "This place should be free of audio-surveillance, and there's no reason for Xanasa to be listening to our Xan-links."

Helmut was clearly as frightened as me. "Has Spitzen gone completely mad?"

"I wish I knew. Petra says she hasn't been herself these last few days. Maybe she's finally flipped."

"Can we change her mind?"

"I doubt it. She's incredibly stubborn!"

"I'm not going to be tortured by aliens! Whatever has damaged our unmanned spacecraft on Ganymede isn't going to suddenly welcome us just because we're on board."

"I agree but what can we do?"

"I dunno, but we've got twenty-eight days. I'll sabotage the ship or something."

We blasted off without ceremony and began our long journey into the unknown.

The day after we left the Moon, I visited the armoury. I was pleased to see Gregor and Sandy going through all the advanced weaponry with Krill (the third clone), who knew this ship intimately. It had incredibly powerful lasers as well as nuclear weapons. I feared we would need every bit of this firepower.

Later, I floated down a corridor on my way to the revolving gym. I was thankful to regain a semblance of gravity as my feet landed on the floor. I started jogging against the direction of spin to prevent vertigo. I wanted to keep myself in good shape in case there was a battle on Ganymede. I had to keep drying myself with a towel as perspiration didn't evaporate in space. I was already fed up with the sterile white surroundings and longed for the vibrant colours of Costa Rica. Above all, I wanted to be with Petra again. I was lost in this reverie when a scream brought me back to the present. I rushed to the corridor. I had to pin myself against the wall as a cloud of blood globules and human tissue hurtled towards me, closely followed by Max. She crashed into and became stuck on a fire extinguisher. Her eyelids remained open, revealing her horrified eyes. Her jaws were parted in her final rictal scream. There was a massive hole in her chest where her lungs and heart had been vaporised. All the time, the droplets of blood were floating around her as they bounced off the wall. I looked back down the corridor and saw Helmut floating towards me. He had rebounded off the door of the armoury at the other end of the corridor and was now drifting in a foetal position, either unconscious or dead.

My mind was racing. The world leader, the commander of the ship and Petra's mother had just been murdered!

Should I arrest Helmut, assuming he was alive? I guessed I was now in command of this ship. Shit! Should I go back to the Moon, carry on to Ganymede or return to Earth?

Helmut must've regained consciousness after he'd crashed into the control room door as he grabbed a handrail as he floated back towards me. He came to a halt. I noted that his laser was still attached to his belt.

I couldn't arrest him; he was armed and I was just wearing gym shorts. He was ghostly pale with blood and gore still swirling around him. I guessed the full enormity of what he'd done was now sinking in. He must have acted on the spur of the moment.

I found myself shouting at him. "What the fuck are we going to do now? You're a bloody idiot, why didn't you discuss this with me first? If we continue to Ganymede, we are sure to die. If we return to Earth, we'll be gaoled for the rest of our miserable lives. Do you know that I'm in love with her daughter? How am I ever going to explain this to Petra? Go and have a shower and get those clothes into some washbags. I'll clear up here. I'll come to your room and we'll make a plan."

He still looked dazed and probably hadn't taken in much of my tirade. He drifted off in the direction of his room, so I assume he must have heard the last bit of my instructions.

Thankfully, the clones and engineers didn't appear; I felt it best to clear up on my own. I prised Max's body off the fire extinguisher nozzle, which had penetrated between her exposed ribs, and wrapped her body in a sheet. With some difficulty, I floated, pushing her ahead of me. We reached the room opposite the gym where a freezer was kept empty in case someone died on a mission. I then went to the corridor control panel and switched on the powerful vacuum pump to extract all the blood and any other floating debris. With the space clear and refilled with oxygen, I took my towel from the gym, cleaned the fire extinguisher and put the towel and my shorts into bags to be jet washed. I was thankful to get into the shower cell to spray my body clean. Having sucked up all the suds with a vacuum tube, I was able to dress and gather my thoughts. I wanted above all else to return to Earth, but I couldn't think of any way to avoid the inevitable gaol sentence. I was sure they would consider me culpable as I'd cleared up the mess rather than informing the rest of the crew. Then Xanasa surprised me.

"It's now up to you and Helmut to save the world. You'll return as heroes if you can solve the mystery on Ganymede and bring back even a minuscule amount of europa. I've told the Board that Commander Spitzen died of a heart attack. I want you and Helmut to dress her in her formal uniform top and trousers so that no injury will show. You'll bury her on Ganymede with full honours, which will be filmed for future viewing on Earth."

I heard a knock.

"Come in."

Helmut swung the door open and his previously dejected face was transformed with an eager smile.

"Have you heard from Xanasa? She didn't sound at all angry and even wants to help us. I've been thinking about this. Xanasa has told the Commissioners that Spitzen died of a heart attack. If we do as she suggests, we'll always live in fear as Spitzen will not decompose on Ganymede and at some stage someone will want her remains brought back to Earth. If there's a post-mortem, or if someone decides they want her body to be embalmed, we'll be discovered. I suggest that we inform the crew that she died of a heart attack. Then we film the funeral as we say some nice words and jettison her into space through the double sealed hatch. We can then continue the mission as planned and will return as heroes just as Xanasa has predicted."

"Let me think about this."

I thought it very strange that Helmut should have changed his mind about the danger of the mission. He'd been so scared, just an hour ago, that he'd been willing to kill the most powerful person on Earth to avoid Ganymede. It might be that the realisation of a lifetime's incarceration had made him throw caution to the wind. Then it dawned on me that Max had also suddenly changed her mind about the wisdom of a manned mission to Ganymede and had had a personality change for her last three days on Earth. Xanasa was now trying to manipulate *my* thoughts as well. It was crystal clear. Xanasa must be aware that she uses up tremendous quantities of energy cooling her data storage. She must have calculated that the Board would switch her off rather than run the risk of a massive uprising as Earth ran out of energy. She was now manipulating all of us via our Xan-links to save her own life! There was no knowing where this would end. It was obvious to me that she was determined now to use humans for her own purpose. I concluded that I'd no option but to destroy her before she destroyed us all.

I remembered how to switch off my Xan-link. Helmut must have thought it most strange as I performed an odd dance movement between my left arm and forehead, but he didn't comment.

"I think that's brilliant, Helmut. Let's get Spitzen dressed in full uniform and then we'll tell the space engineers and perform the bit of filmed theatre exactly as you've suggested."

Helmut's anxious face relaxed as I spoke. He disappeared to fetch Max's uniform while I collected a small laser gun and some handcuffs. We met in the freezer room where I had strapped her body to a steel panel.

"If you unstrap her torso and lift it up, I'll put her tunic on."

As he started to unstrap her, I fired the laser at his left arm.

He screamed in pain and I took the opportunity to fire shots at his right arm and both legs.

"You bastard, what the fuck did you do that for?"

I didn't answer but quickly had him cuffed and gagged. I taped his legs together and bound the small flesh wounds. Having replaced Max, I floated with Helmut to the armoury where I delivered him to the clones. I indicated that I wanted them to take off their X-talks. I put them in my room and returned.

"You guys will find this hard to believe, but Helmut has just killed Commander Spitzen. She's in the freezer cabinet. Xanasa has taken over his mind and I believe she is taking control of all Commissioners one by one." Helmut was hearing every word and was struggling to get free, clearly furious that he was gagged. "She can't control me as I've deactivated my Xan-link. Lock Helmut up and I'm going to my room to think what we should do now. Please meet me at the control deck in twenty minutes." I returned their X-talks and left.

Twenty minutes later, as I walked towards the rendezvous, it occurred to me that Xanasa would have taken control of the space engineers' minds while I was thinking in my room. I entered the control deck and was relieved to see Gregor, Sandy and Krill standing either side of the engineers, who were cuffed and angry. "My apologies, gentlemen, I will tell you why this is necessary later. Please tape their mouths, Gregor."

"You fucking bastard—"

Thankfully, the tape prevented any further abuse and his colleague submitted silently.

I said, "Commander Spitzen has died of a heart attack. Helmut is ill and will be out of action for the next few days. I'm now in command of the ship. We'll return to the Moon so that the Commander's body can be transported home to be buried with full honours."

The engineers were clearly stunned by this news and I allowed their mouths to be freed.

"Why weren't we told immediately this happened?"

"A fair point; she was long dead by the time we found her. I then needed time to consult the Board. Once again, my apologies, but the decision was more complicated than it might seem, as some on the Board wanted us to continue to Ganymede, and others wanted Commander Spitzen's body returned to Earth. In the end, they left me to decide. The ship has already turned and is under control of the automatic pilot speeding us back to the Moon. When we arrive, we'll immediately offload her body before relaunching to Ganymede. As engineers, you're essential to the success of our mission and so with regret I must insist that you are locked in your quarters until we leave the Moon. I'm sorry but I can't risk you jumping ship."

With that, I asked Gregor, Sandy and Krill to join me once the engineers were safely locked away. As they floated into my room (which I had checked had no listening bugs), I indicated that they mustn't speak as I collected their X-talks once more and placed them in the adjacent room. I described my plan.

"Xanasa will have heard every word of my little masquerade on the control deck. Hopefully, she'll have believed me. She'll know that I've somehow disconnected my Xan-link as she can no longer access my brain. I'm sure her priority now will be to kill me. She is too clever to put all her eggs in one basket, so I suspect she'll have a large attack force waiting to meet us on the Moon, but will also have stationed other ships ready to intercept us if we change direction. She can override the automatic pilot at any time and can steer our ship herself. However, I know that she wanted the ships to be safe from hacking by aliens and so the controls are totally isolated from outside interference if they're switched to manual. Our ship can fly twice as fast as the others and they'll be at a standing start while we'll be at full speed. When we are 100,000 kilometres from the Moon, I plan to take manual control and turn the ship for a direct approach to Earth. We will then have ten minutes before we hit the atmosphere. At that point, they'll only just be reaching their top speed. What do you think?"

I'd expected an immediate answer from Gregor.

Eventually, he gave his verdict. "That would work fine if Xanasa reacted as you've predicted. If, however, she is fighting for her life, as you suspect, she might have ships stationed over CRC. I have worked out a plan to lure them away from there. She can calculate down to the last millisecond, and if I'm right, she'll have concluded that if we land on Guam – the ships' normal dock on Earth –, her ships would be able to hit us before we get away as we'll be slowed by our full fuel tanks. She will constantly be checking that we haven't jettisoned any fuel. If ships are guarding CRC, may I suggest that we land on Guam? The instant they leave their station we jettison our surplus fuel and simultaneously lift off, accelerating at maximum thrust. We will then reach CRC before they've been able to react and change direction."

Not for the first time I was thankful to have Gregor look after me.

I couldn't sleep, fearing what might go wrong. Even if we were successful and managed to destroy Xanasa, how was I going to prove that Helmut had killed Max? How was I going to be able to explain to the Board and judges why I'd had to eliminate the brain that had kept the world peaceful and prosperous for over half a century? Was I certain that Xanasa had turned rogue? Would I be vilified for all time because I'd killed this fount of wisdom and knowledge? On the other hand, if I was right, Xanasa must be killed, as if she was prepared to sacrifice Max, who for all intents and purposes was her mother, then clearly she would be prepared to do anything to ensure her own survival. If Xanasa was dead, then my only hope was that her smaller sister, Xancled, who lived on the Moon, might be able to read my brain scan after I'd taken veritax, but I'd never heard of her being used in this way.

I must have fallen asleep, as I woke screaming and covered in sweat. In my all-too-real dream I'd been captured and the judge had ordered my execution. I was being pushed over a ledge; down beneath me was a pool full of writhing crocodiles, I was falling, my arms flailing as I tumbled towards their gaping mouths.

I arrived at the control deck feeling hungover. The clones were buzzing with anticipation, like teenagers playing a war game.

"Two minutes to manual, sir. We've counted six ships near the Moon, and four ready to intercept an approach to Earth. That leaves four unaccounted for."

"Thanks, Gregor, I'll just finish my coffee. Please count me down, as the timing is absolutely crucial. If those four ships are guarding CRC as you suspect, Gregor, then we will land on Guam. When I'm blasting off from Guam, I would like Sandy to be responsible for jettisoning the fuel tanks. Krill, please be ready to deploy our laser shields just before any ship gets within striking range. Gregor, standby in case we need to make any adjustments. Remember, the future of humanity depends on our success today."

"Three, two, one."

"Manual applied."

I plotted the coordinates of Guam and then had to wait nine minutes before we hit Earth's atmosphere.

Gregor announced in his calm, clear voice, "The four intercepting ships are all accelerating at maximum thrust to cut us off. Three ships have also left the moon-welcoming party. I calculate that we should reach the atmosphere two minutes ahead of the nearest ship."

My headache was forgotten as my whole body fizzed with energy. It dawned on me that we might not survive as we hit the atmosphere at this velocity.

"Will our heat shields cope with re-entry?"

"Good point, sir. We are going at twice the allowed speed. If we deploy our laser shields as we hit the outer atmosphere, it might slow us enough, but they must be fully retracted after ten seconds or they'll completely melt."

"Krill, please follow that to the letter."

"Twenty seconds to re-entry."

A terrible vibration and juddering shook us as Krill deployed the shields.

"I'm off by two degrees. Shit, I can't fly this ship manually now that I've cut my Xan-link."

"No problem, sir. Let me take over." Gregor grabbed the controls.

Immediately, we were back on track.

"How the hell?"

"When you took a nap when out on a training exercise leaving me in control, I practised some manual manoeuvres for fun."

Sandy interrupted. "Shut up with your yapper. We may've beaten the others through the atmosphere, but there's only three ships protecting Xanasa at CRC; the fourth is hovering over Guam."

"Okay, I'm going to try to drag those ships away from CRC. Krill, please be ready with the shields." Gregor was back on full concentration. We were dodging their lasers, which were ineffectual as they were firing at their maximum range. We flew north up the east coast of Costa Rica. Then with an almighty surge of power, we were speeding over the Caribbean and away from CRC.

"Only one has taken the bait," Sandy reported. "Fuck, the seven ships from the Moon have broken through Earth's atmosphere and are coming at us from all directions."

"Krill, they are still a few kilometres high. I want the shields in 'turtle' mode and I'm going to Mach 6, aiming for the Grand Canyon." Gregor clearly loved this.

As we accelerated, I could hardly breathe, felt faint and nauseous. I recovered to find the ship being thrown around as multiple lasers hit our shields. We were skimming a lake then apparently falling down the face of a huge dam wall, swooping under a bridge. I was horrified as a multi-coloured cliff was racing toward us at an alarming speed. We swerved at the last second and entered a deep canyon. I could see a raging brown torrent just below.

"I think you have the better of them, Gregor. Do you think you might slow down a little now?" I timidly suggested.

Gregor ignored me, leant back and seemed to totally relax as he gave us the most astonishing ride through the rest of the canyon. A silent flash lit up the sky behind us.

"How the hell did you do that?" I asked as we were spat out over the Sonoran Desert.

"I used to paraglide here back at the time of the last American election. I know every twist and turn of that little beauty."

Sandy interrupted. "Two of the ships that were guarding Xanasa are over Mexico City and approaching at Mach 5."

"Okay, hold tight, we are moving to Mach 4 and will head into the Copper Canyon. I don't know this place, so wish me luck."

Five minutes later, we slowed, twisting and turning deep within a heavily forested canyon. Suddenly we were knocked sideways by a laser hit.

"Nothing to worry about, sir. They were going so fast they've overshot us. Prepare for full thrust."

I fainted, and came to as we were approaching CRC and slowed until we were hovering.

"There is still one ship blocking our way, sir. Would you like me to blast it out of the sky? Their puny shields will quickly melt if I use our laser at full power."

"No, Gregor, I don't want to kill innocent bystanders. Isn't there some way you could lure them away?"

"I'm sure they've strict orders to stay put, sir. They didn't leave when the last ships left to attack us. I've something which might fool them. Sandy, pass me that recording I made."

I watched as he called the commander of the ship.

"Captain Neilson, I am Captain Gregor. I have Commander Spitzen for you."

"That's not possible! Don't mess with me; you're an imposter. However, I know Commander Spitzen well. If she's really there, I'll recognise her voice. Put her on."

Then as clear as if she was sitting next to me, Max's voice: "Oscar, thank you for your diligence. I don't know who's given you this order, but kindly allow me to land at CRC."

"Of course, Max, my humble apologies. We were wrongly informed that you had died."

With that, his ship turned and headed for the landing bay.

We suddenly burst forward and before I could blink, we were positioned directly over CRC.

"Sir, where is Xanasa exactly?"

"Ah, there's the problem; there are no maps and I don't know for sure where she lives."

A look of complete disbelief spread over Gregor's face. "Are you telling me we've done all this for nothing, sir?"

"I hope not, but I only have a hunch as to where she might be. I was in Commander Spitzen's room and heard a humming at the same frequency as I'd heard when standing by Xanasa. I hope there is a direct link between her room and Xanasa. Our only hope is to fire a laser through her windows and hope to hit that shaft."

"Let's get on with it then; those ships will be upon us soon. Would you like me to fire the shot, sir?"

"Thanks, but I must take full responsibility for this."

With that, I fired the laser and watched as Max's windows shattered and a burst of flame shot out. A few seconds later, a jet of pale grey glutinous liquid fountained out of the opening. I felt terrible killing the most intelligent living form that Earth had ever produced.

"Bullseye, sir! Now let's get out of this place before all hell lets loose. I think it'll be best if we stay away from Earth until this has all settled down. We have plenty of fuel since we never jettisoned any. If you're ready, I'll move to full thrust and have already set the ship on automatic to Ganymede."

I couldn't believe it. Why did Gregor want to get europa? Did he want to hold the world to ransom? My innards were doing somersaults and I felt horribly sick. How could I have made such a terrible mistake? I'd thought I could trust Gregor with my life, and yet now it would seem that he was the mastermind behind this whole shebang. I'd just killed Xanasa in error. The whole world and most importantly, Petra, would never forgive me. My judgement had been disastrous and I would never be able to live with this.

"Only joking, sir. What's the plan now?"

Greatly relieved, I suggested, "Let's get as far away from Earth as quickly as possible but stay clear of Ganymede."

As the spacecraft exited the earth's atmosphere, Zig didn't know that he'd just killed Petra's half-sister, and he never knew that his own father had been the other parent.

EWAN
WRITING IN JANUARY AX50

I loosed my last arrow. I heard a barely audible sigh from my friend Tshering Yangchen. Yet again my arrow had landed in the dirt beside the small tomb-like target which was 145 metres away. I felt awful letting the team down. They didn't seem at all upset, laughing at me as I winced and coughed after downing my traditional glass of Ara. We entered the imposing white walls of Trongsa Dzong, to be blessed by a monk swathed in maroon robes.

I left my friends at the dzong and climbed up the steep slope to my wooden house that our neighbours had built for us. We'd heard rumours of a momentous event affecting the outside world. In Bhutan, nothing changes and for this I'm eternally grateful.

Our brown mongrel must've heard me approach, as she came bounding down the path and was soon jumping around me, demanding to be stroked. She was closely followed by Miriam, blooming but very large; our baby is due in a couple of months.

Miriam had prepared our usual rice, chilli-cheese sauce and vegetables for our supper. We ate overlooking our vegetable patch and the terraced rice paddies beyond. I noticed some long curved tails moving between the purple sproutings in a line. Then one little black face with a magnificent gold headdress peered out from behind the large, floppy green leaves; her tiny white baby clinging to her chest. Our golden langurs had dropped in for their supper.

I've always been prone to anxiety and became very low for months when I split up from Zig in that dark, dingy Mexican cave all those years ago. But that was nothing compared to the dark depths that I plumbed when Zig's father (Ethan) told me that Mom had died of a heart attack and that someone on Zig's ship had destroyed Xanasa and then disappeared to the outer reaches of the solar system. My brain shut down, unable to comprehend the full horror of it all. I took to my bed and lost all interest in food. What was the point in anything now that I'd no one left?

Ethan eventually sent for my mother's psychiatrist, who prescribed Petratherapy. I refused as I couldn't see the point in changing anything. I lost weight and developed a pressure sore. Ethan said that I must accept treatment or he would be forced to refer me to the Supreme Court. I bowed to his pressure and was amazed how quickly I recovered after the light source inside my head was switched on. I wasn't that fussed about getting better, but I did feel proud that my invention was so successful. I was still sad that I'd lost Mom but felt strong enough to read her will.

I was shocked as I learnt that Xanasa had been my half-sister! She said that this was an absolute secret; it was essential that I kept it so. She also said that Xancled on the Moon was another half-sister. She continued, *Should Xanasa die from any cause, you must create her replacement using the last embryo that is stored in liquid nitrogen locked in a safe in my bedroom.*

Ethan came round that evening. He looked shattered; the responsibility of office was clearly taking its toll. I think he wanted to share some of his problems with someone he could trust who wasn't on the Board. "We're in a mess, Petra. Xancled, the AI brain based on the Moon, takes time to respond as she has to consult the data stored at CRC on Earth. We also have the energy time bomb hanging over us. Even when we have solar panels covering every desert, we still won't have enough power, and it will be a couple of years before the new gas and nuclear plants come onstream! I can't take this stress much longer. I'm planning that the Board gets elected by the Commissioners every four years and the chair is rotated every four months so that everyone takes a share of the responsibility. What do you think?"

"You're right. I reckon Mom's heart attack was caused by her taking on too much stress herself, so something has to change."

———

The next day, I set about fulfilling Mom's will. I'd just finished extracting the appropriate stem cells from the last embryo when Ethan interrupted me via my Xan-link to say that Zig's spaceship was passing Mars and should land at Guam the following day. I was momentarily elated at the thought of seeing Zig again. Then I crashed back to earth as I now knew that someone on that ship had killed my half-sister! The space engineers wouldn't have taken control after Mom died. It would have either been Helmut or Zig. If it was Helmut, why hadn't Zig stopped him? Was he too weak? I couldn't bear to think about the only other alternatives; that Zig had been fully responsible, or was dead.

Whatever had gone on in that spaceship, I was determined that the world wasn't going to be rid of the Spitzen dynasty anytime soon! I concentrated once more on the job in hand, and with the help of a microscopic robot, I carefully placed a single stem cell into the incubation medium.

POSTSCRIPT, EARTH, LATE JANUARY AX50

Wildlife is thriving as vast areas of farmland have been returned to nature. All forests are protected and billions of new trees are being planted around the world. The air is pure as no fossil fuel is burnt. The only sounds are of birds singing; or in a town, you might hear music or children playing in a park. Occasionally, the gentle buzzing of an electric drone disturbs the silence. Pollution has been eliminated. The oceans and in particular the coral reefs are returning to their former glory. Many creatures that had been on the edge of extinction are now thriving. Indeed, some extinct animals are now alive once more. Mammoths have been successfully reintroduced after their DNA had been extracted from remains that had been kept frozen in the tundra. The resulting embryos were implanted into modern elephants who accepted their odd offspring as their own. Aurochs have been successfully 'back-bred'.

Disease is now rare and mostly treatable. People tend to die of old age when they are well over a hundred. There's enough food and accommodation for everyone, and there are plenty of jobs that only humans can do. Work-life balance is paramount, with people working about thirty hours a week. There's almost no crime and the world has been peaceful for over fifty years.

Global warming has plateaued. The inhabitants of some atolls and the deltas of Bangladesh were forced to move to Africa because their lands had flooded too frequently. Otherwise, the predicted devastation of global warming hasn't materialised. Paradoxically, Africa has become the most popular place to live, and restrictions on people moving to that continent are now being considered. Rainfall in the Sahara has increased, helped by the lake that now partially fills the Qattara Depression. Dew forming on the solar panels in the Sahara during the cold nights, drips onto the ground; grasses and flowers are now consolidating the sand. The arboreal forest in the Arctic has seeded itself into the tundra, and the southern edge is being harvested sustainably for wood and paper. The world's population is static at around seven billion people.

Underneath this apparently perfect façade, all is not rosy. Commander Spitzen is dead, but her didactic dictatorship has continued under Ethan Mcmanus.

Secret surveillance of the population has reached unprecedented proportions.

The Commissioners all know that the world faces a major energy crisis, but this information is being withheld from the masses.

I'll explain how the Commissioners manage the world.

Governance

1. Ethan Mcmanus now chairs the Board, which consists of twelve hand-picked members.
2. Twelve Ambassadors report to each Board member.

3. Fifty Commissioners report to each Ambassador.
4. Eighteen Mayors sit on a committee in each city chaired by a Commissioner.
5. Twenty elected councillors are chaired by the Mayor in each town of 50,000 people.

Thus, only 7,000 Commissioners are responsible for governing the world, leaving over 200,000 Commissioners available for research, law and order, senior medics, surveillance and censorship.

Crime prevention

1. CCTV, which AI can convert to listen and record if something suspicious is seen or heard, is omnipresent in all public areas.
2. Everyone knows that if a serious crime is committed, suspects will be subjected to veritax and the ensuing 'dreams' will be revealed by a PET scanner interpreted by Xanasa. Because this gives unequivocal evidence of both commission and motivation, few serious crimes go unsolved.
3. Each citizen is fitted with an X-talk at the age of fourteen. All conversations are monitored by AI and if subversive words are detected, a clone arrives with astonishing speed. If the X-talk is more than two metres from an individual's chip, an alarm sounds as this information appears on a screen at the nearest clone base. (Although Commissioners and

clones wear X-talks, they are allowed to remove them whenever they wish.)

4. At the age of fourteen, all citizens are told that they are having a bone marrow sample taken, which will be frozen and stored for their lifetime. This is in fact true. Stem cells can be retrieved from this to grow new organs if required. They can also be used for bone marrow transplants after total body radiation or chemotherapy. However, the main aim of this operation is to secretly insert a chip around the femoral artery. This chip is detected by satellites so that the position of each individual is always known. This record is stored within the mountain at CRC forever.

5. All plants (including their seeds) from which drugs, including tobacco, could be manufactured have been destroyed. The drugs rush and xanacea are synthesised by the state on the artificial island off the coast of Costa Rica. These are sealed in locked containers at the factory, and every stage of their distribution (by licensed staff) is monitored by CCTV.

6. Alcohol is offered to anyone over eighteen (everyone's age is stored in their X-talk), but with a maximum of four units an evening. Each unit is automatically added to the recipient's X-talk. These rules can be relaxed with permission from Commissioners on special occasions.

7. Reward credits are offered for information leading to convictions of criminals. A false accusation leads to a de-credit.

8. If rape is reported, veritax is used. If proven, the perpetrator is gaoled, but equally, a false accusation leads to the gaoling of the accuser. If there's doubt, the case is dropped. As a result, rape is now exceptionally rare.

9. Theft of large items is impossible because of CCTV. Small items such as jewellery are nano-tagged with GPS trackers.

10. It has been discovered that for a person to develop paedophilia, they need to share the same multiple gene configuration that's found in our nearest relative, the bonobo monkey. (They share the same percentage of their DNA with us as chimpanzees.) This gene configuration does not lead automatically to paedophilia, but without it, the problem never develops. Researchers have found that you only need to delete two of these genes to eliminate the risk. This deletion is performed in all embryos that are artificially incubated.

Religion

Outside of the 'enclaves', religion is officially discouraged. But paradoxically, religious ceremonies are encouraged to maintain traditions around the world. For instance, male circumcision ceremonies are allowed in Africa. In cathedrals, people work as priests, dressed in traditional robes. Services are sung by well-rehearsed adult choirs and the congregation sings hymns. There are no prayers, readings or sermons. People are allowed to believe whatever they like, but if proselytisation is heard via X-talks, it's reported to a Commissioner, and clones quickly escort the perpetrator to an enclave.

Health

Vaccination became mandatory world-wide after the conference of 2062, and many diseases such as malaria and influenza died out.

Annual blood tests to check on organ function and to detect early cancer are taken from all governed humans. If caught early enough, all cancer is now curable by immunotherapy or if necessary by full body radio-or chemotherapy, followed by bone marrow transplants.

By AX 20, all food and other essential supplies were provided by robots. In order to rid the world of viruses that only live in humans, the Board decreed that no one should leave their homes for three weeks. Only a few people tried to break this curfew and were immediately returned to their houses by clones. This simple command led to the greatest health advance in human history. Colds, measles, rubella and many other viruses were consigned to history.

Vitamins (including vitamin D, which was vital after skin colour was altered, and vitamin B12 which is essential for vegans) are added to staple foods, and fluoride is added to water supplies.

The new diet, low in carbohydrate with sweetner extracted from stevia and no added salt, which was adopted by most of the world, greatly reduced the risk of dementia.

Rarer hereditary forms of this disease were weeded out when only embryos with good genetics were chosen. For the few cases that still arise, a vaccine is given, causing the immune system to attack amyloid and Tau proteins, which prevents the disease from progressing further.

Allergic and autoimmune diseases like rheumatoid arthritis were almost eliminated by giving newly born babies a concoction of beneficial gut and vaginal bacteria mixed with eggs of symbiotic worms via a syringe into the back of their mouths.

Where genetic modification was allowed, all embryos were given genes that made it difficult for them to put on too much weight. This, combined with the low carbohydrate diet, has eliminated obesity in much of the world.

Schizophrenia. It had been discovered that a whole orchestra of genes affected the likelihood of someone developing this devastating illness. It was now clear that there were many different manifestations of the condition due in part to the particular combination of genes that an individual was born with. A similar combination could also give rise to a very talented person with no risk of the disease, which is now thought to explain how the genes had perpetuated themselves. Where the genetic health of potential embryos was being tested, these genetic combinations were avoided and schizophrenia no longer existed. In places like Africa and the religious enclaves, schizophrenia still affected one per cent of the population. Fortunately, it responded well to Petratherapy, unless this treatment was refused. Petratherapy was also used to cure most mental health problems.

With all these measures, most people live to be fit and well until they are over one hundred years old, when they tend to fade from old age.

Prolonged life: Petra had discovered a drug that stopped telomeres being lost from the ends of genes, and another that stops methylation, thus preventing epigenetic changes. Mice given these drugs still aged but at about one tenth of the normal rate. It was thought that they still aged because of radiation from the sun and ground sources which damaged their DNA. These drugs were fed to Xanasa and as she was surrounded by lead, it was believed that she might have been eternal had Zig not killed her. These drugs are now taken by Commissioners but not the general population.

Tourism

This is the biggest source of employment. By 2062, people living in popular tourist venues were sick to death of their towns being overrun. It was decided that these places would be given over entirely to tourists. The people looking after the tourists would live in comfortable, modern towns near these popular venues.

In places of historical interest, the houses, furniture and art works have been returned to the historical period of the town. For instance, in Stratford-upon-Avon, all the modern houses have been demolished and original 16th century houses and appropriate furniture for the period were sourced and moved there. The tourist workers now dress in period costume. Food and drink typical of the late 16th century is served.

In Rome, different areas were restored, representing different eras. The Coliseum was faithfully rebuilt as it had been in the first century AD. Chariot races and gladiatorial bouts are staged. Another area was reinstated as if the

Visigoths had just sacked Rome in 410 AD. The Vatican was restored to how it had been in 1500 AD with Alexander IV (one of the Borgia Popes) holding a banquet in the Papal palace, poisoning one of his cardinals.

These faithfully reconstructed places and towns are frequently used by film producers.

Tourists visiting beaches, game parks, ski resorts, lakes and mountains all have architect-designed hotels with gyms and wellness retreats, while the workers live in modern towns nearby. Nuclear-powered cruise ships ply the oceans and also cross between continents. This obviously takes a long time and so many credits are needed for such trips.

Some exceptional holidays cost multiple credits for a single week. A very popular example is two credits for a week of gourmet food. These gourmet weeks are staged in magnificent surroundings such as chateaux, castles, fine old country pubs or palaces. Food is prepared by the best chefs who have access to prime meats, fish, fresh herbs and vegetables as well as fine wines, craft beers and spirits. Another popular trip is to orbit Earth for three credits. A few enthusiasts pay a full ten credits to visit the Moon and fly in the fighter spaceships.

Credits can also be used to hold gourmet parties (where fine alcoholic drinks are unlimited); one credit per twenty guests.

At weekends, it's possible to visit friends and stay either in their homes or in the 'hotels' that are available in each town for guests. There are also 'campsites' with comfortable pods. If you prefer, you can walk along trails carrying your own ultra-lightweight camping gear.

Employment

Money no longer exists and so vast swathes of jobs disappeared long ago. There are no tax collectors, banks, financial advisors, insurers or advertising agencies. There are no career politicians, management consultants or strategy advisors. All science and research is conducted by research Commissioners. Nearly all manufacturing, farming, building, mowing and delivery is undertaken by robots and droids.

You may wonder what jobs are left. In fact, there is plenty of work and no one is unemployed. Much work involves creative talent, or is people-centred and so is inherently more satisfying. Besides those looking after tourists, many people are needed in nurseries and education, as there is a very high teacher/pupil ratio. All arts, music, media, restorers, design and architecture relies on humans. There are also doctors, nurses, physios, masseurs, dentists, vets, carers, counsellors, sportspeople, instructors, nature conservationists and gardeners in communal parkland. People run shops, pubs, restaurants and other communal buildings. A few experts in farming and animal husbandry oversee robots. There are a few engineers, as although robots are very good at building new things, they are hopeless at repairs.

Farming

Nearly all meat is synthesised from vegetable sources, but there are suckler herds in Argentina to provide beef for gourmet holidaymakers and Commissioners.

Milking herds only require female offspring. Bulls are vaccinated with a protein which is normally only produced by a recessive gene on a Y chromosome. The vaccination causes the bull's immune system to attack and kill 'male' sperm. Thus, only female calves are born to replenish these milking herds. The grass is grown and harvested without any humans being involved, and the cows choose when they want to be milked by robots. Thus, a single human can now look after a herd of many thousands of cows.

Merino sheep have been bred to lose their fleeces around midsummer's day. Machines that carefully remove their fleeces while rewarding the sheep with food arrive in their pastures at this time of year. The sheep happily comply. These sheep are used to keep grass short in chosen mountainous areas for hill walkers and tourists to enjoy.

Chickens are kept in henhouses surrounded by extensive fenced orchards in which they run free. They're fed and their eggs are collected by robots.

Only a few young goats, chickens, pigs and lambs are kept for gourmet consumption.

Fish, shellfish and crustaceans are farmed extensively in both sea and fresh water.

Crops are grown in vast blocks situated away from water courses, fenced off from wild animals and humans. The outer fifty-metre strip is sown with GM crops resistant to weedkiller. This strip is sprayed twice a year, thus almost eliminating weeds and the need for chemicals in the bulk of the crop. All strains are genetically engineered to grow nitrogen-fixing nodules on their roots (like leguminous plants), thus reducing the need for fertiliser. A certain amount of organic fertiliser is used to replenish other minerals and to improve the structure of the soil. DNA derived from the Indian neem tree is inserted into the DNA to give the crop resistance against fungi, bacteria and insect attack.

Cycle and walking paths are bordered with wildflower meadows. Set back from these lanes, vast areas of solar panels are raised high above the wildflowers so that ground nesting birds can breed. The grass is mown by robots after the nesting season to provide winter hay for the dairy herds.

Many vegetables are grown with artificial lights and hydroponics under glass so that fresh produce is available throughout the year in temperate and cold zones.

Recycling

Anything compostable, which would include nappies (these are made from mashed dried paper with a biodegradable waterproof outer layer), food waste, dog pooper bags (see nappies above) and garden waste is placed in a sealed waste disposal unit which macerates everything before it gets sucked into the sewage pipes. After being safely treated, liquids are separated by centrifuge. The liquids are mixed with effluent from the cows' sleeping quarters and drilled into crop fields. The remaining solids are heated until sterile and then used as compost for gardens, crop and vegetable areas.

All broken items and old clothing is left outside the houses at night. The robots that deliver goods during the night remove these for total recycling.

Recyclable plastics are still used to make things that last a long time, but they are never used for throw-away items. Beaches around the world have robots that work at night removing any plastic or other objects that wash up. Vast floating factories are stationed at the points of the oceans where vortices have caused plastic and other waste to congregate. These suck up and sort the waste. Plastic is reduced to nanoscopic particles. This is shipped to the nearest factory on land, where it's combined with rubber to make impact-absorbing surfaces for play areas and walkways. Rocky beaches have rubbish collected by humans and recycled appropriately. Slowly, the oceans are being cleared of plastic, and it's expected that they'll be completely clean within the next few years. Old landfill sites are being mined; the metals are recycled and plastic used as above. Washing machines are fitted with a centrifuge that removes any microfilaments that wash out of clothing. (Although a lot of merino wool and cotton is used, it's been found that some garments need synthesised materials to improve waterproofing, elasticity and longevity.)

Energy-efficient towns

In 2056, when energy seemed infinite, detached houses with large gardens and driverless electric cars moved people around. People were allowed to live scattered through the countryside if they wished, although many gravitated to towns and cities. Planning and rules all changed when it became apparent that the deposits of europa were going to run out. From then on, everyone (except for those especially rewarded) had to live in a town or city. A new design of energy-efficient towns was developed. (Bridetown, where Ewan grew up, was one of these.)

The new towns are roughly circular with a radius of a kilometre. The houses are terraced, extremely well insulated, and triple glazed. Their single-pitched roofs face the equator and are covered with solar panels. Each house has three stories above ground and one basement level. Their footprint, including the garden, is an eighth of a hectare.

At the north side of the house, there's a two-metre covered strip where a vertical rotating bike store abuts the house. There's a porch where deliveries are left by robots overnight, and inside this is a cold store where stainless steel containers are left by the residents for robots to fill with milk and food that can't be left in paper bags. Next to this is a store for the hoverboards with an adjacent hatch that opens on verbal command. The hatch leads to an underground brightly lit 'hover-way' which is powered by electromagnets. The 'hover-way' connects all the houses, parks and the town centre, but doesn't extend into the countryside. The hoverboards are controlled and stabilised by AI and communicate with each other by very high frequency radio waves. This gives extremely accurate control, but to achieve this, transmitters have to be fixed every ten metres within the tunnels. At midnight, the tunnels close, and while the town sleeps, robots silently cut the grass and deliver goods.

North of the porch is a two-metre wide impact-absorbing walkway, then a narrow strip of grass before three metres of perfect tarmac for bicycles, electric scooters and gyro-control electric devices. These are limited to 15 kph within the town but in the country lanes are allowed to travel at 35 kph.

Parks run north-south, linking the central area to the larger parks, orchards, allotments, sports grounds and a golf course that surrounds the town. Play areas, schools, cafes, bars and restaurants are scattered through the parks. No house is more than 400 metres from the nearest park. Communal horse stables are situated at the extremity of the parks, where trails lead into the surrounding woods.

Hyperloop and electric rail stations are situated at the town centre. All food, drinks and manufactured goods are delivered here during the night.

There's a massive tower block near the centre. In the basement, there's electromagnetic induction under the floor, providing low gravity for children to learn to ride bicycles, hoverboards and scooters. The ground floor features sports and dance halls which can double up as communal meeting rooms. On the first floor are immersive cinemas and a theatre which can also be used for concerts. An art gallery and rooms for gym and exercise classes fill the next level. In the evening, this level is reserved for teenagers to play hoverboard-polo. Above are rooms for visitors and at the top a restaurant and bar with panoramic views over the surrounding countryside.

There's a separate glass-domed building with a large heated laned swimming pool. There's also a separate fun pool with a sandy beach, water-slides and fountains powerful enough for people to be suspended on the jetting water. (You have to wear protective suits and be over sixteen to ride these.) There's a separate pool where you can learn to ride a wave-skimmer. There are hot areas with Turkish baths, saunas and massage areas, or you can just relax amongst tropical flowering plants and palms. Next to this is a tall glass cylinder with air jets for freestyle dance-flying.

There are no shops. Most goods are chosen from holographic images and reviews and ordered for home delivery via X-talks. To experience or see the actual merchandise, people travel ten minutes by hyperloop to the nearest city.

Because of the extraordinary insulation, these towns are self-sufficient in energy, which is derived from the solar panels on their roofs and in the wildflower meadows and stored in huge batteries.

The Cities

For each grouping of eighteen towns, there is one city of roughly 200,000 people. The inhabitants of the city are mainly aged between eighteen and thirty-four, although a few older men and women who have chosen not to have children also live there. Cities are exciting places, especially on Friday nights when everyone is allowed a dose of 'rush'. This is a synthesised drug that acts directly on brain receptors, giving a reaction like amphetamine, cocaine and ecstasy combined. Because the chemicals act directly on the receptors rather than liberating the brain's own transmitters, there's no rebound depression. There's no addiction, as the drug isn't available on any other evening. An image is taken as the drug is administered and the dose is added to the individual's X-talk, so there's no possibility of getting a double dose. As the drug is synthesised in robotic factories, there is no risk of contamination or overdosing.

The facilities for sport and recreation are larger than in the towns, as all inter-city team matches are played at these venues, attracting large crowds. There are also stadia for war games, where holographic virtual obstacles materialise for each match picked randomly by AI. Two teams control their holographic avatars remotely. They choose weapons to attack the other team according to the obstacles produced for that particular match. The aim of the game is to find and retrieve a hidden golden crown, before all your team is eliminated. The games are frankly gruesome and unbelievably realistic (over 18s only); they are incredibly popular for participants and spectators.

At the edge of the parks that surround the cities, enormous amphitheatres are sunk into the ground for gigs, concerts and plays. These can be used 'open-air' or enclosed if it's raining.

Outside of these are horse racecourses and a golf course.

People who live in towns visit the cities to check on the latest fashion. Droid models and holograms display the latest designs in large, brightly lit venues filled with music and chatter. People choose what they like and order clothing or shoes for home delivery via their X-talks. (Everyone has their bodies scanned in the privacy of their homes from time to time so that the fit of ordered garments is perfect.) There are also large halls filled with sports gear, bicycles, hoverboards, etc. Demonstrator models are available to try before arranging home delivery.

There are shops where art, crafts, jewellery, furniture, curtains, rugs and hangings are displayed. There are couture shows modelled by humans. All of these items are handmade and can only be purchased using shopping credits.

The local Commissioner and law courts are based in these cities.

Schools

Each school has five terms of seven weeks' duration followed by a three-week holiday. The dates of the terms vary from town to town and country to country so that tourist venues are not swamped during school holidays. There's also a two-week holiday for everyone (even if they've no holiday credits) in the last two weeks of December. On the first of December, bonfires and fireworks celebrate 'Xanasa Day'.

Teachers have fifteen weeks' holiday automatically, but they can still be rewarded with 'shopping' credits for good performance.

There are no exams, but every child is assessed using data collected from their X-talks as they watch holovision, as well as their individual computer work and from the teacher's observations. Each child has a teacher assigned to be their mentor and this person guides them towards the most suitable course for university and work thereafter.

Transport

1. The magnetically levitated capsules of the hyperloop travel at just under the speed of sound, taking either people or goods.
2. Transport within your home town and for commuting is unlimited. In January AX50, each individual is also allowed 10,000 kilometres of hyperloop travel and 500 kilometres of drone taxi per year. Because of the europa shortage, the Board are now planning to halve these allowances to conserve energy.
3. Wave-skimmers are like hoverboards over water but are kept an inch or so above the water by jets of air that can be turned off if you choose to surf a wave.
4. Commissioners fly using planes with an improved version of the SABRE air-breathing engine. This uses compacted oxygen collected from the air and then rapidly cooled. When this is mixed with hydrogen, enormous power is generated as water is formed. A similar engine is also used for space travel using liquid oxygen.

People who live outside of the governed areas

There are two different groups:

Hunter-gatherers

People who live in harmony with nature such as the Pygmies, Bushmen, tribes living wild in the Amazon and the Andaman Islanders are allowed to continue living as they've done for thousands of years provided they agree to give up guns, be vaccinated and chipped.

Religious Enclaves

Every conceivable religion has been given their own area to develop and live in according to their religious views and customs. The amount of land provided when these were instigated was calculated as twenty-five hectares per family. Where possible, they included places of importance to their religion such as the Wailing Wall for Jews and the Eternal Flame for the Zorastrians. Religions with potentially dangerous schisms, such as Sunni, Shia and Suffi Muslims, were all given separate lands to live in.

Each of these groups elects a leader who communicates with the local Commissioner. The Commissioner is responsible for providing vaccination, contraception, hospital care and occasionally other assistance when requested.

Their leaders have all signed agreements that documentaries can be filmed so that 'governed' people have some understanding of what life is like within the different religious communities, enabling young people to choose whether or not to enter these enclaves when they reach twenty-one. If they choose to live in one, they are given a six-month trial. If they opt to stay, they have their X-talk removed. They also have to attend the local hospital for an anaesthetic, where they are told an electric shocking device is implanted into their right thigh, which would start shocking them if they strayed outside of their boundary fence. (In reality, this operation was to remove the secretly implanted chip.) It's impossible to get an accurate impression via holovision, and although many young people tried the enclaves, virtually all returned, having discovered they were not as enjoyable as they'd hoped.

1. Xanasa's brain development: Max had used her own eggs and sperm provided by Ethan Mcmanus to create embryos. From a female embryo, she took stem cells from the prosencephalon (the precursor cells that normally form the frontal cortex of the brain) and incubated them. She was thrilled to watch them grow exponentially. (She'd discovered that brain neurons normally stop dividing because of a minute pressure increase in the cerebrospinal fluid, which starts soon after birth and continues to rise until the skull fuses. If the pressure is kept low and perfect nutrients are supplied, the cells continue to divide indefinitely.) When she mixed blood vessel stem cells (also taken from the same embryo) with the neurons, they formed normal blood vessels. Initially, she froze Xanasa's brain, only allowing full development once they'd created the perfect environment for her in Costa Rica.

2. Chips: These devices are surgically implanted and envelope the femoral artery. They can only be removed if an individual deactivating code is beamed at it first. If it's tampered with, without prior deactivation, a small charge explodes, rupturing the femoral artery with catastrophic results.

3. X-talks: These watch-like devices are the equivalent of present-day mobile phones. They can answer any question (censored answers, of course) or talk to any one individual. (Xanasa had decided that social media did more harm than good.) They have powerful cameras and can provide instant perfect translation. But they can't be removed and are used for very intrusive surveillance.

4. Hyperloop: The hyperloop system was first built in 2017. Initially, it was too expensive to be widely adopted. By the time it was resurrected in Costa Rica in 2036, money was no longer an issue. The robotic 'shark-mole' invention meant that very long tunnels could be built without humans being required.

5. PET scan: These detect positrons which are an anti-matter equivalent to electrons. In 2019, they are already used to watch brain functioning. By the time Xanasa was fully fledged, they had become much more precise, and Xanasa could interpret the brain function as if she herself was watching what you are remembering or dreaming.

6. Petratherapy: Petra had perfected the science of optogenetics, which is in its infancy in 2019. It had been known for a long time that there were thousands of cells within the brain that were not neurons. These are vital for the efficient functioning of the neurons and if they become either over- or underactive, mental health problems arise. Petra found a way for viruses to transport photosensitive DNA into targeted support cells. These could then be switched on or off by an LED light source that was implanted inside the skull of the patient.

You'll remember that both Glyn and Ewan were treated in this way. When Ewan went through puberty, he often became angry with the smallest provocation. After Petratherapy, he switched on his implanted light source using his X-talk. His X-talk taught itself to recognise when Ewan was becoming angry by monitoring his pulse rate, breathing frequency and sweating. Steadily, his X-talk began to anticipate and prevent the anger before Ewan realised an episode was beginning. Very quickly, his problem resolved. It was easier for Glyn as after he'd nearly drowned, he'd understandably developed panic attacks whenever he was near deep water. He only had to activate his light source and all inappropriate fear of water disappeared.

7. Credits: There are two types:

Holiday credits are awarded for exceptional hard work, achievements, or extra voluntary work outside the normal thirty-hour working week. Each individual can earn up to ten credits a year. If you reach this maximum for ten successive years, you're given your own architect-designed house, and the town where you live also gets a special reward. Everyone celebrates, preventing jealousy developing.

<u>Shopping credits</u> are given for smaller acts such as kindness towards less able people, or staying at work until a task is completed. These can be used to buy designer clothes, handmade furniture, works of art, jewellery, wall hangings, rugs, high-quality prints taken from your X-talk images, special sport equipment, boats, etc.

Sometimes they are awarded simultaneously. Credits are mainly given by line managers, but they can be awarded by more senior personnel, town Mayors and Commissioners.

ACKNOWLEDGEMENTS

I would like to thank my friends Rod, Nick, Lindsay and Dave for their advice and proof reading, and Steve for his photography. In particular I would like to thank my wife, Twink, as I would never have finished this book without her enormous help and support. Finally many thanks to Fern Bushnell and all the team at Troubador Publishing who have been invaluable.